D0098224

PRAISE FOR BARBARA O'NEAL

Write My Name Across the Sky

"Barbara O'Neal weaves an irresistible tale of creativity, forgery, family, and the FBI in *Write My Name Across the Sky*. Willow and Sam are fascinating, and their aunt Gloria is my dream of an incorrigible, glamorous older woman."

—Nancy Thayer, bestselling author of *Family Reunion*

"*Write My Name Across the Sky* is an exquisitely crafted novel of three remarkable women from two generations grappling with decisions of the past and the consequences of where those young, impetuous choices have led. A heartfelt story of passion, devotion, and family told as only Barbara O'Neal can."

—Suzanne Redfearn, #1 Amazon bestselling author of *In an Instant*

"With its themes of creativity and art, *Write My Name Across the Sky* is itself like a masterfully executed painting. Using refined brushstrokes, O'Neal builds her vivid, complex characters: three independent women in one family who can't quite come to terms with their fierce feelings of love for one another. O'Neal deftly switches between three points of view, adding layers of family history into this intimate and satisfying study of how women make tough choices between love and creativity and family and freedom."

—Glendy Vanderah, *Washington Post* bestselling author of
Where the Forest Meets the Stars

The Lost Girls of Devon

One of *travel + leisure*'s most anticipated books of summer 2020.

"A woman's strange disappearance brings together four strong women who struggle with their relationships, despite their need for one another. Fans of Sarah Addison Allen will appreciate the emphasis on nature and these women's unique gifts in this latest by the author of *When We Believed in Mermaids*."

—*Library Journal* (starred review)

"*The Lost Girls of Devon* draws us into the lives of four generations of women as they come to terms with their relationships and a mysterious tragedy that brings them together. Written in exquisite prose with the added bonus of the small Devon village as a setting, Barbara O'Neal's book will ensnare the reader from the first page, taking us on an emotional journey of love, loss, and betrayal."

—Rhys Bowen, *New York Times* and #1 Kindle bestselling author of *The Tuscan Child*, *In Farleigh Field*, and the Royal Spyness series

"*The Lost Girls of Devon* is one of those novels that grabs you at the beginning with its imagery and rich language and won't let you go. Four generations of women deal with the pain and betrayal of the past, and Barbara O'Neal skillfully leads us to understand all of their deepest needs and fears. To read a Barbara O'Neal novel is to fall into a different world—a world of beauty and suspense, of tragedy and redemption. This one, like her others, is spellbinding."

—Maddie Dawson, bestselling author of *A Happy Catastrophe*

When We Believed in Mermaids

"An emotional story about the relationship between two sisters and the difficulty of facing the truth head-on."

—*Today*

"There's a reason Barbara O'Neal is one of the most decorated authors in fiction. With her trademark lyrical style, she's written a page-turner of the first order. From the very first page, I was drawn into the drama and irresistibly teased along as layers of a family's complicated past were artfully peeled away. Don't miss this masterfully told story of sisters and secrets, damage and redemption, hope and healing."

—Susan Wiggs, #1 *New York Times* bestselling author

"More than a mystery, Barbara O'Neal's *When We Believed in Mermaids* is a story of childhood—and innocence—lost, and the long-hidden secrets, lies, and betrayals two sisters must face in order to make themselves whole as adults. Plunge in and enjoy the intriguing depths of this passionate, lustrous novel, and you just might find yourself believing in mermaids."

—Juliet Blackwell, *New York Times* bestselling author of *The Lost Carousel of Provence*, *Letters from Paris*, and *The Paris Key*

"In *When We Believed in Mermaids*, Barbara O'Neal draws us into the story with her crisp prose, well-drawn settings, and compelling characters, in whom we invest our hearts as we experience the full range of human emotion and, ultimately, celebrate their triumph over the past."

—Grace Greene, author of *The Memory of Butterflies* and the Wildflower House series

"*When We Believed in Mermaids* is a deftly woven tale of two sisters, separated by tragedy and reunited by fate, discovering that the past isn't always what it seems. By turns shattering and life affirming, as luminous and mesmerizing as the sea by which it unfolds, this is a book club essential—definitely one for the shelf!"

—Kerry Anne King, bestselling author of *Whisper Me This*

The Art of Inheriting Secrets

"Great writing, terrific characters, food elements, romance, a touch of intrigue, and more than a few surprises to keep readers guessing."

—*Kirkus Reviews*

"Settle in with tea and biscuits for a charming adventure about inheriting an English manor and the means to restore it. Vivid descriptions and characters that read like best friends will stay with you long after this delightful story has ended."

—Cynthia Ellingsen, bestselling author of *The Lighthouse Keeper*

"*The Art of Inheriting Secrets* is the story of one woman's journey to uncovering her family's hidden past. Set against the backdrop of a sprawling English manor, this book is ripe with mystery. It will have you guessing until the end!"

—Nicole Meier, author of *The House of Bradbury* and *The Girl Made of Clay*

"O'Neal's clever title begins an intriguing journey for readers that unfolds layer by surprising layer. Her respected masterful storytelling blends mystery, art, romance, and mayhem in a quaint English village and breathtaking countryside. Brilliant!"

—Patricia Sands, bestselling author of the Love in Provence series

THIS
PLACE
OF
WONDER

ALSO BY BARBARA O'NEAL

Write My Name Across the Sky
The Lost Girls of Devon
When We Believed in Mermaids
The Art of Inheriting Secrets
The Lost Recipe for Happiness
The Secret of Everything
How to Bake a Perfect Life
The Garden of Happy Endings
The All You Can Dream Buffet
No Place Like Home
A Piece of Heaven
The Goddesses of Kitchen Avenue
Lady Luck's Map of Vegas
The Scent of Hours

THIS
PLACE
OF
WONDER

a novel

BARBARA O'NEAL

LAKE UNION
PUBLISHING

Text copyright © 2022 by Barbara Samuel
All rights reserved.

No part of this book may be reproduced, or stored in a retrieval system, or transmitted in any form or by any means, electronic, mechanical, photocopying, recording, or otherwise, without express written permission of the publisher.

Published by Lake Union Publishing, Seattle

www.apub.com

Amazon, the Amazon logo, and Lake Union Publishing are trademarks of Amazon.com, Inc., or its affiliates.

ISBN-13: 9781662503702 (hardcover)
ISBN-10: 1662503709 (hardcover)

ISBN-13: 9781542037976 (paperback)
ISBN-10: 1542037972 (paperback)

Cover design by Shasti O'Leary Soudant

Printed in the United States of America

First edition

For the OWLs, with buckets of love and gratitude.

Prologue

Maya

My first impulse was to burn it all down, but no native Californian would ever—even reeling with drink and fury and a desperate need for revenge—set anything on fire.

Instead, I found an axe and carried it out to the vineyard. The night was clear, full of stars. The mountains carved a jagged line across it, and I had to pause to admire the scene for a moment. So beautiful. Such beautiful land. Such a beautiful night. How could things still be so beautiful? Shouldn't everything stop?

A song ran through my head, an ancient pop song.

Before me stretched the tidy rows of vines, so very alive even without leaves. I raised the bottle I carried to my lips and drank of their fruit, sharp and dry, almost perfect. I imagined I could hear the vines breathing, taking in the moonlight and the cold night air, preparing for the new season, their roots drinking nourishment from the soil that I had so carefully tended.

I raised my axe.

And could not bring it down, could not kill the living vines. It would be murder.

Instead I picked up the nearly empty bottle and carried my axe to the wine cave. Rows of casks lined both sides of the center aisle. The most perfect vintage we'd created, seven years of work to arrive here, to the thing I'd always known I could make.

I raised my axe, swung, and brought it home, right through the center of the first cask. Wine burst free, pouring out like blood, faster than I would ever have imagined. For one moment my heart clenched, hard, as if to wake me up.

But I walked down the row, swinging. It was hard, physical, slamming work. I sweat, and paused to capture wine in my palms. Only I would ever taste it. No one else, ever. I wept, and swung, and drank, and chopped open every single cask in that room.

Sticky, cold, swaying, I climbed the stairs to the outside and pulled my phone out of my pocket. "Meadow," I said when she answered. "I think you need to come get me."

AP-Santa Barbara

Famed chef Augustus Beauvais, 67, was found dead in the kitchen of his Santa Barbara restaurant Peaches and Pork early this morning, apparently of natural causes.

Beauvais was well known for his contributions to the American food scene, joining such luminaries as Alice Waters and Dennis Foy in creating the modern farm-to-table movement. He and his former wife, Meadow Beauvais, author of the iconic food history *Between Peaches and Pork: A Celebration of Sustainable and Festive Food*, have long held an illustrious spot in the California foodie world, creating new models for service and sustainable farming. Mr. Beauvais was a guest judge on *Top Chef* for two seasons.

He leaves behind two daughters—Maya Beauvais, a sommelier and vintner who created the label Shanti Wines, and Rory Beauvais—and two grandchildren.

Chapter One
Meadow

I'm sleeping hard when the phone rings. It shatters the dream state and slams me into a state of high alert. Phones don't ring in the middle of the night for no reason. They don't often ring at all since technology has allowed us to shut out anyone we don't want to hear from.

Augustus.

Throat tight, I scramble for the phone. Squinting at the screen, I blink at the bright light, but it isn't a number I recognize. I drop the phone on the bed, nestle more deeply into my fluffy duvet. A cat body, limp and immovable, sprawls over my ankles, and I try not to move so much that I disturb her. Beside the bed, my two dogs snore. Elvis with his big nose sounds like a train. It makes me smile. Better snoring dogs than snoring men, I always say.

The phone rings again, and I suddenly worry that it might be Maya, trying to reach me. I ignored her once, exasperated with her drama, and that led nowhere good. She hasn't been allowed many calls in rehab, but I grab the phone, just in case.

"Hello? Maya, is that you?"

"It's Norah."

I shift hair out of my eyes. Norah is my ex-husband's most recent live-in, and she's never called me before.

A clammy shiver walks down my spine. "What is it? Is Augustus okay?"

"No," she wails. "No! He's dead."

My heart squeezes hard. "What? That's impossible. I just saw him last night." But I'm sitting up, my feet touching down on the floor. "What happened?"

She's sobbing, incoherent, and it makes me impatient until I remember that she's barely thirty.

"Norah, take a breath. What happened?"

I hear her inhale, exhale. "I don't know. Maybe a heart attack or something, they think."

Augustus. For a moment my mind goes still, filling with an image of his big, competent hands. Sensual hands. Strong. "Are you at the house?"

"Yes."

"I'll be right there."

"Thank you," she breathes.

I hang up, and for one long moment I don't move. A faraway howl rises in the canyons of my body, coyotes crying out. The world will not be the same without him. I drop my face into my hands. No tears, only a shattering that creates a kaleidoscope of images arranged over thirty years.

Augustus.

My phone rings again, and this time the call is from Peaches and Pork, the restaurant that made us both wealthy and mildly famous. For a moment, irrational hope flares. Maybe Norah was mistaken, and he isn't dead at all.

"Hello?"

"Hi, Meadow, it's Kara." The restaurant manager. Her voice is hushed. Dull. I press my hand to the middle of my chest, feeling as if I'm the one having the heart attack.

"So it's true," I say before she can. "He's dead."

"Yes. I just wanted to be sure you knew, and see if you want me to handle anything any particular way."

"Meaning?"

"There was someone with him."

"A woman." I don't know why I'm surprised, after all this time, all his infidelities, but I am. It is unexpectedly painful.

"Well, she can't be more than twenty-two."

I would bet a million dollars I know which one. I saw her the other day when I went to deliver some produce—a tall, lean beauty with a perfectly flat belly and breasts like Venus and, of course, acres of long hair. His thing. So cliché. "The new bartender?"

"Yep."

I set the phone on my dresser and press the speakerphone so I can get dressed. "Damn. Obviously she'll have to talk to police, but give her a bonus of $5,000 if she'll sign a nondisclosure agreement to keep her from talking to the press."

"Done. What about the restaurant?"

"Closed for the week until we can sort things out. We can discuss when to reopen once we figure out the logistics of everything else."

"Got it." Kara is an enormously competent woman in her early fifties, square and solidly built, and has run P&P for a decade. "Funeral? Do we know those details?"

This sinks me, and my legs turn to rubber. I sit on the chair, airless, looking out toward the fields, rows of rare squashes and heirloom tomatoes shining beneath the nearly full moon. "No funeral or memorial. He wants to be cremated and scattered over the Pacific."

"Mmm." She takes a breath. "We might want to do something for the employees in a couple of weeks."

I nod, still unable to stand. A fine trembling moves beneath my skin, forehead to shoulders, down my back and chest, my arms and legs, as if I'm freezing. "We can talk about that."

"Once they release the body, where should it go for cremation?"

I frown. "Release the body?"

"Yeah. Cause of death is unclear, so the coroner has to do an autopsy."

"Norah said a heart attack."

"Not clear. The girl said he was weak and fainted."

This visual brings a wave of pain down my spine. "I saw him just last night," I say, and even I can hear my voice is hushed. "He seemed fine. He hasn't been sick, has he?"

"You know Augustus. He would work with an amputated arm and swear he was fine."

I breathe in, slowly, aching in every part of my body.

"Are you okay, Meadow?"

"No. But I will be. How about you?"

"Not really."

We sit, linked by the connection, and stare at the atomic-size hole that's been blown through both our lives. As I contemplate the future, it seems slightly possible that without him, the world will simply stop turning. Finally I say, "I've got to go. Norah is hysterical."

"All right. Talk in the morning."

In the darkness, I hold the phone in my palm, wondering how to break the news to my daughters, Rory and Maya. Especially Maya, who is two weeks away from finishing rehab. Will this derail her completely?

Finally, I get myself together and head for Belle l'Été, the house where I spent twenty years building an empire with my ex-husband. A house I loved and hated leaving. A house where a woman who will have to go now lives.

It gives me no pleasure that he was cheating on her, too.

Chapter Two
Norah

I wait for Meadow in the middle of the night, under a moon that is almost brutally bright, sitting on the balcony of the bedroom I shared with Augustus, smoking actual cigarettes, which are not the same as vaping, no matter what anyone says. I smoke one after another until my mouth tastes like tin and there's not enough water in the world to get rid of it.

Augustus is dead. I can't get my mind around it.

Damn it. Fresh grief and shock move through my gut. For once I'd found something I thought I could call my own, a man who worshipped me from the first moment we met, a man who swept me out of my hardscrabble life into the elegance of his own, into his Spanish-style mansion overlooking the ocean, into a world where I didn't have to worry about my next meal. It was like one of the white paperback romances one of my foster mothers used to read by the hundreds. I never believed it could happen in real life.

I light another cigarette. Inhale, blow it out hard, watch blue smoke rise in a cloud against the moon.

I didn't come to California for Augustus, actually. I came to find Meadow.

Her book changed the trajectory of my life. I knew I wanted to write, and I'd majored in gender and women's studies at the University of Pennsylvania, on a full-ride scholarship. I was a good student—one of the best—and not because anyone had given me much of a leg up, but because I worked my ass off. At the end of my junior year, I was trying to figure out what I wanted to do.

I found Meadow's book purely by accident, wandering through the food memoirs and histories at a favorite bookstore near campus, House of Our Own Books.

I'd read all the classics of food writing by then, of course. In a literature class I read M. F. K. Fisher, and loved her rich, clear accounts of eating. I'd found the original archived blog written by Julie Powell about her one-year experiment with cooking every single recipe from Julia Child's first cookbook and been completely swept away. Her writing was harsher than Fisher's, but also earthier. I found Bourdain, and fell in love with his lusty approach to life and cried for three days when he killed himself.

All of them. And then I found Meadow Beauvais. It had been a terrible day. I'd poured everything I had into attempting to land an internship with a publisher I desperately wanted. Friday, I found out I'd lost it to one of the princes of the universe who peopled the gilded kingdom to which I was trying to gain access.

I still had to go to work at five and sling cocktails for other princes who would tip me and flirt aggressively, but it was still too early to show up and I wandered into the bookstore not far away from the bar. Bookstores can solve any problem, at least for a little while. It was humid and too warm inside, the lights bright against the gray day, and it all smelled of paper and glue and dust and humans and damp wool and coffee brewing somewhere. Only this place of wonders could soothe me.

Meadow's book was on an endcap near the cookbooks, which wasn't the right place for it. It wasn't a cookbook. It was a memoir.

I'd seen the book, *Between Peaches and Pork: A Celebration of Sustainable and Festive Food*, before. The cover is red, tomato red, to match the short-sleeved peasant blouse she's wearing in the photo of her smiling into the camera, an enormous flat basket of herbs balanced on her hip. She's stunningly beautiful, of course, with that long wavy red hair and big pale eyes, and the photographer gave the viewer just a slight glimpse of her cleavage, hinting at the voluptuous breasts that match her juicy lips and the invitation in her eyes. She's holding an apple in her free hand.

You can't help but fall in love with her, or maybe long to rest your head on her bosom and let her sing you to sleep. The ultimate Demeter, mother of all. Naturally I, the motherless daughter, was drawn to her. How could I help it? And even as I intellectualized my longing, slightly embarrassed at my lingering neediness, that little orphan girl picked up the book.

Peaches and Pork. The title of the book, the name of the restaurant. The story of a marriage. Who couldn't fall a little in love with Augustus, the way she wrote about him, the way he loved her?

The marriage had failed by the time I made it to Santa Barbara, as much as you can say a marriage failed after twenty years. Does it only count if it lasts forever? I mean, I'd be pretty happy with twenty years of almost anything.

Anyway. I inhale more acrid smoke. Meadow. I fell for her image, her words, her funny way of writing. I connected with her so very deeply, feeling that she somehow knew me, that if we met, we would be friends.

The book woke me up. If the boys' club wouldn't let me in, I'd make my own way. I changed my focus to writing about women and food, and managed to land a place in graduate school at Harvard. In the back of my mind, I'd always thought to interview Meadow, along with other women chefs, particularly about the ways they influenced the male-dominated world of food.

It took some time to get through my graduate program, working and supporting myself as well as taking classes. I was getting worn down by it all, wondering why I didn't just find a job and get to work, when Meadow landed in my sights again. She was named one of the top food influencers in the country, and Padma invited her to cohost an episode of her television show, one featuring California cuisine.

I became obsessed with interviewing her. At least that's what I said in my email inquiry, which I sent care of Peaches and Pork. What I really wanted was for her to . . . I don't know. Adopt me.

Not really, you know, but if I'm honest, really honest, that's what I wanted. I wanted the sun of her smile to warm me. I wanted to *be* her.

She's also a bit of a mystery.

A copious amount of material has been penned about Augustus, with his big personality and notable charm. In my mind, he was far less interesting than Meadow, whose history was shadowed and not at all clear. Where did she grow up? Why was there so little about her early life? In my reading she appeared to be the impetus for the success of Peaches and Pork, the woman behind the throne, as it were. I had noble, powerful thoughts about elevating her to queen. Empress, perhaps.

Meadow was in Australia when I reached out, so my email was read by Augustus, who invited me to visit the restaurant.

So it was that on a hot, windless day in September, when the threat of fire hung like a portent in the shimmery weight of the sky, I parked a rented compact in the lot of Peaches and Pork and got out, pulling my blouse away from my sweaty back. I'd left my hair down because the sheer volume of it covers my ears, but now I regretted that decision. Better ears that stuck out than sweat soaking my neck.

Too late. I locked the car and approached the front door of the restaurant. In the full light of day, age showed in the ocean-weathered wood facing and the outdated font on the sign. None of that mattered, of course, because the windows and decks all looked over the ocean, the beach sparsely populated on a Tuesday.

I'd read a lot about Augustus, and much was made of his charisma. By then he was well into his sixties, decades older than me, and I was just going through a formality, a stop on the way to Meadow.

The restaurant was not open until dinner during the week, and I had to blink in the dimness as I walked in, pushing my sunglasses up on my head to hold back my hair. The air within was cool and smelled of margaritas and sautéing onions. Music played from somewhere back of the house, and I followed it.

"Hello?" I called, waiting in the dining room for a minute. I'd learned the hard way that some chefs were very particular about strangers entering their kitchens, so I was wary of pushing through the doors to the inner sanctum.

The music was something with a bluegrass flavor. I heard chopping, fast chopping, and the sizzle of something being dropped in a hot pan. A man sang along with the music. Maybe not bluegrass, I thought. Maybe zydeco. I wasn't that familiar, but one version of Beauvais's story had him born and raised in New Orleans. There were many backstories for him, actually, which he seemed to move between at will—the New Orleans childhood, the Montreal years, the French cousins. He seemed like a conjurer, making things up to suit whoever was asking the questions.

I didn't think much of him, to be honest, before I finally pushed open the kitchen door.

He stood in front of a long stainless-steel counter, chopping something that took some effort, effort that showed the sinew of his biceps and shoulders beneath a thin white T-shirt that clung to his chest and smooth belly and showed off the waist of a man much younger. It stopped me, the elegance of his body, the fitness. His skin was a reddish sienna, warm against the white sleeves, and his hands were unexpectedly compelling.

He paused at my entry, raised his head. His pictures had not done him justice. At all. "Hello," he said. "You must be Norah." There was the faint accent, vaguely French, vaguely something else. The voice itself was remarkably deep. Musical.

He wiped his hands on the apron tied around his waist and came around the counter. He was tall, which I'd known, but 6'4" is really quite something in person, and he moved with a kind of loose ease that stirred things in all sorts of places in my body. He engulfed my outstretched hand with both of his, and I stared up at the face that did show signs of his years, but only in the most artful of ways—fans of sun lines at the corners of his eyes, a wrinkling of his brow, white curls overtaking the black in his beard, and of course the famous hair, thick and curling, now salt and pepper.

His aura swept me in, seduced me in seconds flat. He looked down into my face as if I were the most beautiful woman he'd ever seen, and we stared at each other for a full, silent minute. "Have we met?" he asked quietly. "I feel I should remember."

I shook my head. "No," I said, feeling his hot hands around mine. He smelled of chocolate and coriander, of something so delectably sinful that I would eat it no matter the cost.

I forgot all about Meadow.

That, as it turned out, was a mistake.

Chapter Three
Maya

Two weeks before my scheduled release from rehab, my therapist calls me into her office. I have repeatedly asked for a male therapist, but they've made me stick with women because evidently I have some issues with men I need to work on. At first I tried to resist her, but it was like keeping your walls up against Mrs. Claus. She has a small nose and round-frame glasses and a neat pageboy haircut that's entirely white. You could get away with thinking she's a pushover, but behind those glasses are eyes as sharp and steely blue as Paul Hollywood's.

"How are you, Maya?" she asks, settling in her chair, a red-velvet wingback that I lust for and have put on my list.

Curled in the overstuffed, oversize chair where I've grown so comfortable the past eleven weeks, I'm pretty sure she's going to break more details of my legal trouble, which has been on hold while I'm here.

"What's up?" I ask, crossing my arms almost without thinking, then unfolding them on purpose. "Am I going to jail after all?"

"No," she says firmly, but there's something in the way she raises her eyes that makes me realize her news is worse than jail. She folds her hands in front of her. An amethyst ring shines the same color as the print of a jacaranda tree behind her on the wall. "I have some bad news."

A surge of terror rises up through my esophagus, and for a fleeting second, all the faces I love pass in front of my eyes. "What?"

"Your father has died."

"My dad?" I peer at her. My father is the most robust, alive person I have ever met. "How?"

"They think it was probably a heart attack, something they call a widow-maker—very fast and deadly."

I let go of a snort. "That's rich, since he divorced them all too fast to leave a widow." She says nothing and I duck my head, looking at my fingers laced together in my lap. "Sorry—sarcasm."

"Good catch. What's beneath it?"

I take a breath and look toward the windows. Pale-green leaves make a pattern of light and shadow against the glass. "Numbness," I say, and push deeper. "It's not like we had a relationship."

"Mmm. And yet he paid the non-insubstantial fees for your stay here."

I shrug. "Guilt."

"Maybe."

An unexpected pain twists my belly. "I was so looking forward to having it out with him."

She nods.

I think of his laughter, the big sound of it, and how much I adored that as a child. "I'll never see him again."

"No."

Somewhere in my body there must be some grief, but right this second I can't find it. I hold my arms across my gut and wait. "Is there more?"

She shakes her head gently. "Do you want to stay in rehab or get out and be with your family?"

"Oh." I look at my hands. They're so clean, unlike the days when I worked with dirt and grapes and wine. "I don't know."

"How are you feeling about your sobriety?"

Rehab is safe. I'm protected here from temptation, from high emotion, from everything out there that might derail me. Meadow's face comes to me. This will be hard on her. I think of my sister. Harder still on her. "Good enough, I think. My stepmom and sister will need me."

She nods. Regards me another long, soft minute. "If you'll go to ninety meetings in ninety days, I'll sign the release."

It feels both aggravating and like a promise of some possible safety. "Okay."

Slowly walking back toward my room, I wait for emotion to well up, rise, fill my body.

But there's nothing.

Chapter Four

Norah

Of course Meadow banishes me. The night of Augustus's death she comforted me, made me tea, tucked me into bed. It was a great kindness.

Two days later she arrives at the back door of Belle l'Été at eight in the morning, her wild red hair caught back into a braid, her dog Elvis at her heels. In her hands is a thick ring of keys.

I've had only one cup of coffee and haven't even eaten any toast or a bowl of cereal. Too late, I realize that I'm wearing a pair of Augustus's boxer briefs. Her eyes flicker over them, showing nothing, but how would she even know they were his? They're pink plaid. Not exactly what you'd think a man like him would wear. I know I look like hell from crying, and I don't think I've had a shower since I heard the news. "Meadow," I say, and swing the door open to let her in. She breezes by, smelling of grass and oranges. "What's up?"

She takes possession of the center of the kitchen, swinging around with an assessing eye. "I'm afraid I've come to ask you to leave."

I was never going to be able to stay. I have no claim on the house or anything in it, now that my lover of barely nine months has kicked the bucket. I mean, obviously.

The trouble is, I have absolutely nowhere else to go and barely $200 to my name, more if I pawn some of the jewelry I've been carting around since my failed engagement back in Boston. Not even that will get me enough for a plane ticket home. Honestly, even if I fly back to the East Coast, I have nowhere to go there, either.

But this isn't the first time I've faced homelessness. I was shuffled around the foster-care system from the age of two, and aged out dramatically just a few months before high school graduation, whereupon my foster mother kicked me out because she thought her husband was looking at me too much. I'd landed a scholarship to University of Pennsylvania and tried desperately to convince her to let me stay, but she was just done. One of my teachers found me a place to live until I could get to the dorms in the fall, or I'd have been on the street then.

I tuck my hair behind my ears. "Right, of course. I'll be out this afternoon."

She raises her chin. A hard glint lights her eye. "I'm sorry, no. You need to go now."

"Now?"

One eyebrow lifts. "My daughter Maya has inherited the house, and she's coming home from rehab tomorrow. I need to get things ready for her."

"Will she want to come here? I mean, her dad just died. Maybe that's a bit harsh for a newly recovering addict?"

"You're so well informed," she says, narrowing her eyes. "But it's none of your business."

"Sorry. I was trying to be helpful."

"She has nowhere else to go."

We have that much in common. "Can I at least get a shower?"

For a moment I think she will refuse, but Elvis has always liked me, and he heaves a big sigh and leans on my leg right that second. Whenever Meadow comes by, which is way more often than I want to see her, Elvis greets me like his long-lost sister, a behavior I admit I've encouraged. She measures him, then says, "Of course. I'm just going to start stripping beds and get some laundry going."

As if I'm a guest at a B&B and the new guests are coming. I pick up my coffee cup, drain it, and rinse it out. Last coffee in this house. It feels like my ribs are breaking. "Okay."

I head upstairs, bare feet on the cool tiles, feeling something dense start sucking me in, a black hole in the middle of my diaphragm. I look at each step, at the colorful Spanish tiles on the risers, my hand on the carved banister that has known the hands of hundreds of people over the years. My heart sends me a memory of Augustus walking backward, one hand in mine, another on the railing. Tears start gushing out. Again.

All I've done for two solid days is cry.

The primary bedroom sits by itself to the right of the stairs, a big room with french doors that open onto a balcony overlooking the ocean. It's a dull day, but the water is still hypnotically beautiful, moving endlessly. I walk outside, smelling jasmine and sea air, and stand there a long time, knowing I'll always remember it. Remember this view, this house, the man, the whole strange season.

Before she can come up and catch me, I fling open my suitcase and take all the dirty clothes from the hamper, his T-shirts and jeans and underwear, and stuff them into one side. Out of the drawers I take my far more meager things and layer them on top of his. Only then do I go into the bathroom, with its alcoves and tiles, and turn on the shower for the last time. I strip off his boxers and my tank and look at my body in the mirror, thinking of him looking at it, his big hands on my breasts, my ass.

It wasn't supposed to be Augustus. How did I get so caught up in him?

Meadow knocks on the bathroom door. "You all right in there, Norah?"

Some wild meanness rises in me and I yank open the door, fully naked. "I'm fine."

For a long moment she stares at me and I stare back, still wishing I could be her friend, be the one who brought her real story to the world, and that will never, ever happen. She is so disdainful of me now.

Maybe with good reason. I don't know.

We are almost exactly the same height—Augustus was tall and he liked long-legged women—and we stare at each other in a roaring, pulsing silence. In the bright light, the ravages of time show on her skin—in the little lines around her mouth and the softness of her neck. I square my shoulders and she can't help but look at my breasts, which are still high and proud, and something breaks hard on her face. Tears are in her eyes when she looks up again.

She suddenly leans in and grabs my face in both of her hands and kisses me, hard, with full-on tongue. Her lips are soft and full and she knows how to kiss, for sure. I lift my hands to push her away, but she lets me go.

"Now we both know what he tasted." She whirls away. "Leave the boxers," she says, heading for the bed.

I slam the door and lean against it. My limbs are trembling. I cover my mouth with my hand. As I turn on the shower, dive into the hot spray, I'm weeping. I don't know where to go, but I can't stay here.

Or can I? A plan suddenly swims up through my pain and presents itself. It's not perfect, but it will do for now.

Chapter Five
Meadow

Once Norah has gone, I have the house to myself for the first time in eight years. With Elvis, my big black shepherd, padding behind me, I wander through the rooms, reconnecting. Twenty years of happiness were mine here. In the salon, with its leather sofas and fireplace and a wall full of french doors facing the patios and the pool. In the dining room, where we hosted so many dinner parties at the long Spanish mission table, with candles burning on the mantel and the windowsills, Augustus at the head holding court with his big voice, me directing servers borrowed from the restaurant to bring in whatever menu we'd conjured together from my fields.

In the bedroom, where I slept next to him for more than six thousand nights.

My favorite room is the kitchen. Augustus surprised me with the plans for a remodel the day I moved in. They included oceans of counter space for chopping and sorting the produce I was famous for, a sink so deep you could wash a bushel of vegetables, a six-burner gas stove in the arched alcove. We saved all the old touches, the Talavera tile around the stove and along one wall, the handmade wooden cupboards. I'd come from so much nothing that it was extravagant luxury—the kitchen, the house, the man himself.

By the time I met Augustus, I carried a protective shell like a turtle. My childhood was brutal, and I finally freed myself when I was sixteen, running away from home into the even more cutthroat world of the streets. It's not the best part of my story, and I resist telling anyone much about it. It doesn't belong to them, and it would shape the story of who I am more than all the things I've done since to create a better world for myself.

Who I am was born when I was sixteen and found work as a prep cook at a restaurant on the coast. It was mainly a tourist place, campy and busy, but it employed a big staff, and I learned how to prepare almost anything for cooking—cutting wheels of carrots and chopping massive amounts of onions, smashing garlic with the side of my knife to free the skin, breaking down a chicken in under five minutes. All manner of things. It was so satisfying to contribute, to make something, and I had a talent for it, knowing what went with which thing, how to build a base, how to sense a missing note. Trudy, a big woman with hands scarred from years of knives and fires, took me under her loving wing, not only teaching me how to cook but mothering away some of the worst of my scars.

Everyone asked why I didn't work front of the house, the implication being that a woman of my physical presence might make a lot of money serving drinks or food. But I loved the kitchen, the food, the creative aspects of preparation and presentation.

I left the Buccaneer when I was nineteen at Trudy's urging—she saw a call for a position at an organic farm in Ojai, thirty miles away. The position was for a liaison between farm and restaurants, and Trudy thought I would be perfect.

Turned out to be the greatest move of my life. I was on the road a lot in between Santa Barbara and Ojai, but that was fine, good thinking time. At the farm I found childcare for my daughter Rory, who hated when I left her with babysitters. The farm was different. There she could run with the kittens and dogs and chase butterflies and play in the fields.

The farm was where I first met Augustus.

He was the kind of person you felt come into a room, his presence moving ahead of him, an aura the size of a live oak. I was plucking yellow leaves from bunches of radishes when I felt that aura brushing up against my entire right side, as palpable as an actual touch. My skin rustled and I glanced up, thinking it was wind.

It was a man. Not even looking my way. Imposingly tall, built with a kind of loose-limbed leanness, broad shoulders, and graceful movements as he picked through a pile of fresh spring onions. His hair was dark and glossy, too long, a tousle of curls, and he wore a neatly trimmed beard that was as black as his hair. I couldn't see much of his face. His ass was a work of art.

But really, it was that aura that captured me.

As if he felt my gaze, he looked my way and saw me staring. He was older than I thought, and I flushed, but couldn't seem to stop staring. His skin was a light reddish brown, his eyes deep brown or maybe even black. He could have been Greek or Egyptian, Indian or Brazilian, Cuban or Creole or some mix of all of the above. His amorphous heritage, I would discover, was part of the way he spun his story. His nose was large, his face long, and he wasn't the most beautiful creature ever, but it was a face it was hard to stop looking at, like an actor you suddenly see on the street who is both more and less than he seems on-screen, not as handsome, but more compelling.

He raised a single eyebrow, one side of his mouth lifting in a half smile.

Older than me by a decade, I thought, and it turned out to be more. But a fully grown man, one who knew what he wanted. He carried the onions over to me. "Will you wrap these?" he asked in a voice softened with a vaguely French accent.

I smiled.

It was the first beginning.

As I walk through the rooms at Belle l'Été, rooms so familiar and yet slightly off-kilter from the way I arranged them, I feel all the years between then and now. The years of being madly in love, of raising our children, one biologically mine, one biologically his, both of them our daughters, only eight months apart, raised as sisters. The years of intense passion early on that settled into years of solid joy and laughter. The last year, when it all fell apart so suddenly, so ridiculously, so completely.

I head upstairs, carrying a pair of boxes. In the primary bedroom I briskly approach the bureau against the wall, intending to empty the drawers so that Maya can have the room if she wishes. I don't know if she will, but it seems only fair to give her the choice. I'm a little worried about her sleeping in the bedroom of her childhood. Will she regress to that age?

It feels overwhelming, trying to figure out the right thing to do for her. I am terrified of setting a foot wrong, saying the wrong thing, driving her back to the bottle. Losing her completely. One of my employees, Tanesha, who runs the main sales area at the farm, a woman with kind eyes and the history of her life written in the crags of her skin, says it isn't my job to keep Maya sober, that she has to do the work on her own. She keeps telling me to go to Al-Anon, but I haven't yet. Those rooms seem sad, a place for the pitiful. I am anything but that.

What I can do is the task at hand. Clear Augustus's things so Maya won't have to deal with them. It's a daunting task. He's lived in this room for decades and has never been one to throw a lot away. I stand for a long moment with the boxes at my feet and look around at the clutter on his nightstand, the detritus across the top of the bureau. Nothing is left of Norah, thank goodness.

My eyes catch on the painting we chose together. I remember the art fair in Montecito where we picked up the lush nude with red hair flowing down her back. How much he loved it, saying that it made him think of me. Her white breasts, her ruddy nipples, that ample hip and thigh. He never took it down. I love that every single woman he brought here had to see it.

When I open the first drawer, a waft of his scent rises from within, that very particular smell of his skin steeped into his T-shirts even though they've been washed. I slam the drawer closed, walk away, fighting the wild emotion in my chest that threatens to give me the same widow-maker they think killed him. I stagger out to the balcony and take in gulps of salt air. Sun shines on my face and hands. Below, in the courtyard, the turquoise pool shimmers.

The world feels intensely empty without him.

Chapter Six
Norah

I spend the night in the cheapest hotel room I can find, filled with party boys daring each other to shotgun beers and dive off the balcony into the pool. I stay safely tucked behind the door, eating the sandwiches I bought on the way here, drinking the extra coffee and tea I bummed off the cleaner earlier.

The next morning, very early, I sling my backpack over my shoulder and walk back up the hill to Belle l'Été. It's a half-hour walk, a little less along the beach, which seems too risky on such a bright day. I don't want anyone to notice me. I'm the only person on the road, and all the houses are tucked down behind fences and shrubbery, so it's almost certain no one saw me except on the security cameras trained on the street, and I don't care about those.

At the house I let myself in through the gate and check for any cars—cleaners or gardeners or Meadow—but the drive is empty. I have a ready excuse if I surprise Meadow—a necklace I left behind, which is very important to me. It's tucked into my pocket just in case, but nobody is here. I let myself in using the key tucked under a loose brick and turn off the alarm. For a moment I stand alone in the sunny breakfast area near the back door, feeling the loss of him, the loss of *this*, and look toward the pool. I swam nude every morning, the greatest luxury I've ever known, and I can almost feel the water on my body.

But there are more pressing things than a swim. I spent a lot of time alone in this house and know every nook and cranny. Attached to the garage, set into the slope of the hill and reached by a neglected half stairway down, is a little bedroom that must have once belonged to a servant. Judging by the dust, it has been empty for a long time.

I hope it is also forgotten. In the pale-pink light of dawn, I flip the mattress over to make sure there are no rodents nesting in it and open the window, located behind a woody shrub so no one can see it, to let the air into the room. Leaving my bag, I climb back up the stairs, cross the massive garage (someone had a car collection), and walk into the main house, up the stairs to the linen closet, where I find sheets and towels and a duvet, which I dump at the top of the stairs to take down with me.

At the doorway to the bedroom, I pause again, finding my heart squeezed in an iron fist. The bed has been stripped down. It's so painful I nearly can't catch my breath, and cling to the threshold on both sides until my vision clears.

Augustus, Augustus, Augustus.

I pick up one of his pillows off the bed, and although it's been stripped of its case, it still smells of him. I clutch it to my chest. Who will sleep here now? Will Meadow claim it for herself? Or will Augustus's daughter take it? I've never met her.

Back down in my hideaway, I carve out space for food I ferret from the kitchen—things that will keep, like crackers and almond butter and apples. Cans of tuna and salmon, which I hate after endless years of canned fish twelve different ways, but beggars can't be choosers. Cases of San Pellegrino and Topo Chico are stacked in the garage, and who will even notice if I take some of them?

When I'm done, I survey my handiwork. The room is still cold and a bit dark, but it's better than some places I've had to live.

Though, really, I thought these days were behind me. I thought I might finally be getting somewhere.

I shake it off. This is temporary, just until I can get enough cash to make my way back to Boston. I'll find a job slinging hash or cocktails and it will take only a couple of weeks. In the meantime, I'll pick back up the work on my dissertation about Meadow. I don't need her permission, and in fact maybe it's better if I don't bother. Then I won't be trying to earn her love and I can write whatever I find.

There are still so many questions about her. About her past, and her life, and her secrets.

I sit down on the now-made bed and lean back into the pillows. It's fine. It's comfortable, actually. I've been so tired, and grief has hollowed me out. The smell of Augustus rises from the pillow I stole from the bed, and I close my eyes. Just for a minute.

Chapter Seven
Maya

My sister, Rory, picks me up from rehab in her truck. When she first greets me, we hug and hug and hug and hug, her arms so tight around me that I can barely breathe. Tears spill from her eyes to the hollow of my neck, and I realize with a shock that we have entirely different responses to the death of the man we both call Dad. "I am so wrecked about this," she cries.

I hug her tightly, rubbing her back. "I know. I'm so sorry." It makes me feel like a monster because I'm still not feeling that much.

Funny that the biological child is so chill and the adopted one is falling apart. It's a mean thought, but I've discovered over these months in rehab that I have a pretty wide mean streak, one of the millions of things I drank to cover up.

We drive up the highway with the windows open to the mild air, her red hair escaping its artful messy bun to fly in tendrils around her lightly freckled face. Everything about her is like that, as if she's starring in a lifestyle essay in a Stampington & Company magazine, all the time, at every second. She has an adorable hipster husband who makes distressed cabinetry and doors from rescued pieces he discovers up and down the coast, and two little girls who are as pretty as their parents, and they all live together in a cute little Craftsman cottage that was dated and awful when they found it. #winningatlife.

Except that she's not that smug. She's just pretty and nice and kind and good, and I feel irritated with myself that she's come all the way out here to pick me up and I'm doing my usual cynical thing. "Thank you," I say. "Meadow has a lot going on."

"I really don't mind, Maya. You don't have to keep thanking me." She signals properly and changes lanes. Through the window on her left is the Pacific, roiling and tossing against the rocky coast of central California, the sky a sunlit blue, as if to offer the perfect complement to that hair I've always envied. She glances at me. "I love you, you know."

"I do know." I shift my gaze to the sea, thinking I don't deserve it. I'm prickly, snarky, cynical, a cactus. She's a flower, and I'm not sure which one is better.

We don't chitchat. There are too many big things going on for that. We sing along to the radio, and it's not really very long before she's on the twisting road to the top of the bluff where my father's house stands, a Santa Barbara mission style built in the twenties by a Hollywood director. Rory and I spent most of our childhoods here after Augustus married Meadow. We ran up and down the tiled staircases, and played all day in the pool that overlooks the ocean, and slept outside on the balconies when the weather was hot.

Belle l'Été. Beautiful Summer.

My father had three wives, none current, so the house came to me. I'm not sure whether he meant that to happen or if his usual lack of attention to detail meant he just never got around to changing his trust, but either way I am now full owner of not only the house but also the restaurant and every part of his empire.

Great choice, Dad.

Rory and I get out, me carrying my meager belongings, and stand in the curving driveway, looking up at our childhood home. "You should have it," I say. "You're the one with the family."

"Don't be ridiculous. The farm is my legacy. This house was always going to be yours."

We both look at the whitewashed walls and blooming bougain-villea, the wrought-iron balconies and tiled patios. I'm flooded with memories. Rory and I have spent many happy years here, but what does a newly recovering, single woman with no means need with a fifteen-room house on the ocean?

"It feels like a punishment," I say before I realize I'm speaking aloud.

"Maybe you could think of it as a totally fresh start."

A fresh start. Starting what? From where I stand, my entire life looks featureless, empty, without markers of any kind. This house feels like going backward, but honestly, where else could I go? I've chopped down any pathway to my old life, not that Josh was going to be per-suaded one way or the other. He is so furious over the lost vintage that he'll speak to me only via lawyers.

A waft of memory, the vineyards on a foggy morning looking soft and painterly, burns across my vision, and I feel like I can't breathe. So much lost.

Rory touches my arm. "Let's go inside and get you settled."

I open the big arched door and enter, shouldering my bag. The air is cool within, despite the heat of the day, and I smell basil and tomato and garlic, the signature notes of my stepmother Meadow's cooking.

When she rounds the corner, no one would have to tell you Rory is her daughter. Her long red hair is barely touched with gray, except for a single white streak on the right side of her face, a body that's gone cur-vier and curvier over the years, a face that still makes people stare. She's the woman my dad stuck with the longest, twenty years, and technically my stepmother, but she's the only mother I've known. My biological mother is a thin memory, a caricature of neglect, a fact my therapist called me on more than once. "Why," she asked in her mild way, "if you don't remember anything, did you name the winery for her?"

Anyway.

A teddy bear of a puppy rests in the crook of Meadow's arm, no doubt one of her rescues.

"Surprise," she says in her lovely, husky voice, coming over to kiss me. "I wanted to be sure you had a proper welcome."

I drop my bag and fling my arms around her shoulders, relief flooding me as I fall into her softness. Her skin smells of lavender. Her hair brushes my face, and her arms cradle me close, and I manage, just barely, not to cry. "I'm so glad you're here," I breathe. "Thank you."

"I have missed you so much, sweet girl," she murmurs into my ear. The puppy wiggles between us, making a protesting little noise, and we both let go, giving him some space. She keeps a hand on my shoulder, touches my face, brushes my hair back. "How are you holding up?"

"Good."

She knows that's not true. Everyone knows I'm a long way from good, but she smiles.

It's only now that I realize she doesn't look that great herself, that she's aged a decade since I saw her last, after the debacle at the winery. New tracings of lines show between her eyebrows, along her mouth, and the circles beneath her eyes are heavy and dark. "How are *you*?" I ask. "You look so tired."

She tsks. "Never tell a woman she looks tired, Maya. You know that." She kisses my head and pulls back. "Meet Cosmo," she says, holding the puppy up higher on her hip for my inspection. "That's his name for now. You can decide what you want to call him."

The puppy is a husky mutt of some kind, with thick gray and white fur and a retriever face with floppy black ears and the ice-blue eyes of one of his parents. He meets my gaze and gives a soft woof, not at all little or puppyish.

"Nice try, Meadow," I say, shaking my head. "I don't need a puppy. I haven't even been taking good care of myself."

"You don't have to decide right this minute," she says. "I'm going to stay with you for a little while, until you get on your feet."

"No," I say. "You don't have to stay." I really need to learn how to be on my own again. Be present with being single, with being in recovery, with the fact that my life has changed irrevocably.

"Not for long," she says. "Just a few days."

Again I notice the strain in her face, and it makes me feel guilty. How much has worry about me contributed, and how much is grief over my father's death? They've been divorced eight years but continued to be business partners—friends, even. In my opinion she never really got over him, and he would tell anyone who listened how leaving her was the greatest mistake of his life.

"I just want to help you get settled," she says, touching my shoulder, running her hand down my arm. I have so craved touch. It eases something deep within me. "Keep you company while you get your sea legs. Is that okay?"

I stroke Cosmo's ears, and they're softer than a velvet throw. Sensing my weakness, Meadow lifts him into my arms. I take his surprising heft without thinking, and automatically bend my face into his fur, inhale puppy smell and puppy breath as if it's the elixir of life. Maybe it is. He licks my ear, then again, as if it's his job to clean me up. "Can he sleep with me?" I ask.

"It's your house." She turns to Rory. "Can you stay a little while? I made lasagna."

Rory bends down to hug her. "Not today. The girls have ballet at three."

"Bring them afterward."

"Not today," Rory says firmly, and straightens, brushing a lock of her mother's hair over her shoulder. "I think Maya needs a chance to get her bearings without two wild girls."

"Fair enough."

I offer my cheek and Rory kisses me, her keys still in her hands. She's thinking of her own family; the dinner that's no doubt in the Instant Pot or the oven or the fridge; and the long antique dinner table she found at a garage sale, one that her husband refinished and distressed; and a meal with just the four of them, mom and dad and two girls, talking about their days. All the things we didn't grow up with. We ate plenty of spectacular food and sat around a table often, but never just as an ordinary family unit doing an ordinary, everyday supper. "Call me if you need anything at all," she says.

"I will."

She looks me hard in the eye. "Promise?"

I draw a cross over my heart and raise my hand, palm out. "I swear."

"Okay. I'll be back tomorrow." In my ear, she says quietly, "Don't let her bully you into anything."

"I won't," I say, but I'm not one for making my wishes known, which is probably why I took an axe to thirty-six barrels of painstakingly handcrafted wine. As my therapist pointed out, maybe it would be better to speak up before things get so dire. The puppy wiggles against me and I kiss his face.

"Including this adorable creature," Rory says.

When Rory leaves, Meadow swings around. Everything swings with her, lightweight skirt, hair, earrings. She's over fifty, but you'd never know it unless you got close. "I made the beds, all of them. I wasn't sure where you'd want to sleep."

I think of my old bedroom with all the posters and high school tchotchkes. Anxiety rises, too many things I don't want to deal with just now, not to mention the depressing aspects of returning to a childhood bedroom, even if it is because I inherited the house.

"How about the primary?" Meadow asks. "It's cleared out completely. Or you can sleep in the old guest room. Or Rory's room. Whatever you want."

"I haven't been here in so long," I say instead of making a decision, and carry the puppy to the long line of french doors that look out toward the tiled pool and the ocean beyond. Puppies can drown, I think, and hold him a little closer. "I thought it might be creepy, but . . ." I look around. The round table in the breakfast nook is the same, and the floors, and the big kitchen. "It's not."

It feels like home. Something in my body lets go. I can't afford to keep the house, but for now I can crash here. Get my life together.

"Let's go look," I say.

At 1:00 a.m., I'm lying in bed listening to the rise and fall of the waves. Cosmo sleeps next to me. I run my fingers through his fur, taking pleasure in the feel of his ear, his throat, the spiky hair along his shoulders. His belly is hot.

Outside, waves crash to shore. The sound comes in through the french doors, along with a cool breeze that whispers over my skin, brushing its fingers through my hair. The bed is deep and comfortable, a king that barely fits in the twenties-era room. The covers smell of fresh air. Meadow's touch, no doubt. She has a gift for homemaking, all those little things that make life just that tiny bit better—line-dried sheets, ironed cup towels, really good scented candles, the best soap, homemade bread tucked into a basket with one of those ironed cup towels. I don't have the gift, which women say now like a badge of honor, as if there is something suspect or maybe even laughable about homemaking, but I wish I did. I am just not domestically inclined, but I do appreciate it when someone else is. Rory has inherited it, of course. She likes to pick up antique linens when she finds them, and embroidered doilies, and old sheets and pillowcases that she sometimes dyes for the fun of it.

I just would never *think* of doing that. Or making all the beds for a returning child, like Meadow. Or inventing some fabulous dish like my dad.

I never had a passion until I discovered the alchemy of wine, that incredibly beautiful mix of soil and light and climate and grapes and time. It was the one thing that felt like it belonged to me. I have a palate and a nose, and from much too young an age, I could tell a great wine from a merely good one.

But I have to admit that being a vintner, especially the past few years, mainly gave me a great excuse to drink. Drink a lot. *Drinking* was my true passion, not the wonders of wine. From the very first sip when I was eleven years old, I felt that burst of relief. *Oh. This.*

The longing for it burns in my chest right now. I can close my eyes and imagine it, that sharp citrus flavor pouring down my esophagus, easing every nerve in my body, head to toe. Making everything go away. Stop. Making it all stop hurting, making my thoughts stop whirling around with such urgency.

I can't believe I will never—

My sponsor's voice nudges me. *Stay where your feet are.*

My feet are in this bed, in the room that belonged to my father until recently. It's not as weird as I thought it might be, again thanks to Meadow, who scrubbed him out of the space with a thoroughness that surprises me. It feels like a hotel room, smelling of lemon verbena and peppermint, the wooden floors gleaming, the little bathroom tidy, even to small wrapped soaps on the sink. My father might never have lived here at all.

None of which helps me fall asleep.

I haven't been able to sleep very well, not for ages. I thought this would get better with giving up the booze and getting into healthier habits, but that does not seem to be true.

What I do know is that lying here, trying not to think about drinking, is counterproductive. Trying not to think about anything is impossible. Leaving the puppy asleep, I swing my legs out of the bed and putter toward the door in my pajamas. They're soft, pretty, and I have a dozen pairs thanks to Meadow and my dad, who sent care packages every week with all kinds of things like this—pajamas and soft socks, organic lip care and expensive oils for my hair.

The house is dark. I tiptoe past Meadow's door, wondering again if I made the right choice. Should I have let her sleep in the bedroom where she spent so many years? I worried that it would make her sad, and I also really didn't want to sleep in my teenage bedroom and feel all the things that would bring up—the roots of my talent for obsessive love affairs, for obsessive thinking, ruminating, unhappiness. I've got enough feelings to sort out without facing my own teenage angst.

The stairs are cold underfoot. There was talk for years of installing underfloor radiant heat, but the cost was prohibitive. When I lived here I wore slippers with rubber soles because the tiles are not only cold but slick. Tonight I'll just live with it.

In the kitchen, the light is on over the stove. I open the fridge and just stand there, staring at the well-stocked shelves. Pellegrino and Topo Chico and other bottled water I know costs a fortune. The cheese drawer is full. Plump red grapes fill a yellow glass bowl, and small plastic containers hold portioned celery and carrot sticks, deli turkey, pickles, and condiments.

Not a single bottle of wine or beer or hard seltzer, which is what I'm subconsciously searching for. When I realize it, I sigh and reach for the grapes instead. The glass bowl makes a clank against the counter, and I remind myself to be careful here. The kitchen counters at the house at the winery were softer, polished wood. Another memory flashes, me and Josh on a random summer evening before the pandemic, listening to the calm melodies of Fleet Foxes or sometimes Bach or other baroque music, which Josh loved. On my own I tend toward female singers, everyone from Joan Baez to Pink, but I never insisted on my music with him. I didn't *mind* his choices, after all.

I stand there, wanting. Wanting, wanting, wanting in a way that's both pointed and vague. Wanting the life I destroyed, and not wanting it at the same time. Wanting one more day in the before times, wanting to yell at my father, wanting—

Well, wine, mainly.

Rubbing my tongue over my teeth, I turn and start going through the cupboards, looking for something. Anything to ease this hunger for the thing I can't have. Riffling through the pantry I poke through jars of rice, pasta, odds and ends that only a serious cook would bother with, preserved lemons and black cardamom and tinned tiny fish.

Where the *fuck* is the candy?

Finally, I find a Christmas tin, stuffed away forgotten in the back, and pop the lid off. Mother lode! Butterscotches and peppermints twisted into cellophane, some chocolates that have gone pale on the edges with age, an unopened bag of ribbon candy, and another of the old-fashioned hard candies that look like they've been sliced. I carry the whole big metal box out to the kitchen and pour it on the counter, spin open a butterscotch, and greedily pop it into my mouth.

Oh. Yeah.

The outside has that slight stickiness of age, but the sugar washes through my mouth, down my throat, hits my pleasure centers, and immediately some of the anxiety slides out of my body. Sucking on it happily, I turn the bags over to check the expiration dates: 6-3-17.

The chocolates are dead, then. I toss them in the trash. The rest are hard candies and should still be okay. At least until I can get something else in here.

Somewhere behind me or below me comes a sound. A soft thud and then something I can't quite identify—a little animal noise, maybe. I pause to listen, the hair on the back of my neck rising.

When I was a kid, I thought this place was haunted. It has so many alcoves and arches and rooms all opening one into another, the kitchen to the dining room to the salon to the patio to the living room to the stairs, that you could almost imagine a shadow running ahead of you into the next room. It was the biggest house I'd ever walked into, never mind lived in. When my mother died, we were living in a one bedroom with a galley kitchen, which would have all fit right into the salon.

When I listen, nothing more comes, and my greed overcomes my fear of walking spirits. I pick out another handful of candies to try—a long wavy piece of red ribbon candy, a bunch of the little slices, more butterscotches, which I stuff in the pockets of my pj's.

Another noise alerts me—this time more of a creak. I frown, listening hard, not chewing so I can hear, but it doesn't come again. Is it the puppy?

No. Coming from another direction. Probably the old house settling.

Or my dad, hanging around. "Don't even think about it, Dad," I say. "I still won't talk to you."

The room is silent. With my pockets stuffed full of candy, I head through the patio doors to the pool area. Outside, the sky is clear and starry, the edges washed out at either end by light, but in the middle is a host of stars. I think of the desert, shockingly filled with stars, so many it's hard not to get dizzy. As a city girl, I almost fell over the first time I saw the stars over the desert.

Out here the air is warmer than the house. I sit by the pool and look through a window cut in the shrubbery for this purpose. Popping hard candies in my mouth as often as necessary, I stay with my feet and look at the sky. For the moment, all is well.

It won't last, but right now I'm okay.

Chapter Eight
Meadow

After dinner, Maya goes upstairs and I wander out onto the balcony of the guest room. She decided on the main bedroom, which was appropriate, but it makes me feel a little lost, too. Lost again, maybe. I pride myself on being a survivor, but the well of sorrow over Augustus, then and now, seems almost insurmountable. That's the thing about grief. It spirals up and up and up, revisiting us again and again, reaching out with electrified tentacles to sting us when we least expect it.

I look out over the swimming pool to the constant waves. The noise of the ocean will drive me crazy overnight, rolling and rolling and rolling. Some people love it, but the endlessness of it, the knowing it will never stop, makes me restless. Only the house, settling in like a grandfather made of stone, calms me; only being inside the rooms I know so intimately eases me.

Perhaps I want to be with another version of myself, the me who learned to love the sound of the ocean as I slept next to my husband. Augustus bought the house with the first big money he earned, snapping it up thanks to a customer in the real estate business. He couldn't live here, and had no time to clear it out that first year. It was in bad shape when we first toured it, packed to the ceilings in some rooms with paper and books and scripts and things nobody wanted to examine too

closely, the kitchen both brilliant with all the tile and alcoves and hor-
rendous with neglect. The pool had been empty for decades, the living
room so dusty it was clear no one had entered the room in just as long.

The place captured me instantly the first time he showed it to me.
I saw the promise shining below the dust and mess.

We were young enough to tackle the renovations, doing them a
few at a time as we could afford them. As our success grew, the farm
and restaurant and my book, then our shared guest appearances on
everything from *Good Morning America* to *Top Chef* and guest spots all
over cable and the Food Network as that world exploded, brought in
money by the fistfuls. We poured much of it into our businesses and
the rest into the house, making it into the showpiece it deserved to be.

In the dark, I walk downstairs to the salon, turning on the lamp I
always liked, a Van Briggle blue ceramic shaped like a nymph. Soft light
falls over the sofa, a sturdy oversize velvet that I chose myself, not caring
if it lasted or not, but it did. The turquoise fabric is still cozy as I sink
into it, the color so extravagant. Opposite is a fireplace, cold and dark
just now, but split logs are nestled into their spot alongside.

It's quiet. I tuck my feet under me and pull an ultrasoft blanket
around me. Through the windows comes the sound of the sea, and the
furnace kicks on, blowing with gusto through the cast-iron vents.

How I loved this house! I never felt I belonged anywhere so much
as this, with Augustus and the girls and my glorious kitchen, and work
that made me happy. It was the best part of my life, from the second
time Augustus and I got together through the end of our marriage,
more than twenty years later.

Oh, Augustus, I think, wishing he could materialize for just a few
moments and sit with me here in this place we built together. I would
build a fire and hold his ghostly hand one more time.

Foolishness. I close my eyes and settle more deeply in the couch,
and imagine instead that I am back there, long ago, when the girls were
small.

In the late nineties, the girls were still in school, the farm was exploding in popularity, allowing me to pay off my benefactor, the widow who carried my loan, in record time, and Augustus worked all the time. Peaches and Pork was not yet at its zenith, but it was very busy. Both his ambition and his need to build something monumental kept him within the restaurant's walls for fifteen hours a day or more, and he rarely made it home to bed before midnight. I heard him come in, quietly, his keys clinking in the dish on our old colonial-style dresser, his belt rattling as he stripped off his jeans. I barely stirred most of the time, weary myself after long days at the farm, at work on my own empire, tending the girls, herding goats, and making meals for my family and myself.

I just liked hearing him go through the motions of leaving work behind and coming home to us. Whatever consumed him out there was left on the floor with his clothes, and he crawled in beside me, his big body sinking the bed. His feet touched mine, our toes greeting, before he plumped up his pillow and fell asleep, snoring gently through an open mouth.

Often, he slid his palms over my body, over a breast or hip, and teased me awake. His mouth fell on my shoulder or my neck, kisses warm and slow. He stroked my hair, slid my nightgown up and found my flesh and nestled his in it. It seems I remember the moon shining in through the french doors, painting us white. I remember the sound of the ocean, restless and crashing, nearly drowning the soft groans and murmurs of our lovemaking.

And then he would sleep, his face buried against my shoulder blades, one heavy arm over my hip. In the darkness, I listened to his breath, and mine, and the sound of dogs snoring on the floor, and a cat creeping back up to her place on the bed, draped over my ankle, and the girls safely asleep in the rooms down the hall, and the fields stretching out in abundance, and all was well. So very well.

Chapter Nine
Maya

Since there were legal charges over my winery debacle, one of the requirements of release from rehab was that I had to have a job lined up. Obviously my previous careers as sommelier, then vintner, were out. I couldn't face the restaurant business with all the attendant alcohol, and although Meadow offered me work at the farm, I declined. The work would break my heart, close as it was to the vines I'd lost.

But my family has long tentacles through the communities along the coast. Rory's husband knows the owner of the coffee shop on the edge of Santa Barbara. More than a shop, actually. They roast their own artisan blends and serve light meals, salads, and pastries baked down the block by the owner's sisters.

The day after I arrive home, I'm scheduled to start training at the café at 1:00 p.m. I need to make a meeting, in accordance with the rules of my early release. To do either, I will need to pick up my car at the restaurant, where it's been living since Meadow fetched it after I went to rehab.

First, however, Meadow makes me a breakfast of scrambled eggs and toast and then props herself on the cushiony kitchen stool. I sit at the end of the island so I can see the ocean. Cosmo is sprawled on the cool tiles next to Elvis, Meadow's big black shepherd. He tolerates the puppy, who has sneaked up close to his belly.

Yesterday I was eating in a cafeteria with a bunch of other people in a beige room with posters on the walls with slogans like "Nothing Changes if Nothing Changes."

Well, I think, blowing on the cheesy eggs, *I have made changes.* Everything has changed, actually, and a lot of it feels okay. Sunshine, the sound of the sea, the puppy at my feet. Meadow chatters brightly about the beautiful day and a friend of hers and all kinds of other inconsequential things. I've fallen out of the habit of small talk. A taut sense of . . . something—Impatience? Irritation? Anger?—starts to build in the connective tissue of my body. My neck starts to get tight, a clear warning signal.

"What are you even talking about?" I say aloud. The words are too sharp, and I know it the minute they leave my lips.

Her expression shows dismay for the space of a breath; then it's gone, covered up. "Sorry. Am I babbling?"

"Kinda."

She tucks a lock of hair behind her ear. Nods. Folds her hands in front of her. "I just don't know what to say."

"It's okay not to talk."

For a long moment, she stares at me. "What is this 'not talking' you speak of?"

I smile, as she meant me to do.

"It's a bad habit," she says, looking at her entwined fingers. Her ankles are tucked around the legs of the stool, and something about the girlishness pierces me. "I try to smooth things over with chatter. I know I do and tell myself not to, and then I keep—" She breaks off. Raises her brows. "Going."

Even this admission irritates me. Looking away, I tell myself it's mean to push her away after all she's done. She's trying hard to be upbeat for me.

What are you feeling?

I want her to go home. Leave me here to figure things out. But even as I think the words, think of ways to gently ask her to go back to her own house, she picks up a small statue of the Buddha in her palm. He's fat and jolly, and I immediately think of my father laughing his big laugh at the head of the table, telling some story to entertain us all. A sudden, searing pang burns through my chest, and I raise a hand to the place.

Tears gather in Meadow's eyes, and although she tries to blink them away, they fall down her cheeks. I try not to resist whatever it is that's coming up, this sense of my father, the one I missed, not the one I was so furious with. I say, "No one ever laughed like him."

Meadow shakes her head, dashes away the wet on her cheeks. "Sorry. It's not your job to make me feel better."

I reach for her freckled hand on the counter. "You also don't have to pretend not to feel anything."

"We bought this on one of our very first trips."

"Yeah?"

Her thumb moves over the belly, intimately. "We drove up to San Francisco, following the coast, checking out a list of restaurants we wanted to try on the way. We ate so much," she says. "Learned a lot, too. Your dad got the idea for his citrus carnitas on that trip, from a little hole-in-the-wall near Carmel."

I've heard part of the story before. It's even in her book, but one of the things I learned in rehab was to make space for people to talk. It wasn't really my strong suit before. Maybe it never will be, but it felt good to just listen to people without judgment. I can do that here. "You met Alice Waters and she took you to one of the farms she bought produce from."

Meadow smiles. "I'm sorry, I've told this before a million times."

"It's all good. I don't mind." I touch the Buddha's head. "I haven't heard this guy's story, though."

"Really?" She sets him down on the counter in a bar of light. "He was in a little Asian imports shop. I bought a blouse, and your dad bought me this and tucked it in my pocket." She sobers. "I was so in love with him."

"How old were you then, Meadow? Like, twenty or something?"

"Nineteen. Rory was just little." She sighs, more fervently. "I don't know what I was thinking."

I was just little, too. My sister and I are only eight months apart in age. On that day I was at home with my mother, who was at the time my father's wife. I don't bring this up, either, but I suddenly feel as if my dad is right there in the room with us, taking up all the space and air. I narrow my eyes, looking around, but of course the room is empty.

Meadow looks at the end of the counter, then back to me. "Something wrong?"

"Nope." I straighten, pushing away from the counter. "I need to get my car, if you wouldn't mind."

"I can do that."

———— ✑∿✒ ————

The car has been parked behind Peaches and Pork since I went to rehab. Meadow and Augustus drove up to the winery while I was passed out in Meadow's guesthouse and picked it up for me. As I unlock the car door, I get a sudden flash of myself that night, sticky with wine. I wasn't in blackout, amazingly enough, so I remember every detail of Josh's betrayal—his confession that he'd fallen in love with the woman whose name had been eternally on his lips for six months, Sophie—and then every step I took to destroy what we'd made together.

Such a beautiful wine.

A hot yearning stirs in my gut, a longing for the swirl of that beautiful pale yellow in a glass, the crisp sharpness on my tongue. It seems impossible that I will never taste that again, that I will never *make* it again. I am so good at it, and so not good at almost anything else.

Wine I know. Wine I understand.

The vines are still there. It just won't be me who makes the next batch. Josh will, with his great love, Sophie, the French winemaker who so besotted him. I had to "sell" my half, including the house, back to make up for the cost of the lost vintage. The only thing that makes me feel better is that he was always the business half, not the talent. Without arrogance, I know there are few people who have my nose, the innate ability I have to taste and smell the smallest variations in blends. Even the great Sophie, born and bred in Alsace, would not have my nose.

But I will never use it again.

Never ever again.

Grief breaks through my belly like shards of glass. I take a breath, bring myself back to this moment. It occurs to me that I feel terrible sorrow over losing my career, and the loss of my beloved wine, but almost nothing over the death of my father.

What kind of person am I?

The parking lot is weirdly empty, but of course, without Augustus there's not really a restaurant. I wonder what they're going to do with it now.

Them.

For the first time, it hits me. "Them" is me. It's mine. Not a responsibility I ever wanted and will have to unload, but that's also not something I have to deal with today. The manager is competent, and Meadow knows everything about it. I wonder why he didn't leave it to her.

Along with the house, which Meadow loves so madly and missed bitterly after the divorce. I don't want the responsibility of it, either, but at least it gives me a place to be until I figure myself out.

I look around for a minute at the patched asphalt, the saltwater wear on the wooden building, the outdated font on the sign. It's not seedy, not yet, but it has an air of weariness, a sense of time gone by.

"It used to be so glamorous," I say.

"Yeah. It really needs some updating. Probably the menus need an overhaul, too." Meadow hands me the key to my car. "I'd be happy to help you do that if you like."

I stare at her. "I'm not keeping it."

She swallows, looking at the building, and I think there are tears in her eyes.

I look away, ashamed that I feel nothing.

"Maybe you can give it a few weeks before you make any decisions."

I nod, tucking my hair behind my ear, then lean in and kiss her cheek. "Love you."

"Love you, too, baby," she says. "Text me later."

The car is a boring blue Prius, and even though it's been sitting, it starts right up. I turn to raise a hand to Meadow to let her know I'm okay, and she's standing in the empty parking lot, staring out toward the ocean under the morning gloom. Her skirt whips around in the breeze, and she reaches up to pull hair out of her mouth, and she looks so sad and broken that I turn off the car, step out, and cross the pavement to wrap my arms around her. This time she buries her face in my shoulder, and clings hard to my back, and I gently rock her, saying nothing. I can feel the dark hole of her grief right on the other side of her silence.

After a minute, she pats my shoulder blade. "You'd better get going."

"Yep. Text me and let me know you're all right."

She gives a little laugh.

I researched meetings before I got here, and although the most important thing is to get my ass to a meeting, I'm glad to have found a women's group at an Episcopal church. I sail in a few minutes late and slide into a chair in the back. I was afraid it would be in a circle, which means you have to face and look at everyone the whole time, but the rows are arranged to face the front and a speaker.

They're reading the opening, then take turns reading the steps. As I hear the familiar words, something in me lets go. It's a motley crew, from the very well-tended mom-type with her fancy manicure and yoga pants to a ragged girl next to me with unwashed hair who is chewing on her fingernails and doesn't look old enough to be in the meeting. She stares at me for a long moment when I come in, and I give her a lift of my chin. "Hey."

She turns back to the meeting. The speaker is a beanpole, and tall, with the serious, but shimmery and natural, face of an academic. Her story is one of high functioning that ended in a DUI where she blew a .34 BAC, which is pretty close to dead if you don't know.

She finishes and people speak, including the girl next to me, who is five days sober today.

"Good job," I say when she sits down again.

"Thanks." There's something so haunted about her, the circles under her eyes, the jutting of her collarbones, that I am transported to the face I saw in the mirror three days after I arrived at rehab. Scared, skinny, lost.

When the meeting ends, I give her my phone number. "Call or text if you need to talk."

"Yeah, thanks," she says, and stuffs it in her pocket.

"My name is Maya," I offer.

"Sunny," she says, looking over my shoulder toward the door.

"See ya," I say and step aside.

A handful of women greet me, offer the slogans that seem so corny unless you need them: *keep coming back; it works if you work it; easy does it.*

As I leave my shoulders are looser. My head is higher. It's like working out. Getting to the gym is sometimes hard, but it feels so good when you've done it.

The Brewed Bean Café is a bit off the beaten track, too far from the university to appeal to students and far enough from the tourist track to get only a few stragglers. It's a local joint that's established a very good reputation over the past eight years. I've been in only a couple of times—let's be honest: I'd never have chosen coffee if beer were available—but the minute I walk in, that annoyance I've been carrying along the back of my neck drops away. It smells deeply, richly, intensely of freshly roasted coffee. Small tables line the big windows that face both toward the bluffs to the south and the ocean to the west, though there isn't really an ocean view, at least from this level. There's a sidewalk, then a street, and then a row of palm trees and scraggly oleander bushes.

Inside the floors are warm, worn wood, and the bar looks like it spent a few centuries in a pub, carved of more of the same shade of wood. Industrial-style cage chandeliers fitted with old-school light bulbs hang from the ceiling. At this in-between hour, there are few customers—a pair of businessmen in the corner; a woman about my age with fabulous long, shiny hair hunched over a laptop; a weary-looking man by the window who makes me think of Irrfan Khan, a Bollywood actor I love.

"Hi!" A woman in her forties, with short dark hair and a turquoise apron over her jeans and T-shirt, greets me. "What can I get you?"

"Hi. My name is Maya Beauvais. I'm here about the job?"

"Oh sure! I'm Jessica. I'm the manager—and Jacob's wife. We've both known Nate since kindergarten." She waves for me to follow her through a doorway.

"You must know my sister, too, then. Rory."

She looks over her shoulder, startled. "You really don't look like sisters."

"No."

We move through a small kitchen, which I notice with approval is fantastically clean. A girl wearing a hairnet and plastic gloves is portioning salad into what look like earth-friendly containers. "Renee, this is Maya. She's starting on second shift this week, front of the house."

She nods at me, and I think she might be stoned, or maybe just into the task. "Hi."

I wave, hurrying to catch up with Jessica. She leads me up a set of old wooden stairs to a small office outside a big open room with windows looking toward the alley. Burlap bags of what I assume are coffee beans are stacked on shelves. A big metal machine that makes me think of a still dominates the room. I breathe in the heady, thick scent of coffee. "This is where you roast?"

"Yeah. It's pretty cool. Have you ever done it?"

"No. Looks intriguing."

"I'll have Jacob pull you up here the next time. I don't have the knack, but he can always use a spare pair of hands."

"Cool."

"Have a seat," she says, and pulls out some paperwork from a file cabinet. "I just need you to sign a W-2."

It's weird, becoming an employee again, but it also feels like something I can manage. Making lattes. Clearing tables. A J-O-B, they call it in recovery lingo. I scribble my name on the form and pass it back.

"I'm sorry about your dad," she says.

"Thanks."

"He was quite a character. So charming and good looking."

"Yep." I wonder if I should seem more distressed, but I can't start with lies. "We weren't actually that close the past decade or so, honestly."

"I get it. I worked at Peaches and Pork for a while in high school."

I give a half laugh. "Yeah, me too."

She smiles. "Well, we're not quite the operation it is, but we're proud of what we've built here. The café is on the main level, which is where you'll be working, as a barista. This is the roasting area, obviously."

Eyeing the bags, I ask, "Do you sell a lot of your own beans?"

"We do. It's our main source of income, actually. We use the coffee in the café, but we also sell it in bags, half pound, one pound, more by special order. Several restaurants in the area have standing orders for their own roasts."

"Really." It's a comment more than a question. And even though that snide part of my brain wants to dismiss the artisanal part of it—Rory's set are all hipsters—I'm intrigued. "Like wine, in a way."

"Exactly what my husband says. Maybe you'd be good at it, with your history. It's really fascinating, honestly."

I appreciate her not avoiding the elephant in the room. "Interesting."

She stands. "Let me show you around. Have you ever been a barista?"

"Nope."

"C'mon. I could do with a good espresso."

Chapter Ten

Norah

I recognize Maya the minute she comes into the café. She moves like her dad, with the same long, loose limbs, and her face is a feminine version of his, the heavy brows and wide mouth, and the same sprinkle of freckles over her nose. It sends a little stab through my heart, and I can't help staring. She sees me looking at her and gives a quick smile.

It makes me feel guilty.

Long before anyone in the house was stirring, I slipped out with my backpack and washed in the outdoor shower, hidden from the windows behind a wall of shrubbery. I dried off with a towel I'd taken from the linen cupboard, and squeezed my hair, shivering in the gloomy morning. For the moment, I have plenty of clean clothes, but I'll eventually have to figure out how to do my laundry.

Not today. I tucked the towel away on a branch behind the guesthouse to dry and headed down the hill toward town, feeling absurdly good. I'd forgotten how great the payoff could be in the survival stakes. Not that I want to stay in this difficult space, but I take pride in my ability to be adaptable no matter what. I can eat for days on five dollars, get shiny clean in a gas station restroom, hustle a job from almost anyone, anywhere.

I spent most of the morning at the local library, doing research in the local newspapers from the seventies and eighties and nineties, trying to trace the story of Peaches and Pork and whatever other news I could discover about Augustus, or Meadow, or both. It gives me something to do besides freak out over my precarious situation. And maybe I'll find a story in the whole thing.

One thing I found was their wedding announcement.

LOCAL LUMINARIES WED

Local restaurateur Augustus Beauvais wed organic farmer Meadow Truelove in a ceremony on a moonlit beach last Saturday. In attendance were the daughters of each, Rory Truelove and Maya Beauvais, with Jared Humphrey officiating.

The bride and her attendants wore simple white lace accented with red velvet, and bare feet, with head-dresses of white dahlias and red roses. The groom's suit was hand-tailored by Georges Durant, Montecito.

The couple met at the farm, discovered kismet, and joined forces in celebrating the growing farm-to-table movement in Central California.

Neither couple has living parents or grandparents, but they were held in love by their restaurant and farm families. They will reside in Santa Barbara in the famed Belle l'Été house, built in 1922 by director Simon Greenfield and occupied by him until his death in 1990.

One color photo showed them kissing against a setting sun, Augustus so much taller, his stance so possessive that I felt an unexpected surge of jealousy. She's dipping slightly backward, trusting in his embrace, her left arm falling toward the earth, her hand holding her bouquet, as if she's been chased and captured somewhat unwillingly. Augustus pulls her pelvis into him, bending forward to kiss her. So hungry.

The other photo was one I'd seen before in innumerable articles about them, Augustus standing slightly behind her, his arm circling her rib cage, right below her breasts. She leaned back into him, secure, her face serene. Her red hair sprayed across his black shirt, glittering. He looked sensual and commanding. She looked like Demeter, taming the god of the underworld. Hades? Poseidon? I can't remember.

This was the photo that gave me a girl crush on her. They're both thirty years younger than now, Meadow in her twenties, Augustus a decade or more older. She was impossibly beautiful in that way that's hard to pin down, her skin fresh and perfect as milk, her eyes long and blue, her lips full and red. A fairy-tale being, a creature from another world.

So very, very sensual, both of them. It oozed from their pores, the slight upturn of their lips, the placement of his hand, the angle of her arm, reaching up behind her.

I felt it again, the surge of longing. For Augustus, my lost lover, but also for Meadow. Not exactly sexual, but not exactly not sexual, either.

My gut started to rumble with hunger and I caved, packing up my notes and carrying my backpack to the coffee shop I like. I checked the balance on my debit card—$241.32. I had to find a job as fast as possible, and plan to make the rounds at restaurants after 2:00 p.m., the classic dead time.

Damn. Restaurants. I thought I was finally free of them.

Whatever. For today, I had enough for a meal. At the Brewed Bean, I ordered a hefty sandwich and a bottomless cup of coffee with cream to give me more time to sit.

Settled, I pulled out my notebook and leafed through the pages, trying to puzzle out the answers to certain gaps in Meadow's life. I mean, maybe I should be mad at her over the way she kicked me out, but I get it. If I were her, I wouldn't like me, either.

Over my generous sandwich of thinly shaved Black Forest ham and chicken and slices of provolone, stacked with sprouts and cucumber and tomatoes, I went through my notes—sketching out the timeline backward. Now, of course, she's the highly regarded ruler of a small empire of organic farms, author of a famous history and a cookbook, and former wife of Augustus. The story of her life in central California is well documented, especially in conjunction with Peaches and Pork.

But in months of looking, I haven't been able to find a single shred of anything about her before she arrived in Carpinteria, her very young daughter in tow. No school records, no marriages, nothing. It's not such an ordinary name that it shouldn't have connections to something.

I'm starting to think she made it up. Which leads to the question, Why? What did she leave behind?

As I'm assembling a set of clear questions, a woman breezes in through the door, ringing the bell. I know her instantly. Maya Beauvais, Augustus's daughter. I'm not sure what I was expecting from someone who has such a reputation for drama, but not this calm-looking person who introduces herself to the owner. Her hair is her best feature, thick and curly, just this side of out of control, and she covers it with a yellow paisley scarf to go to work. I like the way she works efficiently, without hurry, someone who knows her way around the food business, because of course she does.

Observing her from the corner of my eye, I wonder what it was like growing up with such big personalities, people who were obviously a bit obsessed with each other. Augustus didn't talk much to me about his past or his family until Maya crashed and burned three months ago, and then it was his main focus. Getting her into rehab, making sure it was the best available, working on her legal issues, trying to find ways to get back into her good graces. One of the great regrets of his life was that he'd left Maya to her addicted biological mother when he married Meadow. He never told me the whole story, but I could piece some of it together. Upon the breakup of her marriage, the mother succumbed to her addiction to booze and pills. It didn't even take quite a year before she killed herself, and Maya went to live with Meadow, Augustus, and her stepsister, Rory.

I lean against the window and take a sip of cold coffee. What was that year like for a little girl? When Augustus told me the story, I kind of hated him for leaving her. How could he have done that? Why didn't he take her with him? I said it aloud: "You abandoned her."

Augustus only nodded, looking at his hands, as if the answer to why were written on his palms.

My watch dings on my wrist, reminding me that it's time to go see about finding a job. I gather up my things, and reluctantly leave yet another fascinating Beauvais. At least I have a face now when I hear her moving around upstairs.

Briefly, I wish we could be friends. We're close in age. We have some things in common, the food business, me writing, her doing. And she must have loved Augustus on some level, even if she hadn't spoken to him in eight years.

Which is exactly why we will never be able to be friends. I sling my pack over my shoulder, glancing back just once to see she's absorbed in making a coffee.

Onward.

Chapter Eleven
Meadow

After Maya drives away, I let myself into Peaches and Pork. The manager, Kara, is going to meet me here so that we can go over what the next steps should be, both for handling employees and for the near future of the restaurant. Technically, all but my 10 percent of the restaurant belonged to Augustus, but practically, I've participated at least peripherally forever, even after the divorce.

It's hard to let go when you've been married a long time. It felt as if we had to find every single one of the threads that connected us and snip each one individually. A long and trying process. Some of the threads were more like steel cables that couldn't be severed.

Like the restaurant into which we'd poured so much of ourselves, and my first book, which is not only a history of the foodie world in the area and Peaches and Pork, but our love story. And of course we couldn't divorce the girls. He could no more stop being Rory's father than I could stop being Maya's mother.

The restaurant is cold inside, the chairs upturned on the tables so the staff could sweep and vacuum after the last service. The bar is tidy, with only a few glasses on the drainboard, the evidence of after-work drinks. A red wineglass, a highball, a pint glass. I look in the bar fridge and see that the beers have been stocked. Containers of limes and cherries and other bar standards stand at the ready. They'll be slimy by the time service starts again, but that's not my concern.

It's luxurious to be here by myself. I always like a restaurant after hours, seeing the bones of the place, moving freely, and this one is deeply familiar. I wander through the bar, adjusting a couple of bottles—Jim Beam and Johnnie Walker Red—then move into the kitchen.

I'm not prepared for the mess. No one has been here; the restaurant has been closed since his death. Unlike the dining room, the kitchen is strewn with paper and muddy footprints, everything out of order. Most of it is the detritus of a lifesaving operation, discarded medical supplies, the rolling pass-out bar shoved out of the way. A plastic container that must have been sitting on the counter has been knocked over by the walk-in, shriveled carrots spilling out on the floor. An enormous skillet is upended nearby, and piles of bar towels, some stained, some not, are scattered everywhere. I don't know whether I should enter to pick things up.

Probably not.

I creep closer, frowning. For a heart attack, there is a lot of mess. Discomfort swirls in my belly, and I move a little closer, trying to see if there's evidence of anything. Muddy footprints smear the white tiles, and there's a touch of blood on the floor, too, but not much. Maybe he hit his head on the way down.

Otherwise, I don't see anything out of the ordinary. The stainless-steel counters are clean. The kitchen, like the front of the house, had been put to bed.

I wander into the office. It appears to be undisturbed. The surface of the desk is cluttered with papers, but most of the rest is fairly tidy—notebooks lined up next to the computer where he kept his notes, pens and pencils in empty jars, olives, peppers, capers, all normal size, not restaurant-huge. This single detail knocks the wind from my lungs and I sink into his chair, close my eyes.

Augustus.

All at once I smell him, that particular scent of coriander and promise. A sense of pressure weighs against my body, as if he's sitting on top of me. For a space of seconds, I'm frozen, feeling as if I'm suspended within the essence of the man himself. I want to hang there, breathing him in, but the pressure grows heavier and heavier, and I open my eyes with a gasp.

Nothing, of course.

How can he be gone?

An envelope catches my eye. *Maya Beauvais*, it reads in his curiously beautiful handwriting. I pick it up and there's heft to it. Was he writing to her at rehab? Setting her up for success when she reentered the world? I shuffle around on the desk, looking for another letter for Rory, but there isn't one. It gives me a pang to imagine how she will feel when she realizes he's slighted her. To protect her, I pick up the letter to Maya and tuck it in my bag. I'll give it to her privately.

"Hello!" a voice calls from the other room. I stand up to greet Kara. She's a square, solid person with shorn black hair that's bleached out on top and combed into short spikes. Her brown arms are covered with full tattoo sleeves illustrating the history of her life. "How you doing?" she asks.

"Okay." I lift one shoulder. "You?"

Her face has aged a decade overnight, giving her bags under her eyes and jowls that are suddenly soft, as if she hasn't slept since Augustus died. "Not good. I mean, he was a dick, but he was like my brother, man." Her face crumples and she covers it with a hand, trying to hide her grief.

"Oh, Kara," I say, flowing toward her, gathering her close. "Sweetheart, I'm so sorry."

She resists at first, taut and aloof, but then a cry rises from her throat and she leans into me, her arms tight around my body. I hold her as harsh sobs explode from her like they're ripping holes in her skin. In all the years I've known her, she's never once wept. It makes my heart burn, but I don't offer any platitudes or meaningless phrases. Sometimes there's nothing to say. The best I can do is give her some room to let go.

After a long while she sighs against me, then straightens, wiping her face with her palms. I reach for a box of tissues from behind me in the office and hand them over. "Thanks," she says. "Sorry about that." She wipes her face, almost harshly, leaving behind a couple of pieces of lint.

I pluck them off. "Don't be sorry."

"I guess you loved him as much as I did, once upon a time."

"Yes." I look toward the area where the medical debris is scattered, thinking of his body lying there lifeless, and a pain burns through my lungs. "Did they release his body yet?"

"I don't think so." She blinks.

"Is there a cause of death?"

"The EMTs were pretty sure it was a heart attack, but I guess you never know."

"There were no drugs or anything in evidence?"

"No, I made sure to look. And I paid off the girl. I don't think she'd been with him before, so she was really freaked out. I sent her packing with an NDA, so we'll be fine." She eyes me. "Though I'm surprised you cared about protecting Norah."

"Not Norah." I shake my head. "Maya and Rory."

She snorts softly. "You think they don't know their daddy was a player?"

"They know," I say. "But why rub it in their faces?"

"You're a good mom," she says. "Let's get some coffee and sit down. Make a plan. You think we can keep the place open?"

"I have no idea. We need to look at the books and figure it out."

Kara heads into the bus station, where the coffee machines are, and I start to follow, but something catches my eye, a flash of red by the stove, and I turn, startled. For a moment I stand there, sure I saw something. Was it a rat? Something that fell from the counter? I step closer, looking, but there's nothing.

Maybe only his aura, left behind where he spent so much time. I shake my head and follow Kara.

We pour coffee and spread out at one of the tables in the dining room. Kara has opened her laptop with the accounting spreadsheets and we're talking about the possibilities of reopening. "We need a memorial," she says.

"He was adamant. Nothing like that. We discussed it only a few weeks ago."

Her gaze sharpens. "You did?"

I lie easily, even though he doesn't strictly deserve it. "It came up when Maya went to rehab. He really doesn't want a funeral."

"That's a mistake." She takes a sip of coffee. "Your daughters, the employees, the press—everybody will want to pay their respects."

I lay my hand over hers on the table. "You want a memorial, and I get it, but I just feel like he'd haunt me."

"Is it written down somewhere? Because I'm really not feeling it, to just let him go, do nothing."

Here again, I run into the reality that I just can't get used to, even after so long—that I don't actually have any legal sway over anything to do with him. "I don't know."

She drinks coffee. "When they release the body, what then?"

"Cremation."

"And the ashes?"

"He wanted to be scattered in the ocean."

"Fair enough." She ducks her head to hide the tears that shine in her eyes again.

"You can be there. When we do it."

She sniffs, and I can tell she's formulating her own plans. A wake, I'm guessing, full of raucous toasts and a lot of hard drinking. "All good."

I let it go. "Let's see about reopening."

The numbers are far worse than I expected. I stare at the columns grimly. "This is pretty bad."

"Yeah." She sighs. "I warned him that we needed to overhaul the menu and freshen the joint up, but he was stubborn."

I'd had the same conversation with him. It would have been perfect to use the quarantine periods to do this work, but he wouldn't hear of it, insisting that his employees needed the money he'd spend on the renovations.

Which was partly true, but if there was no restaurant, there'd be no employees. I rub my eyebrow.

A cop wanders into the room from the kitchen, startling us both. He's a tall, good-looking guy with super-short black hair. "Hey," he says. "I let myself in the back door."

Kara drawls, "Well, come on in, Officer. How can we help you?"

"Hi," he says, offering a hand to me. "I'm Officer Vaca, investigating officer."

I incline my head, a whisper of unease blowing through my body. "Meadow Beauvais."

His eyes sharpen. "Wife?"

"Ex," I correct. "A longtime ex."

"When did you divorce, ma'am?"

Ma'am. Ugh. "In 2014."

"But she's still involved in the business," Kara adds.

"Did you inherit the restaurant, then?" he asks.

"No, I own a portion, but most of it went to our daughter. His daughter, actually. My stepdaughter."

"You're okay with that?"

I shrug, meeting his gaze evenly. "I have my own business, Officer, and it's a lot healthier than this one."

"Mmm. What's that business?"

"Meadow Sweet Organic Farms."

"Really?" He looks up at me. "Oh, hey. You wrote that book."

"Yes."

He scribbles something down, underlines it. "I just have a few questions. It was pretty chaotic the night Augustus died, and I know we talked to you"—he nods toward Kara—"that night, but I need to go over a couple of things, if that's all right."

"Sure."

"Are there any cameras or anything on the property?"

Kara nods. "Several. One on the parking lot, one on the front steps, a couple from different angles in the dining room, in case of disputes."

"Nothing in the kitchen?"

"He didn't want anything in there. Kitchen work can be pretty freewheeling."

"I see." He looks first at me, then Kara. "You're the manager, right? Kara Williams?"

She nods.

"Where were you that night?"

"At home with my wife, as I've already said several times. I came down here when the ambulance was called."

"And who called you?"

"He was here with an employee."

"Oh, right." He flips back to a previous place in his notes. "Emma Sunderman."

Kara and I exchange a glance.

"How about you, Ms. Beauvais? Where were you?"

"Home alone in Ojai until Norah called me. His girlfriend," I supply before he can ask. "She was hysterical, so I talked to Kara, then went to see if I could calm Norah down."

"Did you?"

I shrug. "I finally got her to take an Ambien and she went to sleep."

He nods. "When was the last time you saw him?"

"That afternoon. I dropped off some produce from my farm, and we spent an hour talking about arrangements for our daughter's return from—" I stop, realizing that she might not want me spewing about her addiction.

"From?"

I glance at Kara, who gives me a bare nod. "From rehab. She was about to be released."

"And was she?"

"Yes. She's living in the house he left her."

"That's the house on the mesa?"

"Yes."

He snaps his notebook closed and tucks it back in his pocket. "All right. That's all I need for now."

"Can we clean up the kitchen yet?" Kara asks.

"Should be all right. I'll double-check and give you a call in an hour or so."

"Do you know when they'll release his body?" I ask. "We'd like to make arrangements."

"I don't actually know the answer to that question. Toxicology sometimes takes a couple of weeks."

I frown, unsettled. "That seems long. I thought it was a heart attack."

"Sudden death has to be examined, by state order," he says. A beat of something, then: "I'm sure it'll be done soon."

"All right. Thanks."

He salutes us and wanders out.

Kara says, "That was weird."

"Very," I agree. I stare at the door where he exited, wondering what's really on his mind. What are they looking for in the toxicology reports?

I shake it off. "Never mind. What's next?"

Chapter Twelve
Maya

After work, I walk from the café to Rory's house for dinner. I can tell Meadow and Rory have set up a rotating shift of babysitting me, and tonight is her turn. She invited me to supper, and I'm grateful. The tag-teaming will have to end, but tonight I'm hungry and happy after the shift, looking forward to a good meal, glad to have done something useful with my day. My purse is safely stuffed with bags of Jelly Belly beans, my drug of choice. As I walk, I pop them into my mouth one at a time. Pear. Dr Pepper. Tutti-Fruitti. Never licorice, because I pluck them out. Licorice is an abomination.

It's the little things.

The house sits on a street lined with jacarandas that are spectacular when they're in full bloom. Right now it's roses, and in Rory's yard they climb up the wall in a profusion of pink. I open the gate, and a big mutt the size of a Saint Bernard but with the curly fur of a chocolate poodle comes loping around the house to greet me. I bend and kiss his head. "Hi, Nemo."

The door bursts open and my nieces spill out to the broad porch, then down the stairs toward me. "Aunt Maya!" they cry. "We misseded you!"

I kneel to welcome their hugs, and they slam into me with the full force of their small bodies, arms and legs flinging around me, hair in my face, in my mouth, the smell of sunshine and dirt and play filling my nose. I am engulfed by them, and close my eyes. "I missed you guys so much!"

Polly, older at five, with wispy blonde hair and Rory's beautiful blue eyes, pulls back and puts her little hands on either side of my face. "Mommy said you were sick. Are you better now?"

A quick rush of tears stings the back of my eyes. I hate, hate, hate that this has spilled over into their lives. "Almost," I say.

"Good." She leans in and kisses me on the lips. Nathan does this. Kisses everyone on the mouth—child, acquaintance, whoever. His philosophy of kisses is that if you love someone, you can kiss them on the mouth. I love it so much.

"Me too!" says three-year-old Emma, pursing her lips. She's as perfectly round as a baby doll—round eyes, round cheeks, round yellow curls. I bend in and kiss her wet little mouth and she says, "Mwah!"

For one second, the harsh doom of *almost* hangs over my happiness. *You almost lost this forever.* I feel winded and just look at them both for two seconds, which seems almost too long. Shaking it off, I take a hand in each of mine. "Let's go in and see your mom."

The house is not large, a Craftsman bungalow painted pale green with white trim. A fabulous porch sports dozens of pots—cacti and small shrubs and things I don't know the name of, all color and shape and California. The entire neighborhood is made up of bungalows in all their beauty, mullioned windows and wide porches, those graceful Arts and Crafts details. It would have been out of reach for a young, newly married couple if not for the generous assistance of Nathan's parents.

Rory appears at the screen door, her coppery hair glittering in the long slant of sunlight reaching from the western sky. "Hey, girls, let her up!"

I kiss each head. "They're fine."

"How was your first day?" she asks. Her feet are bare beneath a yellow sprigged sundress, and her toenails are painted bright green.

"Great, honestly."

I slide in when she holds the screen door for me. The living room spills into the dining room into the kitchen, where my brother-in-law, Nathan, stands, a white apron around his body. "Hey, Nathan," I call, raising a hand. I feel off-kilter, unsure of what I should do. I haven't been here in quite a while, haven't seen Nathan since New Year's Eve, when he escorted me out of a party and poured me into an Uber. I flush, remembering. By then, the high-level but still acceptable drinking I'd maintained for more than a decade had spilled over into messy and obvious, and I couldn't seem to get it back under control no matter what I tried. I made a million rules: Only one drink. Or maybe only one drink per hour. A glass of water between glasses of wine. Switch to beer. Use a small glass. When the moderation techniques inevitably failed and I awakened in the morning with yet another debilitating hangover, I'd vow that today I wouldn't drink. Just for today. My afternoon self would argue that I deserved wine, that it was my business, my *talent*.

The memory of New Year's Eve shames me, lighting heat along my cheekbones. But Nathan comes right over and envelops me in a bear hug. He's big enough to make it count, tall and broad shouldered, his blond hair smelling of ocean. "I'm so glad to see you, Maya," he says, squeezing me and rocking me. "We're all so glad you're okay."

As he releases me, he kisses my mouth soundly.

"Thanks for the job hookup," I say.

"You are so welcome." He pulls me by the hand to sit at the counter. "You started today, right? Did you like it?"

"Yes," I say honestly, and pluck a chip from the bowl. "I'm intrigued by the roasting process and how it works."

"Yeah, well, I know Jacob is deep into it, so I'm sure he'd love to regale you with every detail."

I nod.

"We're making tacos. Is that good?"

"Sure." The kitchen smells of cumin and chili powder. He picks up a pint glass full of beer. "We have some NA beers for you. Couple of them come highly recommended."

My throat aches with longing for the amber ale in his glass. A slight foam floats on the top as he takes a sip, and I can feel it in my mouth, sloshing into my belly. I swallow, reach into my pocket for some Jelly Bellies, and pop one in my mouth. Cotton candy. Or maybe bubble gum. "Can I just get some water or something? I'm kinda worried the NA beer might be triggering."

"Oh. Oh, sorry. Should I . . . ?" He points to his beer as if to pour it out.

I really want to say yes. *Please pour it out and don't drink in front of me right now. Just for a little while, just until I get used to this.* But I don't, just as I always let Josh choose the music. "No, it's all right."

"Topo Chico?" Rory says, reaching into the fridge to pull out two slightly blue bottles of Mexican soda water. "That's what I'm having."

I'm grateful. "Yes. No glass." It's cold and very fizzy and remarkably satisfying when I glug it down. I seriously doubt she'd be having water if I weren't here—she's a card-carrying member of the Mommy Wine Club—but I'm grateful.

Sitting there, in a place I've eaten hundreds of times, I feel like an outsider. The square. The uncool one. Unenlightened.

I spill a handful of jelly beans on the counter and pluck out a light-blue one.

"How's it going with Mom?" she asks, her eyebrows twitching.

"Mmm. Okay."

"So she's hovering?"

"Yeah, but she means well."

"Of course, but she's also clueless sometimes." She reaches for the speckled pink jelly bean, and I slap her hand away.

"Tutti-Fruitti is mine."

"Scuse me." She leans on the counter. "I know you have more."

I've always had a candy habit. As a kid, it was all the dissolvable varieties, Smarties and SweeTARTS, candy cigarettes. Rory was more discerning—she liked more sophisticated things, such as Heath bars and Toblerone. She struggles with keeping her weight down, just as Meadow does, so she doesn't indulge much. I raise an eyebrow. "I didn't want to tempt you."

"I'll watch my own weight, thank you very much." Her eyes widen as I pull out the gigantic Jelly Belly bag. "Jeez, Maya. You're going to give yourself diabetes."

Miming scales with my hands, I incline my head. "Cirrhosis, diabetes."

"Good point." She straightens. "Have you talked to Josh yet?"

My ex, both romantic and business partner. "No. Probably the only talking we'll do from here on out is by lawyer."

"That's kind of sad. You guys were together a long time."

"Yeah." A pang moves through my heart. Unbidden, I see his bright blue eyes, the way his cheeks crinkled when he laughed. We met in college and shared a lot of really big dreams, including the one I destroyed in my drunken rage, a virtually perfect sauvignon blanc. "I guess. But we really had already broken up, you know. I hung on way too long before . . ."

"You took an axe and gave the wine forty whacks," Nathan says, grinning.

"Haha," I say, but it's good to be able to joke about the whole thing.

Rory says, "I thought you'd offered your share of the winery to make up for the damages."

"He wants to keep the name and label." Which is my mother's name, Shanti, and my label design, which is a beautiful logo, meant to appeal to women browsing the shelves. It worked. I've given up a lot, but I'm not giving that. "It's up to the courts to decide."

"I can't believe he's being such a dick," Rory says.

"Well, to be fair, the entire vintage was destroyed."

"Man," Nathan says, shaking his head half in wonder, half in admiration. "That had to be one big mess. Did you swim out?"

I pick out a red jelly bean, letting the night rise up in memory, the bits and pieces that I have—flashes of swinging the axe, of putting out my hands to catch the wine spurting from the barrels, of being as sticky as a child after a carnival, of sloshing through wine to go to the stairs. The cold, starry sky overhead as I dialed the phone. "I definitely needed waders." I take a sip of my drink, touch the pain in my chest.

"We don't have to talk about this," Rory says. "Plenty of time for that."

"Dinner's ready," Nathan says, and takes a big gulp of beer. I watch his throat swallow, then look away.

Rory links her arm through mine. "Sorry about that."

I'm not alone, I think. Rory will always be in my corner.

The dinner is simple and straightforward, family food, kid food, the fresh tacos and lettuce and chopped fresh tomatoes that taste of sunshine and summertime. "These tomatoes must be from Meadow Sweet," I say, unable to stop shoving them into my mouth. I have such greed for things now, weird things, but my therapist tells me to just go for it. Better than wine.

"Yeah, she starts them in January in the greenhouse."

"So good." I spoon another hefty helping into a fried soft corn tortilla and eat it plain.

Polly says, "You really like tomatoes, huh?"

I pause midbite to give her wide eyes. "You don't?"

"Not like that," she says with a raised brow.

"Dude, the shade!" I wipe my fingers, blot my mouth. "Try again."

"No, I'm good."

"Do you have a whole one left, Nathan?" I ask.

"Sure." He pops into the kitchen area and brings back a beautiful red-and-yellow heirloom with deep creases cracking the top and bottom, along with a sharp knife.

I hold up a finger to Polly. "It's all in the presentation." I slice a beautiful chunk from the tomato and sprinkle it with salt and pepper very lightly. "Now try."

She gives me a look, pulling back her chin like she'll be infected. "No thanks."

Emma holds out her round little hand. "Me! I will."

I give her a big smile and hand it over. She slurps it with great enthusiasm. Polly rolls her eyes. "She's only doing it for you."

I smile, slicing another piece of tomato for myself. "That's okay."

Rory has a funny expression on her face.

I take a bite, incline my head. "What's up?"

"You just reminded me of Dad right then. You have a lot of his mannerisms."

A wave of emotion swells through my gut, resistance and recognition rolled up together. "He was good at getting us to try things."

"Remember the artichoke challenge?"

I smile, reluctantly.

"Tell us," Nathan says, loading another taco.

"He made them forbidden," Rory says. "We weren't allowed to ever eat them. Ever. He told us they were only for adults, and then he and Mom created an artichoke garden."

I laugh. "With a fence around it, so we couldn't get in."

"And then, at the end of the season—must have been what? July?"

I nod. "They 'allowed' us to watch them harvest them."

"And cook them."

"And by this time, of course," I add, "we're dying to taste artichokes, and the air smells of garlic and spices and fresh lemon." My mouth waters. "They sat down to eat and we're watching them with our usual dinner in front of us. I say, 'C'mon, you guys, are you really not going to share?'"

"So Mom looks at Dad and he looks at her, and they say something like, 'The artichoke committee wouldn't like it,' but of course they shared."

"And they were so insanely great." The craving for that flavor wells up in my mouth, so intense that I'm going to have to stop and buy artichokes on the way home, even if they're not yet in season. I shake my head. "So good."

"Artichokes are disgusting," Polly says.

"Yeah, that's what you think," Rory says. "You never had them the way your grandpa cooked them."

"When is he coming over?"

I look up, alarmed.

Rory shakes her head at me, fiercely. "I don't know, baby."

Nathan drains his glass. "Man, that was an elaborate scheme to get kids to like a particular vegetable."

"Yes," I say, but I'm reeling with the recognition that Rory hasn't told the girls that Augustus is dead. I give her a wide-eyed look, and she shakes her head back at me, like *back off*.

Nathan, oblivious, rests his fingers on the ring of the glass. "You guys had a weirdly happy childhood, you know that?"

"Some parts, for sure," Rory says.

"For sure," I say in agreement, but I hardly know how to sit there with such a yawning thing sitting between us. I look at my nieces, oblivious to their great loss, and it makes me want to howl. I stand. "I guess I'd better get back."

"So soon?"

"Yeah, I just . . ." I can't think of an excuse. "Mom," I say, waving my hands.

"Okay," Rory says.

"Walk me to the street?" I ask.

She gives Nathan a look, then stands and follows me out. In the yard, I turn and face her. "Why aren't you telling them?"

"I will," she says, and dashes tears off her face. "I just . . . I don't know. I just can't tell them yet."

"You're *lying* to them!"

"For God's sake, Maya, what difference does it make? He's gone either way."

I see the misery in her eyes, the way her lower lip trembles, but all I feel is the lie. "I have to go."

"Maya!" she protests as I start to walk away. "Don't be such a dick. We all grieve different ways, or maybe you're not going to grieve at all, huh?"

I turn. "Maybe not." But I don't really want to leave on such a mean note. I pause, shake my head. "I'm just freaked that they don't know." I kiss her cheek. "I really do have to get back to Meadow."

"Fine," she says, and wipes away a tear. "It's not just you that everything has happened to, you know. It's happened to all of us."

"Has it?" I ask, and walk away before I say something even meaner.

Chapter Thirteen
Maya

The first thing I do every morning is walk. Before coffee, before anything. I swing my legs out of bed, shed my pajamas, and don leggings, a long T-shirt, and a hoodie. My shoes are by the back door, so I sit on the bench there and tie them on, then head out. Meadow must be awake, but she's nowhere in sight. The puppy is nowhere in sight. He must have slept with her. I find I'm disappointed.

Mornings are often gloomy this time of year. Farther south, the summers are bright and sunny, but in the Santa Barbara area, a marine layer often hangs low over the ocean until much later in the day. I grew up with it, and love it, love the softness it lends the air.

I bypass the swimming pool, finished in colorful tiles from the twenties, and unlock the cedar gate that opens at the top of a long, steep set of stairs that wind through succulent plants to arrive at the beach. Sixty-seven steps, exactly the age my father was when he dropped dead.

The beach is nearly empty so early, and the house is far enough from the towns to the north and south to escape tourist curiosity. A big swath of the mountainsides burned a couple of years ago, erasing hiking trails that used to lead here. Lucky for me, I guess.

Walk. One foot and then the next. Air moves over my face, my neck. I breathe it in a few times, filling my lungs to remember that being alive is not to be underrated, and then . . . I just walk. I don't bring podcasts or music with me. I want to hear whatever the earth has to tell me.

It started in rehab. A lot of people do hard exercise to sweat out their demons, but I wasn't exactly in the peak of health, and I'd broken a rib somehow when I chopped open the casks. Walking was all I could manage. I walked the grounds and garden—let it be noted that for all his flaws, my dad ponied up big-time for the best rehab around—and while it was not a lot of area, you can do a lot with loops.

Walking was *possible*. I could do it when it didn't feel like I could do anything else. I couldn't think. I couldn't have functioned at all in the outside world. I can't sit still all the time. I can't always focus enough to read. Even when I'm walking, things pop up, memories and regrets and shame and guilt, but they don't stick around and needle me the same way.

At the foot of the stairs, I take off my shoes and socks and leave them, and make my way to the hard-pressed sand on the edge of the water, walking close enough that waves ruffle over my toes and ankles now and again. The water is very cold, but I never mind that. A wind is blowing from the north, cleansing my face and neck. Seagulls and little plovers poke through the leavings of the tide, and a pair of brown pelicans soar overhead, peering at the surface of the waves for breakfast. A dog and a person walk in the distance, but I'm otherwise alone. It's the great thing about this location. It's lonely, but it's also never crowded.

Lonely. That I am. Not as bad as I was during the pandemic, when Josh was stranded in France for months on end and I couldn't see anyone. The drinking had been heavy before that, but the loneliness and isolation sent my habits into overdrive.

Meadow and Rory are great, but neither of them understands what happened to me. They don't realize that this wasn't some bad choice I made and I'll "get through it." I think for a long time they both expected that I would quit drinking for a while and then be able to drink like other people. They're terrified now that I'll pick up. To be honest, I am, too. There's something in me that's just broken.

We're all broken, says my therapist's voice. I somehow have always felt more broken than most, but maybe that's not actually true.

Keep your head where your feet are.

The sand is cold beneath my feet. I taste salt on my lips. Something eases down my spine.

Only Josh—and my dad, actually—really saw what was going on with me. Even though I refused to speak to Augustus, he was around on the periphery of my life, there when each of the girls was born, present at family parties. He mostly respected my boundaries, but I felt him watching me.

Seeing me. That was his gift, after all: seeing people. It's why we all had our own nicknames, why he knew how to give gifts that were so perfect, how he managed to hire and keep staff long term in an industry rife with turnover.

Across the screen of my memory, I see him looking at me with concern at some gathering or another.

I shove the visual away. Josh rises in his place. Handsome and ordinary all at once, an all-American boy I met in college, both of us studying viticulture. It was tempestuous from the beginning, which I realized in daily therapy sessions at rehab was my MO: I was drawn to slightly aloof men, men who made me work hard at gaining their attention, relationships that would be intense, passionate, full of sex and fights and making up.

Josh met every single one of my requirements. He loved me, but sometimes he was hard to reach. He adored me, worshipped my body, and then couldn't stand to talk. He drank way too much, which put my college drinking into perspective. My parents never really liked him. They thought him too privileged, too arrogant, too prone to fits of high emotion.

Our fights, starting near the beginning, were legendary. Not physical, unless it was fight sex, brutal and wildly satisfying but vicious. I was known to throw things. He was known to yell. Twice, we nearly got kicked out of the dorms or school.

But we also shared a genuine, deep passion for the art of wine, and that connection, that dream of having our own label, bound us together for a long time. After graduation we settled into our relationship, learned how to avoid setting each other off. Together we traveled the world, tasting wines and partying with all the other young, ambitious vintners we met. Through those years of exploration and travel, when we applied ourselves to learning our craft and plotting how to make our own wine, we were wildly happy. Even during the first few years of making our own wine, we were mostly good. We still broke into extreme fights followed by extreme sex, but I told myself that was just the DNA of a relationship between two intense people.

We were in trouble long before he left for Paris. Some of that was me. The more I drank, the more volatile I became, and although he drank as much as or more than I did, it never seemed to affect him the same way it did me. He didn't want to fight the whole world. He didn't want to burn things down and start again.

But he was not blameless. His rigidness, his focus on doing things exactly as they'd always been done, his powerful need for rules and order aggravated the hell out of me. It was constraining. Claustrophobic. It roused my battle instincts.

Looking back, I see that it's possible we had outgrown our relationship. We got together in college, after all, and people don't always stay together. We were bound by the big dream of making perfect wine, but what was underneath that? I didn't know then. I don't know now. Maybe I honestly don't even care.

Still. Why did he have to *cheat*? He knew this was one of my hot buttons, that my father cheated on not only my mother but then my stepmother. I hadn't spoken to Augustus in years because of the affair that broke his marriage with Meadow.

How could someone who said he loved me have done the very thing that would hurt me the most?

A derisive voice in my head says, *Well, it wasn't like you were exactly a great catch.*

I bow my head, letting the wind toss my hair. It will be a mess to untangle, but the sudden heavy heat of shame weighs me down so much I just can't worry about hair.

What is wrong with me?

Stop. The voice belongs to my sponsor, a woman with a heavy cigarette smoker's voice. *How is this helping?*

I lift my head, take in a deep breath, pull my shoulder blades down my back to straighten my spine. *Stay where your feet are.* I'm here now, walking on the beach. Looking at seagulls. A plover pokes her beak into the wet sand. Overhead, a heron swoops by with powerful wings. I can smell ocean and seaweed. My lips taste of salt.

Here. Now. In this small space of nowness, I can breathe. I don't have to be anything to anyone.

Take a step. Take a breath. Look.

At an outcropping of rocks, I start to go around the front on the tiniest sliver of sand. It's always dicey, this bit, and it's not really navigable except at low tide. Judging by the foam line, it's on its way back up, and I won't make it on the sand. I have to make the passage over the boulders fallen from the cliff above. Using a hand to brace myself, I lean on a gritty rock and slip along the sand, feeling the suck of air pockets beneath my heels.

I see the cresting swell before it hits me, but there's no time to get out of the way. I leap to the top of the nearest rock, raising an arm to protect my face. The rock below takes the full brunt of energy, but the spray leaps into the air and onto me with a great splat. It's cold and salty and takes my breath for a second, and by the time it retreats, I'm soaked.

And laughing.

"Are you all right?" a voice asks from my right. A man is coming from the cove, and he's taken a side hit, but only his shoulder and one pants leg are wet.

I look down, shaking my hands, wiping my face. "It's only water. You?"

"Fine."

We're at a bit of an impasse, him coming my way, me going his, and both of us trapped by the sudden swell. The rocks are biting into my feet and I sit down, pulling my knees close to my chest. "Do you have enough room to pass?"

He shakes his head. He gestures toward a flat rock nearby. "Do you mind?" His accent is British, mixed with something I can't quite place. "It will recede in a moment."

"Go ahead. It's not my rock."

"Nor mine," he says, settling. His hands are long fingered, the skin a warm brown. His feet are much lighter, bare, beneath khaki trousers rolled up to above his ankles. His hair, like mine, is curly and black, and it tosses around his face. It makes him seem friendly. "Are you visiting? I haven't seen you before."

I take a breath, wondering how much to say, but there are not really many ways to phrase it. "Not exactly. My father died and I inherited his house."

"Ah. Your father was Mr. Beauvais."

The "mister" makes me smile inwardly. "Yes, that's right. Did you know him?"

A one-shouldered shrug. "Not well. Only as neighbors." He points down the beach. "I'm four houses to the north."

"The glass house. That's a beauty."

He nods, but there's an aura of sadness about him. "Yes. My wife quite loved it."

The past tense is stark. I don't know how to respond, and the sound of the sea rises between us. Finally, I say, "Do you? Love it?"

His fingers are laced together, forearms resting on his knees. He looks out to the sea, shakes his head. "No."

"I love my dad's house," I volunteer. "I grew up there."

"But?"

I watch four pelicans ride air currents high above us. "I hadn't spoken to him in years. It feels wrong to take the house."

"I see." He looks at me. His face is long, dominated by large dark eyes, and I think he must be a decade or more older than me. "Do you suppose he'd want you to have it anyway?"

The question pushes some button, and I have to look toward the distance to let the emotion recede. It hasn't left my voice when I answer. "I don't know," I say, and let that hang in the air.

Then I tell the truth. It's a muscle that's hard to use when you haven't bothered for so many years. "Yes."

He nods.

A wave splatters us lightly and I shiver. "I wonder if I should just go back."

"I am considering the same thing." He inclines his head. "Did I see you at the coffee shop yesterday? Are you going to work there?"

I look at him, but he doesn't look familiar. "Were you there?" He looks off to the sea, and his nose in profile reminds me—the Irrfan Khan look-alike. Up close, the resemblance is not so pronounced, but he does have the same large dark eyes, the sad mouth. "Wait. I do remember. You were sitting by the window, not working on your open computer."

This wins a half-hearted smile. He tosses a rock toward the water. "Yes. That is unfortunately the story of my days—not working."

"What are you not working on?"

"A novel."

"Really." I look toward the house on the cliff. "You must be a very successful writer to live in that house."

"It was my wife's. She was an actress."

I'm intrigued, drawn in by the pearlescent details he brings out. "Hmm. Does that mean you met on set? Are you famous, Mr. Not Working?"

"No. We met because she wanted to make the movie of one of my novels, but it never came to fruition."

"Now you have to tell me your name."

He meets my gaze. A lock of hair falls in his eye. "Ayaz."

I repeat it, to remember. "Ayaz."

"And what am I to call you?"

I take in a breath, feeling the freshness all through my lungs, and let it go. I think of oysters and grit. "Call me Maya."

"All right, Maya." He eyes the water, creeping ever higher. "I believe I shall now make my escape. And so should you."

We stand, and just for a minute, I don't want to turn away. Something about his sadness draws me in.

But I lift a hand. "See you around, Ayaz."

My bare feet make wet marks across the patio, and I smell something baking as I push open the door. Meadow is awake. She's playing light Celtic music through the Bluetooth speakers, and her hair is swept up into a messy bun. I see gray streaks in the hair of her nape. "Good morning," she calls, busily chopping. "Did you work up an appetite?"

"I thought you'd left," I say, and point to the bowl on the counter. "I was going to make artichokes."

"For breakfast?"

"Why not?"

"It's too early for local artichokes. They must be imported from Mexico," she comments. "Sorry, not judging. Just observing."

Snapping annoyance rises up my spine. As if he knows it, Cosmo rockets out of the salon and dives into my ankles, all squishy adorability, and looks up at me with the worshipful gaze only a dog can offer. His little mouth smiles widely. What can I do? I bend down and scoop him up, kissing his nose as he wiggles and licks my face. Irritation subsides. "Rory and I were talking about the elaborate scheme Dad set up to get us to eat artichokes, and I got a heavy craving."

"Your dad didn't do that," she says, slicing a chunk of cheese from a block and handing it to me, high above Cosmo's eager nose. "I did."

I break off a tiny bit of cheese and give it to him, popping the rest in my mouth.

"You shouldn't feed him anything except in his bowl," Meadow says.

"Right. I notice how well you follow that rule."

She shrugs.

The easy green globes of artichokes gleam in their blue bowl. "I mean, yes, you grew the artichokes, but Dad was all about making it into this big thing."

"Nope." Calmly, she scores an orange. "It was my idea."

I feel a ping somewhere in my body, a recognition, and I pause, reaching back through time to find the memories. The fenced garden, the way my father teased us with the adult nature of artichokes. Meadow is nowhere, but that's impossible. "You have to be right," I exclaim. "My dad never grew a single thing in his life. Why do I remember him at the middle of it?"

A small, wistful smile touches her mouth. "Because he was Augustus, I suppose."

Cosmo squirms to get down and I let him go, glancing toward the doors that lead to the pool, which are closed. "Yeah."

"He was a big personality," Meadow comments. She drops a handful of thinly sliced red peppers into a pan and they sizzle.

It smells great and my stomach growls in anticipation, but I also feel a weird tenseness in my neck. Still. I wish, very badly, to be completely alone. Rehab was such a crush of people, all the time.

To be honest, I am also a little afraid of myself, of what I might find—do—if I'm alone. At least Meadow means well, and just wants to take care of me. I should let her. "What are you making?"

"Herbed biscuits and scrambled eggs with chives and parsley."

My stomach growls so vividly in approval that Meadow laughs. "I'll make you a fresh cup of coffee."

Her cooking is a tsunami of love. I give in to it, sinking into a chair at the island to watch her cook. She's plump now, an hourglass sort of plumpness that is perfect for two little granddaughters to curl into. The kettle has been held at a simmering temperature, and she pours hot water into a french press. "These are some beans from the Brewed Bean," she says.

"I learned a bit about the various kinds of beans yesterday," I offer. "It's fascinating, honestly—how the different beans from different places have particular flavors. And did you know that every single bean has to be picked by hand?"

"I did not know that," she says, but I get the feeling she did and is humoring me. Which is aggravating in a way, but would I rather she acted like a know-it-all, which is her usual fallback?

I take in a breath, let it go. Stick with the moment. "Which beans are these?"

"Uncommon Sumatra."

"Smells so good."

"Are you working today?"

"Yes, same time. One o'clock."

She sprinkles chopped chives into a bowl of eggs that she beats gently. "Good. A J-O-B, right?"

"What's that?"

"An AA thing I picked up somewhere, I don't know."

85

It irks me. "Don't do that, okay?"

"Do what?"

"Spout platitudes about AA and my program and all that. It's not your program. It's mine."

A slight flush burns up her pale white cheeks. "Sorry. I'm just—I don't know. Sorry."

Now I feel like a shit. "No, I'm sorry. It's okay."

"It isn't. You can tell me the truth. I'm not some delicate flower."

I pause, taking her in. Really look at her. The threads of gray curling through the red of her hair, the wrinkles around her mouth from smoking long ago, the age spots on the backs of her hands and up her arms from spending so much time in the California sun. A nugget of truth surfaces. "I think you're more delicate than you give yourself credit for. Especially right now."

Quick tears spring to her eyes, and she looks down to hide them. A ripple of compassion moves through the stiffness in my lungs, giving me space to breathe. To love her as she is. "Am I? I don't feel like I am."

"Your daughter just chopped down her life like a big tree, and the man you loved for a long time has just died. That would make anyone vulnerable."

"Maybe," she says, and clears her throat, busying her hands with breakfast.

My mind returns to dinner the night before. "Did you know that Rory hasn't told the girls that Dad died?"

She takes a breath. "Yes."

"And you think this is okay?"

"No." She rests her wrists on the counter. Looks at me. "But I'm not their mother, and I have to let Rory do what she thinks is right, at least for a little while."

I narrow my eyes. "Uh, it's not like they're not going to notice." Like all the children in the world, they worshipped him.

She stirs the eggs again, turns around to pull the pan off the burner. "Look, she's handling his death differently than you are."

"Obviously. She's been close to him all along."

"Let's just allow her a few days to figure it out, okay? Give her some space?"

It irritates me for no reason I can name. I think of the girls waiting for their grandpa and him never coming again, and a little crack works its way down my armor. A memory of myself waiting for my father to reappear surfaces, pinging me uncomfortably. "It just seems so sad."

"That he died?"

I sigh. "No. I mean, yes, obviously. He was too young and all that. But . . ." I can't find the words to articulate what I'm feeling, and a hard, intense desire for wine bursts through me. "She's lying to them!"

"Well . . . I mean, not really."

My emotions swell, fill my throat, enormous and overwhelming. I don't know what to do with them. *Speak up,* says a little voice, and I'm so pissed off that my eyes are filling with tears, but I say, "Yes, really. It is an *actual* lie. They think he's still alive, and he's dead. That is a lie."

"Maya," she says, ever so gently. "She's grieving. People grieve in many different ways."

Fury burns along my skin, in the crooks of my elbows, along my shoulder blades, and I feel like I might explode, like I might pick up an axe.

I stand up. "Meadow, this isn't going to work."

"What?" she says. Genuinely clueless or giving a good imitation.

A ripple of nervousness edges along my ribs, but I hear my therapist in my head. *Only you know what your boundaries are, Maya. You have to find them.*

"I need to be alone to figure things out. I need you to go home."

"Honey, I didn't mean—"

"You're okay. You're not bad or wrong or any of that. I just need to be alone, in my own head, in my own space. You're hovering."

"Oh, am I? I'm sorry. I'm just—"

I hold up a hand. "I know. You're worried. You're afraid I'm going to fall off the wagon. All of you are, and I've given you good reason, but—"

"It's not that," she says.

"You poured out every drop of liquor in the entire house," I say. "Which had to have been quite a bit."

"Well, of course. I wanted to make it easier for you."

The nervousness amps up to anxiety, snaps and crackles up my spine. "I know. I appreciate that." Taking a long, slow breath in through my nose, I hold it for a moment, then let it go. "But I need to do this myself. You can't save me."

Tears spring to her eyes, making them even brighter blue. "I do know that. I mean, I want to. I always want to make things easier for you. Fix it."

"I know." I round the counter and hug her, feeling my own emotions rising up like a tidal wave again, ready to swamp me, knock me down. *Feel what you feel,* says a voice in my head, but how can I let all this in? All of it? It's so much.

We cling to each other for a minute. Her fingers are tight on my back, and her smell is sunshine and lavender and all things good. I loved her so much from the start, even when it made me feel disloyal. I pull back. "I wish you could. But I need some space."

"Oh! Okay. I have to be somewhere anyway." She steps back. "Do you want me to clean up?"

I shake my head. "I'll do it."

She pauses. Her face shows the edges of her fear that I will disappear, that I'll be lost in a bottle forever. "You don't have to do everything alone, Maya," she says. "That's partly what got you here."

"Pot," I say, pointing to her, then back to myself. "Kettle. Believe me, I know that. And I promise I'll call you if I need you, but the best thing you can do for me is give me some room to breathe."

She sucks her top lip into her mouth, something she's done my entire life. "Okay." She closes her eyes, straightens her back. Takes a breath. "Okay. I'm going right now. I'll be back later."

My gut sinks. I meant really be alone, really leave, but how can I say that? One step at a time. I just nod. "Take Cosmo. I won't be here to watch him."

———— ❧⁓⁓❧ ————

After Meadow leaves, I sit at the counter for long moments, aching in some strange way I can't even pinpoint. My chest, my thighs, my forehead. I want—

A drink.

It's just that, of course. The same thing as ever, the same thing as always. Wine, beer, shots of tequila. Whatever it takes to kill the feelings. My therapist said that the reason alcohol is so hard to give up is because it works.

Other things can work, too. Standing up, I round the counter and clear a spot for a fresh cutting board, then pull the bowl of artichokes over. They're gorgeous, as big as footballs, the leaves well formed and hydrated. I smell one—dust and day and chlorophyll—then center it on the cutting board and cut the end off. The knife slices right through, as if the tough skin is made of cheese, and I look at the beautiful knife for the first time. It's a Japanese Yoshihiro chef's knife. Of course. Everything in my dad's kitchen is going to be perfect.

I cut the ends off all of them, then trim the leaves with good scissors, noting the pleasure I feel in the good tools, and slice them all in half. The heady scent makes me dizzy and hungry.

Somewhere in the house, I hear a door slam. I lift my head. "Meadow?"

No answer.

Leaving the artichokes, I pad into the hallway and stand there, listening. "Hello?"

Nothing.

Maybe it was the wind.

That longing for booze sweeps back, harder this time. Rum, wine, Blue Moon (oh, yes please, a Blue Moon, with a thick slice of orange). The thirst builds and spreads through my body, burning up the back of my neck, on my tongue, creating an itch in my brain in a place I can't scratch.

Tools, I think. *Remember your tools.*

I pour a glass of cold water and drink it down fast. It hits the same centers as alcohol, the back of my throat, the mid-esophagus, cooling. Calming. The craving eases. I take a deep breath, blow it out, focus on preparing the artichokes. All of them go into a steamer for twenty minutes while I make the grilling sauce.

Play it forward, says the voice of the group leader in my head.

I don't want just *one* drink. It's a cliché, but it's also true. I was always amazed to see leftover wine in a glass, an unfinished cocktail on a table in the restaurant. Who does that? Walks away from alcohol?

Turns out, lots of people do. Just not me.

The first time I tasted wine, I was eleven years old and already a worrier. I worried about everything—whether my father loved me, if a meteor would hit the earth, if Meadow would get cancer and die like the mother of a friend of mine. I had a constant case of mild gas (which went away only when I gave up milk in college), so I worried about farting. I worried that my teeth were too big, that my hair was too crazy, that I laughed too loudly, that I was too awkward to be anybody's best friend. I picked at my nails and often had skin rashes of various kinds.

When I was eleven, our parents threw a party for someone's birthday. Rory and I dared each other to steal a bottle of wine and run upstairs with it. On the balcony of our parents' bedroom, we poured a good red into highball glasses and imitated the people we'd seen smelling, swirling, sipping. It smelled amazing to me, fruity and full of something that made me think of chocolate bars, but Rory wrinkled her nose. "Why do they do this? It stinks."

"I love it," I said honestly, and stuck my nose in farther, not even knowing what I was doing, but aware that there was something here. Something richer than I expected.

Then we drank, little sips, and smacked our lips together, and then great big gulps, on dares.

Oh. My. God.

The wine hit the back of my throat and the middle of my chest with a great zinging blast of something unexpected.

Quiet.

Quiet that spread from that center of my chest upward and sideways and downward, rippling out to my brain and my lower back.

I drank again. And again.

It was amazing. All the noise, all the anxious wishes to please, all the memories I hated cropping up—all of it just . . . stopped. It was an amazing discovery, that anything could do that.

Rory passed out, but I sat there on the balcony drinking the rest of the wine and watching people below. I sadly poured the last drops into my mouth and wished for more, but I didn't trust myself to steal another bottle and get away with it.

But I knew there would be a next time.

Chapter Fourteen
Meadow

I try not to show it as I gather my things and leave the house with Elvis padding behind me and Cosmo in my arms, but every cell in my body is stinging with rejection. The rational part of my brain knows that it has nothing to do with me, that Maya just needs to be alone, but it goes against every instinct I own to turn away from her at this moment of need and leave her to it. For more than thirty years, she's been at the very center of my life.

The first time I met her, she was barely four. It was a still July day that crackled with heat. Augustus and I were on a hunt for the best mangoes in the county. I wanted to buy some fresh, to make a dish I'd learned at a job I first took when I left home, prep cook at a Thai restaurant that paid me next to nothing but let me bring Rory when her day care filled up or closed for no reason (or for reasons that made no sense, all the same).

That particular day, Rory wasn't with us, though I can't remember why. I must have wanted to go out with Augustus myself. Did I know Maya was coming? Was I disappointed when I saw her? Maybe a little. Augustus and I had known each other only a few weeks at that point, and couldn't keep our hands off each other.

I'd never wanted to have sex with anyone. They teased me about it at work, laughing when I rebuffed all advances, from boys, girls, everybody. The very thought of someone kissing me was disgusting. My experiences with sex had not been appealing, to say the least.

But from the first second I saw Augustus, I wanted him. He turned a switch inside me, off to on. On, on, on.

A few weeks in, I was obsessed. Obsessed with his mouth and the long, slow, deep way he kissed me. Obsessed with his big hands and the ways they explored my body, everywhere, all over, up and down, in and out. I loved his body, his ribs and tongue and penis and legs. The sheer number of hours we spent naked and exploring each other was a revelation.

But that day, he brought Maya with him. She was not the slightest bit beautiful or cuddly. She'd entered the scrawny years of childhood, and had her dad's long, long limbs. Her hair was unwashed and unbrushed and wildly curly, but Augustus explained that her mother loved partying more than she loved her daughter, so he wanted to take her out, give her other experiences. At the time, it made me love him all the more, but now I know addiction isn't so clear cut.

She eyed me warily, with an expression I would have called cynical in anyone but a four-year-old. Her eyes were a watery green in a cat-shaped face, and she had eyelashes so thick they looked fake, and a lush mouth just like her father's.

I was smitten, but never in my life—before or since—did anyone make me work so hard for approval. The one thing she liked was my hair. It was almost to my waist, thick and wavy, and Maya loved to brush it. Once I found that secret, I tucked away pins and barrettes and soft fastenings in my pockets so she could play with my hair whenever we were together.

No one ever believes me, but I honestly didn't know Augustus was married to Shanti. He wore no ring. He was up-front about the problems with her addiction. We never went to his place, only to mine, but he told me it was because he lived too far out for it to be realistic, the opposite direction from the farm.

I was nineteen and madly in love. Of course I believed him.

I drive back to my farm outside Ojai, just over forty minutes from Belle l'Été. Bright, hot sunshine breaks through the morning gloom by the time I pull into the driveway, marked with a hand-carved sign, a rising sun over a meadow, and the words MEADOW SWEET ORGANIC FARMS.

My pride and joy, though it has begun to feel hollow the past decade or so. I still take pride in growing organic produce and supplying restaurants for a hundred miles around. I love the experimental crops, the annual tests of new heirloom varieties of squashes, tomatoes, beets, potatoes. Sometimes they're successful, sometimes they're not. Two years ago, a purple Incan potato proved so popular, I moved out a half acre of reds, but then the Incas succumbed to a fungus and I lost the whole crop before it ripened.

That is the farming life. Unpredictable. Plants are living things, vulnerable to all kinds of threats—storms, insects, fungi, and more and more often, fire. Today, a crew works along the perimeter, chopping out scrub and grasses for fire mitigation to give us a chance if an ordinary sort of blaze sweeps down the mountains. Nothing can stop a firestorm of the sort that has become more common in recent years, but we do our best. The hills are tinder after a dry winter, and the Santa Anas will start blowing in a couple of months. All it takes is a spark—lightning, a bad muffler, an arsonist with a match—to gulp down vast swaths of land. The past five years have been a horror up and down the state, through the whole West, really. We are learning to live with the threat of catastrophe, like lobsters in a pot on the stove.

A small crew is packing up strawberries that were harvested early this morning and loading crates into trucks for delivery to various restaurants. I wave and the crew leader waves back. A man is bent over a central irrigation unit with wrenches and screwdrivers to fix a problem that showed up last week.

I herd Cosmo and Elvis into the house, and stop to give the other animals some love, kissing the cats and rubbing Joe the ancient border collie's soft belly. My assistant, Tanesha, works in the office attached to the house, so they have plenty of attention, but they miss me anyway.

I poke my head into the office. "How's everything?"

"Good. We're supposed to be at the grade school in two hours. Will you be ready?"

"Sure. I'll just pop in the shower."

"I had a phone call from the Carpinteria police," Tanesha says, turning to offer me a slip of paper. "They want to talk to you again about Augustus. I told them we'd be that direction this afternoon, and they said that would be fine. Just stop in. Ask for the guy on the paper."

I frown, feeling a ripple of unease. "Did they say why?"

"No."

"Did they say if they've released the body?" I hold the paper lightly between my thumb and index finger. "Rory is not coping very well."

"He didn't say." She clicks a program closed on the computer and swings around to face me. Her feet are bare beneath a pair of well-worn khakis, and her ankles are dusty from working in the fields earlier. A pale line shows where her socks stopped. "How's Maya?"

"Okay, I think." A rippling sting reminds me of her request that I leave her alone. "I worry that she's not very stable yet, and she doesn't want me living there, but . . . it's early days."

"People do get sober, Meadow."

"Do they?" I ask, mostly rhetorically. I think of Maya the night she called me to come pick her up from the winery. I couldn't go by myself because I couldn't drive that far along the coast at night with my bad eyes. I called the only person I could, her father. He drove us there in the dark night. He was the one who helped her up from the ground, where she'd more or less passed out, covered in wine, her hair stiff with it. I could only weep, shattered by her crash.

Thinking of it, my heart aches. I would spare her this, all of it, the deep suffering of addiction, the losses she's racked up, take it all on myself so that she could have a life of happiness and joy. Pressing a palm to my diaphragm, I take a breath. "I just want her to be okay."

"You can't do it for her."

I take a breath. "I'm trying. I just haven't seen people be successful that often, and to lose her dad like this, right before she gets out . . . I mean."

"She has tools. She can do it." Her hands are folded in her lap. "Have you looked up Al-Anon meetings yet?"

I shake my head.

"I'd offer to find a list of meetings, but I think that's something you need to do yourself when you're ready."

"Yeah." I lift a hand. "I'm off to shower."

When Augustus and I pooled our talents and passions, our fortunes rose like a comet. The book I wrote out of an overflowing sense of love for both the farm-to-table movement and all the things Augustus and I were creating together became a bestseller and went back to print over and over. Peaches and Pork became an *It* destination, worth the trip from cities north and south to sample the tender wares of Augustus Beauvais, whose star rose right along with mine.

Money poured in. I wanted to use some of it to create projects that would teach the concepts we believed in—sustainable food, ecology, eating from local gardens. We admired Alice Waters's Edible Schoolyard Project, and after much discussion, we settled on the Plant It Forward foundation, which helps create community and school gardens in challenged neighborhoods up and down the central coast. It has been very successful and, after almost twenty years, has gained national attention and provided models for other regions and cities.

I've learned to share some of the administrative tasks with other people, and some of the community outreach, but I never tire of working with a gaggle of kids on a plot of land. There's something sacred about growing food, about planting seeds and watching them sprout, about pulling a radish from the warm earth, about harvesting an ear of corn and popping it into a pot. I taught Rory and Maya to garden, as my mother taught me, and now I teach other children.

This morning, Tanesha and I drive to Hermosa Elementary, located in a neighborhood of battered ranch homes too far from the ocean or the mountains to be gentrifying. With funds from Plant It Forward, they've plowed a large section of playground under and this spring planted their first crops. I like to regularly visit the newest urban farms to make sure we catch problems early, and this is one of my babies this year. The first project leader disappeared halfway through the plowing, and we scrambled to find another member of the community who would be willing to take it on. A young teacher volunteered and has been doing a great job, but I know she's in a little over her head.

As I step out of the car, I see her in the midst of knee-high corn, wearing a pair of denim overalls and a bright yellow scarf over her hair. She's pointing to a small knot of children, obviously giving them tasks for the day, then spies us and waves us over.

"Hi!" she says. "Kids, you remember Ms. Beauvais, don't you?"

They greet me by rote, but one boy, about ten, pops up a hand. "Ms. Beauvais, you said we could grow anything, right?"

"Within reason."

"What if we want to grow marijuana?"

I raise my eyebrows. "Um, no."

"It's legal. My uncle's growing some."

"He's an adult and can make that choice," I say. "But you are a child and you may not."

He snaps his fingers in exaggerated disappointment, and gains the attention he sought when his friends laugh.

It reminds me abruptly of Augustus. He always knew how to play the crowd, bring in approval, charm his detractors.

For one long moment, standing in the hot sun with a gaggle of children amid knee-high corn, I am swamped by a heavy wave of loss. A tangle of things rise in my mind—the spark in his eye, the way he waited for the return on a joke.

And more. I acutely miss the taste of him, the scent of his skin. Swaying in the sun, I curse myself and my weakness.

Oh, sweet Jesus, why did I allow it to begin again?

Chapter Fifteen
Norah

I awaken too late to get out of the house ahead of Maya and Meadow, unfortunately, and have to lie in the bed I've made of Augustus's clothes, listening to them talk overhead. Meadow walks with a sturdy, no-nonsense step that I can follow throughout the house. Maya is lighter of foot, though I can still hear her.

Meadow leaves first. I listen, playing with my phone, eating a KIND bar, waiting for Maya to follow. It takes a while. She putters around the kitchen, clanking pans, and my stomach growls over the scents filling the air. After, water runs, probably for a shower, and I squirm in anticipation.

Finally, I hear her walk through the house and close the heavy side door that leads to the garage. Her car is quiet, but I can see a part of the driveway and watch it drive away. I give it fifteen minutes in case she forgot something, then finally escape my little prison. The cleaners won't come until tomorrow, so I should be relatively safe. I walk through the garage and into the house, smelling something garlicky and exquisite, which turns out to be grilled artichokes. Two halves are left in the fridge, and of course I can't eat them, but I slide back the cling wrap and pluck a single blade free. Heaven.

On the counter are bananas and a loaf of bread. Easy stuff. I make toast with honey and a cup of tea and eat a banana sitting at the table, reading my phone, just as I always have. I fancy the rooms welcome me, that they haven't forgotten me.

Stomach sated, I wash and dry and put away my dishes, then collect food that will keep for tonight's meals and carry it out to my room. I haven't washed clothes for a few days, but that will have to wait. First, a swim and a shower.

My favorite thing in the world is that pool. It's long and narrow, about the width of two lanes, meant for laps and sunbathing. The tiles are beautiful, handprinted, turquoise and green renditions of sea creatures like octopuses and mermaids and fish, and I kept the temperature at seventy-eight degrees, which is heavenly if you're human, barely cool.

Part of the pleasure of it is this: I drop my clothes to the concrete, the shift I was wearing, and my panties. I dive in naked, the water flowing along the parts that never get fresh water on them like this, the silkiness moving over my breasts and bottom, sliding between my thighs. I swim for many laps, never counting, just feeling it, and then when I'm done, I roll over on my back and let the sun warm my parts, too.

As I'm lying there in the sun, my brain starts to turn over the pieces of what I know about Meadow and how I might be able to find out more. The farm and her book emerged from the union with Augustus, but what happened before that? Her book is very light on details about her young years, starting basically when she began working at the Buccaneer, a local tourist trap, with Trudy Nickels, with her daughter in tow.

What happened before that? I feel like the answers to Meadow's drive and ambition are more about the past than anything she's written.

A pair of birds are squabbling in the bushes, and I open one eye to see if there's anything to be worried about. Nothing. Only the bright, hot blue sky and the edge of the shrubs.

For a moment, I let myself imagine that Augustus is still asleep upstairs, the doors open to the breeze. I could go up and wake him, kissing his long back, nuzzling into his neck. He would stir, and roll over and make love to me, and then we'd shower the sweat away, and he'd go off to work and I'd—

What? What have I been doing the past nine months?

Not much. Lying here now, I'm ashamed of myself for dropping everything, all my fierce ambition and quests. I didn't even think about it, just took up the mantle of kept woman as if I'd been training all my life. I dived into the ease he offered, the long, lazy days walking on the beach, swimming in the pool, reading in a way I've never had the luxury to indulge.

But is shame the right emotion? The truth is, when I arrived here, I was exhausted from years of foster homes, where I had to stay on my toes, then scrambling through undergrad, then grad school, trying to figure out how to make a name for myself, make a mark. Survival takes a lot of work if you're an orphan woman in America.

I was lucky to have so many opportunities, the scholarships and awards, but it also takes a lot to keep your chin up in those glittering worlds of privilege. My hard work opened doors to rooms that were filled with people who only pretended to accept me, who made me all too aware that I was not from their ranks and no matter how far I rose, I would never be one of them.

I took comfort in the writings of women throughout history, and the ways those writings made me see my life. I'd grown fascinated with the tipping points in the sixties and seventies and eighties, when women moved from not being able to open a credit card account in their own names to running successful businesses of all kinds, like Meadow Sweet Organic Farms, one of the best farm-to-table establishments in the country.

What I feel now, lying in the hot sun, is gratitude. Augustus gave me some space to rest and heal. I will miss him terribly, but it's time to get back to living my own life. I'll get my research done here, earn enough money from the restaurant gig to get myself back to the East Coast, and then dive into my thesis.

A book about Meadow Beauvais, the woman I came to find, a woman who found a way to achieve big goals, just as I hope to do.

I shower luxuriously with all the best-smelling travel-size sundries Augustus kept in a bin in the linen closet, using a fresh towel I'll take downstairs with me. There are so many, no one will notice. As I wash my hair, I mull over how to find out where Meadow came from. It feels like she's hiding something. Maybe just a lackluster childhood, but most people don't walk entirely away from their parents. Maybe she, like me, was a foster child. Maybe that was one of the reasons I was so drawn to her, sensing a lost little girl who was much like the one I carry around inside me.

I was a foundling child, left at a fire station in Pittsburgh. In the years between then and the time I aged out of the system at eighteen, I lived with seven families. One lasted nearly six years, and I would have stayed forever if I could have, but after that I was shuffled around a lot. No one likes to foster teens. I kept my focus on getting out.

And I did. Full-ride scholarships, always working, plus classes and homework and whatever jobs would keep a roof over my head. Restaurants were a bonus because they fed their employees, so I could be sure of getting one good meal a day anyway.

I really thought I was over that part of my life. That's what you get when you let down your guard, start to depend on anyone but yourself. I knew better.

I dress and dry my hair, then carry my things down the hallway. The doorway to one of the girls' rooms is open, and a suitcase lies open on the floor. For a moment I pause, then drop my stuff in the doorway and poke around. It's Meadow's stuff. She likes embroidered peasant blouses and bright colors. A pair of magazines populate the bedside table, *Saveur* and a journal for organic farming.

Don't underestimate her. Which I did for a while, lost as I was in the intensity of my connection to Augustus. She dropped from being a fascinating person I felt a connection with to the rather dismissible position of ex-wife to the man I was in love with.

The first time we met, she'd brought bags of produce to the house. I'd been living here for only a month or so, and when I saw her sitting in the kitchen, talking to Augustus as if they were still married, still deeply connected, my stomach twisted hard.

Living as I had in so many slightly and not-so-slightly hostile environments, I had learned to take the measure of human interactions very quickly. The mood between two parents in a family could influence every single aspect of my life, and I needed to be able to read them fast. It was my superpower.

What I saw as I came into the kitchen was Augustus focused entirely upon Meadow. His body was turned directly toward her, his shoulders back and chest forward like a bird puffed up for mating, and just as I entered the room, he shoved his hands through his hair, leaving tousled curls. He touched his beard, smoothed the hairs, then touched her hand with his other fingers. Something she said made him laugh, vividly, in a way that was deep and smart.

She, too, was completely engaged. Her upscale peasant blouse showed off a remarkable amount of cleavage, and she was positioned just below him on the barstool to give him an unobstructed view of all that flesh. Her lips were slightly parted.

If these had been my foster parents, I would have expected them to make an excuse to go somewhere and screw like bunnies.

A cold sweat broke over my skin. It had never occurred to me that they might still be lovers, that he might have more women in his life than me, but the evidence here was hard to ignore. In that moment I was so vividly in lust with Augustus that I couldn't bear to let him go, not yet. I squared my shoulders and wandered into the room casually, wearing only my bikini and a kimono I'd found that probably belonged to her.

She saw me before he did. "Hello," she said. "You must be Norah." Not a single note of jealousy marred her expression, which showed only slight amusement, as if I were a toy he'd brought home.

To my relief, Augustus held out one arm and I flowed to his side. He dropped his arm around me. "Norah is a writer," he said. "As a matter of fact, she's quite interested in your work, both as a farmer and a writer."

She gave me a Cheshire cat smile, which I knew right then meant I'd never get anywhere with her. "Is that right? We'll have to have a chat sometime." She stood. "Right now, I've got to go. Walk me out?"

Augustus dropped his arm and followed her, his body fairly shouting his attraction to his ex. My throat was hot and something stung my lungs. She was twenty years older than me, and if not exactly fat, definitely not thin. I touched my flat belly to reassure myself as she swayed out of the kitchen with her ample hips. At the door, they exchanged something more, and she pressed a hand against his chest, making a point I couldn't hear. I picked up a cracker and put it in my mouth, feeling stupid and too young. Augustus bent down and kissed her full on the lips, then patted her ass.

Right in front of me.

"What the hell?" I said when he came back.

He grinned. "Don't be jealous, *chérie*," he rumbled, exaggerating his accent and lowering his lids to skim down my body. I let him lift me up on the counter, and peel back my bikini top to show my pert, if not lush, breasts.

I pushed him away. "Are you sleeping with her?"

He met my gaze, his hands on my thighs. "Do you want me to?"

"Of course not!"

"Not even," he said slowly, his hands running up the inside of my thighs, "if I bring you with me?"

All these months later, I delicately look through her suitcase and touch her bras and wonder if that's what was on my mind all along. Do I long for her body, her kiss? Is it a carnal hunger I feel? I test the idea, imagine touching her body, kissing her again, as she kissed me in the bathroom, and I feel no desire. That's not it.

It's something else. Something warmer, calmer.

A mother. Of course. I drop her lingerie and force myself to swallow the longing, which eternally rises: *a mother a mother a mother a mother*. How old will I be when I finally stop?

Firmly, I shove the hunger down deep and refocus.

I want to know what makes Meadow tick. What drove her to the heights she's attained? And what happened between two people who obviously had such an abiding passion for each other?

Chapter Sixteen
Meadow

On some of the school visits, we harvest and serve food from the land, but today nothing is quite ready. The lettuces and radishes bolted weeks ago, and the squashes and tomatoes are too small. After a couple of hours, we've done all the checks and answered all the questions the children have about the community garden.

Tanesha walks with me to the car. "Can you drop me at my brother's house?" she asks. "Unless you want me to come to the police station with you."

"I'll be fine."

I drop her off and head into the city center to the police. I have the piece of paper Tanesha gave me, but I'm very clear on who wants to talk to me: that square-jawed man who stopped in at Peaches and Pork. Officer Vaca. I feel clammy as I enter, and wipe my palms on my jeans.

I give my name to the desk sergeant and sit in a plastic chair against the wall, waiting. A woman in her late twenties wrings a shredding tissue between her fingers, but she's the only other person here. I find myself smoothing my jeans, brushing a lock of hair out of my face, worrying over the dirt under my nails. What will he tell me? Ask me?

He takes his time. I've been there nearly twenty minutes when he strolls from the back somewhere. "Hi, Ms. Beauvais. Sorry to keep you waiting."

I stand. "No worries. How can I help you?"

"This way." He leads me to a room with a single table, and closes the door, gesturing for me to take a seat.

I frown. "Is this an interrogation? Do I need a lawyer or something?"

"What would you need a lawyer for? It's just busy as hell out there."

Mollified, I sit down, but gingerly, on the edge of the seat. I think for the first time in years of my stepfather. He had the same sharp jaw, the same regimented haircut. "What can I do for you?" I ask.

"We need to piece together the events of the night Augustus died," he says, flipping open his notebook. "You said you saw him in the afternoon? Or was it evening?"

"Evening. I brought a flat of strawberries from the farm."

"That's in Ojai, isn't it? Kind of far to drive to just drop off strawberries."

I flush and look down at my hands to hide the truth of what I was doing there. "It's not unusual. I make the drive daily. Sometimes twice a day."

"Mmm." He peers at me with ice-blue eyes, and pauses a long time. I try not to, but I squirm a little. Look away.

"Did you have a sexual relationship with the deceased?"

"We were divorced," I say.

"That's not what I asked. Did you have a sexual relationship?"

It's embarrassing. I feel my ears heat up. "No."

"Really?" He leans back. "Because we have video from the restaurant that says otherwise."

"What are you talking about?"

He flips lazily backward in his notes. "The night of May eighth, an encounter on the bar? Ring any bells?"

A memory of that night walks over my skin, touches my inner thighs. "Yes," I admit. "So what? We were married a long time. It happens."

"Did it happen a lot?"

"No. Our daughter went to rehab and we were both very upset about it," I say, and sigh as I pull my hair out of my face. "It was comfort."

"What about his girlfriend?"

I shrug. "He's always had a lot of girlfriends."

"Do you know where she is, the girlfriend? We'd really like to talk to her."

"Talk to her about what?" My pulse goes thready, and I'm suddenly worried that there's more to this than just establishing a timeline. "Do you think someone killed him?"

"It's inconclusive at the moment." He taps his pen on the table.

Cold freezes my spine. "What do you mean? I thought it was a heart attack?"

"It was the logical conclusion at first, but the coroner hasn't been able to nail it down. It wasn't a classic heart attack for sure."

"He hadn't been feeling very well for a few weeks."

"Did he see a doctor? Did he talk about his symptoms?"

"Not really. He didn't have a lot of energy."

He writes something on his paper. "And you don't know where Norah Rivera is?"

I shake my head. "I kicked her out."

"Kicked her out of where?"

"Belle l'Été, the house on Cliff Road."

He nods, blank faced. "Did you have the authority to kick her out? Do you own part of the house?"

"No. It belongs to my daughter."

"The one in rehab?"

"Yes. She needed a place to live, and I knew Augustus had left it to her."

"She was in rehab the night he died?"

"Yes. I'm sure that's easily verified." My stomach is burning with tension. "Is there anything else?"

"Did you have sex with Augustus that night?"

I take a breath, meet his eyes. Lie. "No. I just brought him the strawberries."

He scribbles on his notepad, his handwriting so tiny I'd need a magnifying glass to read it.

"Can I go now?"

"That should do it. For now." He meets my gaze with his cool blue eyes, and again I feel a shuddering reminder of my stepfather. "Thanks for coming in. I appreciate it."

Back in the car, I realize that my hands are shaking. For long minutes, I sit with my hands in my lap, staring out the windshield at the past.

Did you have a sexual relationship with the deceased?

The third time we started again, Maya had been settled in rehab for five days. That night, I sat in my garden beneath the moon trying to absorb the light and ease my jangled nerves, my tangled emotions. I drank my own special herbal tea blend, made with lemon balm, peppermint, and chamomile. In the darkness, I smoked a joint that had come highly recommended by the clean-shaven guy behind the counter at the local pot shop. He promised it would be mild and mellow and, maybe because my eyes were practically swollen shut from crying, added that it would probably help.

I hadn't been high for decades, but my entire soul felt shredded, so shredded I feared that it would not come back this time. I was desperate to escape my own experience. Nothing on earth could have made me

109

drink a glass of wine. After rescuing Maya, soaked inside and out with the wine she had so painstakingly created, that pleasure was ruined forever.

So I sat in my garden, smoking with lazy attention, waiting to see what happened between inhales. So far, he was right—a soft blurriness crept up my limbs, and the heavy weight of the past few days finally dropped away. I had my feet propped up on a table, and tilted my head to admire the bare shape of them, high arches and long toes. *Nice feet,* I thought.

Both dogs sat with me, alert for things to chase, or invaders, or a cat who might tease them. Elvis growled low in his throat, and I said, "It's all right, baby."

"*Calmez-vous,*" said a deep voice in French. *Settle down,* to the dogs.

Augustus. I looked at him, then back to the garden, unwilling to allow my anger to rise again, anger so bitterly, blisteringly hot that I'd had to walk away before I struck him in the kitchen of Peaches and Pork. His great flaw was carelessness—carelessness with me, with his life, with his daughter in particular.

"Will you share?" he asked, and without asking permission, sat in the chair beside mine. I handed over the joint.

"What are you doing here?"

The joint glowed orange as he inhaled. I waited. He exhaled in a gust, the smoke making a cloud against the stars. "I can't sleep, thinking about her, wondering if she'll be okay. If . . ." He paused, pressed his thumb and forefinger against the bridge of his nose. "How I could have changed things." He handed me the joint. "I wish I could go back in time," he said.

Tears stung the back of my eyes. "Don't," I whispered. "I can't cry anymore or my eyes will fall out."

We sat in the dark in silence, smoking. In the place where the movie of Maya's crash had been running, a softness filtered in, erasing the edges. "I do blame you," I said quietly.

"You are not alone," he said, but stopped short of claiming responsibility. He left her—for me, it's true—but still.

"My mother was an alcoholic," he said, out of the blue.

I peered at him. At that moment, I had known him for thirty-three years. We had spent thousands of nights together, had whispered hundreds of secrets to each other in the dark, from pillow to pillow.

He'd never said this aloud even once. "What?"

"She was a sex worker in New Orleans. She drank herself to death, and I became a ward of the state, as they say."

I was too high to take this in. "I thought she died of cancer. And your aunt in Montreal?"

His mouth turned down as he nodded. His hands were loose between his knees. "That was the story I told."

"But I always thought you told *me* the truth." The anger was boiling again, right below my skin, threatening to burn me, burn him, burn us all up.

He looked at me. "I was ashamed. And once the lie started, how could I change it?"

The moon washed over his extraordinary face, the long nose, the full lips, his heavy brows. "Are you really Creole?"

"In part, but I did not know my father, or any of my family. I don't know."

"So Maya—"

"Is the granddaughter and the daughter of women who died of alcoholism."

I closed my eyes, thinking of her passed out on the ground, an axe at her side. I thought of her when we finally rescued her from Shanti, a little girl with tangled hair and a dirty face, so skinny that I could see both bones in her forearms when I bathed her. I bent my face into my hands, sorrow rising again.

When his big hands fell on my upper back, I allowed the contact. I am human. I need to touch others as much as anyone else, and maybe of all the humans in the world, Augustus would know my sorrow over all this. We had failed her so terribly, both of us.

When he rose and came to kneel before me, I allowed myself to fall into his arms, leaning into the curve of his shoulder, where I inhaled the comforting scent of his skin, and we wept together over our broken daughter.

When he lifted my face to kiss me, I met his lips as if they offered a sacrament. The same wildness broke through us, the same tenderness. When he unbuttoned my blouse and freed my breasts, lifting them to his mouth, I allowed it. When he laid me down in the grass, I allowed it, and opened myself to him, to his ministrations. We shared our sorrow, and the simmering longing we shared for the taste of the other. Our tears and our kisses mingled. Our limbs tangled. We clung to each other as if lashed to a mast in a storm, then lay in each other's arms in the grass, covered only by moonlight, and for the smallest time, there was peace again in the world.

That was how we began again, for the third time.

Chapter Seventeen
Maya

I'm weirdly nauseated when I get home from work. It worries me, how often my stomach is upset lately; I keep fretting that I've completely ruined my liver. Gingerly, I rub the spot on my side, but it doesn't hurt or feel enlarged. There was a woman at rehab who had such an enlarged liver you could see it at a hundred paces.

Meadow hasn't yet returned, so I head down the stairs to the evening beach. It's more populated than the morning, but there still are very few people around. The sun hangs like an orange disk above the ocean, casting shimmers of oily red over the sea. On the horizon, an industrial ship moves against the sky, its speed deceptively slow.

It has been a warm day, and the sand is an agreeable mix of hot surface, cool underlayer. I walk toward the edge of the ruffling water. The tide is low. Birds call into the air. Tension spills out of my body, and it occurs to me with a little shock that I have *really* missed living near the ocean.

The things I didn't know about myself, or didn't acknowledge, keep surprising me. That I missed the ocean, that I wasn't really in love with Josh and hadn't been for a long time. That I get hungry. That I need sleep. That I'm actually a morning person who wakes up cheerful if I don't go to bed drunk.

Who knew?

The fresh air is good, but my stomach is still slightly upset, and I keep swallowing, wondering if I should have had a glass of oat milk or something before I came out. Upset stomach or no, I owe my sponsor a call for the day, and this is as good a time as any. She answers on the first ring. "Hello, Maya. How are you?"

"Not bad," I say honestly. "Walking on the beach, breathing fresh air." I pause, watch some birds wheeling around. "Looking at birds."

We chat about this and that. She asks if I've been to a meeting and I can reply honestly that I have. I didn't see the girl Sunny today, but that doesn't mean anything by itself. Still, I looked for her.

Deborah asks about the job, which I like and feels like the right place to be. I told her about Rory last night, and we talked through the things I could do next time if I was uncomfortable with people drinking around me. Leaving is always an option. Bringing my own drinks. Giving myself more time before I enter those kinds of social situations. "Or," she said, "what would happen if you just tell the truth about how you feel?"

Which is what she's going to say to this next thing. "I asked Meadow to go home," I say.

"Well. That's a big step. How did it go?"

"Not that great." A soft wind blows a scent of brine over my face. "She didn't quite get that I wanted her to move out completely. She thought I just meant for the day."

"And?"

"I didn't have the heart to get more pointed. She's grieving and she's worried about me and I know she just wants to help."

"Mmm. How does that feel?"

I pause, feeling it in my chest, tense and hard. "Not good. I really want her to go home. I need some space to figure things out, and as long as she's around, I'm never testing myself."

"Is that what you want to do? Test yourself?"

"No." I pause. "Maybe? Or maybe I just want to be alone. I haven't been alone for months, really."

"It is your house."

"Well, kind of." Hair tangles around my face, and I pause to pull it out of my mouth. "She lived there a lot longer than I did. I moved out at eighteen. She lived there another nine or ten years." I think about the way she moved the paintings around, returning them to the way they'd been. "Maybe I should just give it to her. I can't possibly pay the upkeep on a house that big."

"Maybe," Deborah says. "But not right now. Don't make any decisions for at least a few months. All you have to do right now is stay sober."

The phrase sweeps away about 85 percent of my anxiety, giving me space to take a breath. One thing: stay sober. I don't have to solve any other problems right now. "Thank you."

"Call me tomorrow."

I hang up and text her a big care emoji, then tuck my phone in my pocket and clamber over the rocky division between two beaches, the place I got stuck the other day. Rory and I spent hours and hours on this beach, walking, talking about our big dreams, boys we had crushes on, assignments in class, and places we wanted to travel. In the end, she chose to stay close to home, while I wandered the vineyards of the world.

As I reach the top of the rocks, I see the sandy stretch on the other side. A man is doing slow movements in the lowering sun. Light the color of persimmons washes over his face and arms, and I pause to watch, recognizing Ayaz only as his movements turn him my direction again. He's deeply focused, hands in stylized positions, arms slow and deliberate. It's powerful and beautiful. I rest where I am until he finishes, then step down on the sand. He gives me a nod, not exactly smiling or not smiling. "Hello again."

"Hello. What was that you were doing?"

"Tai chi."

"Isn't that for old people?"

"Not at all. It's one arm of kung fu."

My stomach is roiling again, and I swallow, nodding. "Do you—" I have to turn and run toward the water, where I barf up the contents of my belly. And again. And again, until I'm leaning on my knees, breathing in slowly.

Ayaz offers me a bottle of water. "I haven't opened it."

The nausea is settling, and I drink some water, spit, and drink again. "I'm so sorry. That was embarrassing."

"Not at all."

We move away from the water, washing our feet farther along. "Are you all right now?"

I nod. "Thanks. I did some damage to my stomach with my drinking, I think. It's just taking time to heal."

"Would you like a cup of ginger tea?"

I look up at his kind, dark eyes. "Yes, actually. That sounds amazing."

This time, there is an actual smile, very small, around the edges of his mouth. "Good. Come."

I follow him up the stairs. A house looms over us, all glass and wood, an aggressive show of wealth that Meadow hates. My father always mildly commented, "To each his own," and I felt the same way. Why did the houses all have to be the same? What new thing will someone build in the future over here?

"Here we are," Ayaz says, unlocking the heavy gate with a key and pushing it inward. "Sorry about that. We had a lot of trouble with paparazzi."

He allows me to pass into a fenced garden with a pool. The space smells of roses and jasmine, as if I've wandered into a fairy tale or the Arabian nights. I suddenly feel faint and refocus on the conversation. "Paparazzi," I repeat. "Intriguing."

"Not really. They're parasites and ruined my life for a time."

"Your wife must be quite famous."

"She was," he says. "Now she's dead."

I'm taken aback and it must show on my face, because he adds, "I'm sorry. That sounds far more harsh than I meant it. Only that fame and life are fleeting, and the focus of those little armies of photographers is a very foolish pursuit." He locks the gate and gestures for me to follow him across the garden and into an anteroom, then up a set of stairs with three landings, which leads us finally to the main floor.

"Oh wow," I say. The room is open to a wall of glass two stories high, showing miles of water and shoreline. I'm drawn across the room as if by a siren, standing close to the glass to look and look and look. Below, the restless surf, in the distance the lowering sun and horizon. Something in me quiets. "It feels like floating, like you're a bird."

"Yes."

The kitchen is situated toward the back of the room, with a big island and gleaming white walls and counters, as clean as a clinic, and I join him, sitting on a comfortable bar chair upholstered in white leather.

"Ginger or mint?" he asks. The kettle is on. His hair boasts a glossy shine, the sign of health, and now that I have time to look at him, I see that his body is lean, his waist small. He's not much taller than me, but every inch is well made. A distant, almost forgotten part of my body stirs. *Remember?* it whispers.

"This is not the kitchen I would put you in," I say.

He looks around. "It's very white."

I smile. "I ran a winery," I offer. "The blending rooms were like this. All stainless and pure cleanliness."

"What sort of kitchen would be a better setting for me, do you say?"

"Hmm. Something older, maybe. With more color?"

He nods, a faint smile on his lips. "That would be my preference."

"Older, or more color?"

"I'd like an old house," he says. "Edwardian. With an AGA."

"An AGA," I echo. "What color?"

"Oh, something blue, perhaps." He gathers a cutting board, a knife, a knob of ginger that looks fresh and hearty. "A winery," he says, inclining his head. "Not anymore?"

"No." I suck my top lip into my mouth, debate telling the truth. But what the hell. I have to be real with who I am. "I'm afraid I'm fresh from rehab. Wineries are out of the question for me now."

It startles him, but he doesn't look away. "I'm sorry."

The simple expression somehow slides through my defenses, and I feel a sudden, ridiculous swell of tears. The fact that I've lost the thing I genuinely loved in all this gets lost sometimes, but I did love making wine. I was great at it. A roar of loss sounds in the distance, and I swallow. "Thanks."

"I've never drunk alcohol," he says, "so I am not sure what you feel, but it must be difficult to lose such a business."

"I mean, I guess." I take a breath. "I was so bloody tired by the end that I would have done almost anything to stop."

Again those soft, accepting eyes. Into a saucepan he grates fresh ginger. His fingers are long, tipped with oval nails. He leaves space for me to talk, which is unbelievably rare. When I don't speak, he asks, "How long have you been out?"

"Three days," I say, and laugh at my newbie status. "I was in for almost ninety days."

"And how do you feel?"

I take a moment to consider. "Pretty good, honestly. Sleep is hard to come by and I can't shake my Jelly Belly habit, but . . ." I shrug. "All things considered, I'm better."

He smiles. "That's good."

"It is."

He places a small plate on the counter and shakes some rice crackers onto it.

I pluck one up and taste it. "Why don't you drink?"

"I was raised in a Muslim family and neighborhood. Never saw the point, really." He rinses his fingers. "Why did you drink?"

I meet his gaze. His heavy, dark brows are slightly lifted, his mouth turned up slightly in a faint smile. "I guess that's a valid question." I shrug. "I don't really know. Everyone drinks, don't they?"

"You don't. I don't."

"True." I switch directions, suddenly weary of my only topic of thought or discussion revolving around my drinking or not drinking. "I didn't google you, by the way."

"You don't know my whole name, do you?"

"Oh please. I could have your real name in three minutes flat."

"Really?" He sounds genuinely surprised.

"You're kidding, right?" I pull out my phone, about to demonstrate, but he reaches over the island and touches my hand. Shakes his head. Intrigued, I tuck the phone back in my pocket. "Okay. But it's kind of surprising that you wouldn't know that."

"I'm an analog sort of man." His smile is wry.

"Ah."

The water begins to boil. He takes the kettle off the burner and pours it into a pot, then adds loose tea. The scent of ginger rises sharply. My stomach growls. Loudly.

I hope he hasn't heard. He says nothing, but reaches for a dish on the counter and passes it over. "Dates," he says.

"Mmm. Perfect." They are very fresh and fill my mouth with a density of flavor I never remember noticing before. "My God, these are good."

"Perhaps you're simply hungry."

"Maybe, I mean, considering."

He laughs softly, and there is something in the sound that washes through me, a sense of quiet. "I don't have anything interesting, but I roasted a chicken last night that I would be happy to share."

"Thank you, but I've imposed enough."

"I insist."

I'm tempted. He has such kind eyes and a voice that flows along my nerves like some magic elixir. I'd rather be here than with Meadow, who is no doubt bustling around the kitchen making some fabulous supper. "That's kind," I begin my refusal, and then my mouth says, "Roast chicken sounds great."

He smiles.

We eat at a table by the big window, looking out toward the twilight ocean. The meal is simple, just roast chicken and roast carrots with a spice I'm not familiar with. "Za'atar," he says, nudging a dish of yogurt toward me. It's some of the best food I've had in months, the chicken perfectly tender, the carrots sublime, the ginger tea a perfect accompaniment.

I'm so hungry that I eat like a teenager, spreading butter on fresh bread, devouring the chicken. "Did you *cook* all of this food? It's amazing."

"Thank you. It's simple fare, honestly." He butters a slice of bread himself. Again I notice his beautiful hands—the hands of an artist or a surgeon or a pianist. "Do you like to cook?"

"A person could not grow up in the house I did without learning to love cooking. Both my father and stepmother are serious foodies." I realize what I've done, and a startling, cold wash of grief splashes through me. "I guess that's 'were' now," I say, and to my horror, tears well up behind my eyes. I look down to blink them away. "Sorry," I say, clearing my throat.

He raises a hand. "It is very fresh."

"We weren't close."

"As you said. But a father is a father nonetheless."

"I guess." I take a breath. "Do you mind if I ask about your wife?"

"That depends on the question."

I feel censured, which is ridiculous. Not everyone tells everything to everyone, as I have been known to do. "Has she been gone long?"

"Six months. She drowned." He gestures toward the water surging into waves. "You probably read about it. She was quite famous. Alexandra Zaitsev."

I blink. "Oh. She was in the spy movie, the anti–James Bond thing, right?"

He nods.

It's a little disconcerting, especially since I've been feeling that bloom under my skin, that first whisper of attraction. Zaitsev was an acknowledged beauty, and her death caused quite a stir. "How terrible. I'm sorry."

He peers toward the horizon, then back to me. "Like you, I am ambivalent. We had been estranged for a few months, and I was quite angry with her, but one never wishes to see an untimely death."

"Even harder to be a husband than a daughter," I say.

"Is it?"

I watch a wave rise and begin to crest. "I don't know, I guess. My sister is so brokenhearted she hasn't even been able to tell her children, and my stepmother looks like she's aged a decade." I shake my head. "And all I can think is that I had something I really wanted to get off my chest with him, and he up and died, the bastard."

Ayaz gives me a slow, sad smile. "Things are often not what we expect."

"No." Outside, darkness is falling, and I'm mindful of the walk back. "I suppose I should get going."

"You will walk on the street, not the beach, won't you?"

"Ah. Good thought. Yes." I touch my belly. "Thank you, both for the food and the company. You're easy to be around."

"Thank you. Why don't you leave your phone number? Perhaps we can have a meal another day."

I hesitate, wondering if I need to articulate my position on dating or men or connections or whatever. My sponsor has been quite clear that I should not even consider dating until I've been sober a solid year.

But he's newly widowed, from a woman so beautiful I feel like a toenail in comparison. He almost certainly doesn't want anything, either. We can be friends. God knows I need people who don't drink. When he waits, his fingers over his phone screen, I give him the number. It rings when he calls, and I type in *Ayaz*.

He walks me to the front door, much more modest on this side, and I can see the age of the place in the seventies-era redwood foyer. I start to open the door at the same moment he does, our inner forearms making contact in a weirdly intimate way. I smell faint soap and cedar, and the scent electrifies my nerves, setting them alive from scalp to toes. I look up, surprised, and his face is close and I can't help but look at his mouth, and I'm very flustered, my ears hot, before he finally rescues the situation by straightening a bit.

But I notice that he's looking at my mouth, then back to my eyes, and for one dizzying moment, I really think we might end up kissing.

Which would be against all the rules of sobriety, and we're both in a messy place, and I really need a friend, not a lover. "Thanks," I say, and dash out the door.

"Good night."

Chapter Eighteen
Norah

In the morning, I get out before I hear anyone moving, bringing with me the clothes for work, my notebook, and my laptop. I grab a cup of coffee and an everything bagel with extra cream cheese to keep me going, and settle in to get my head in order. I landed a job as a server yesterday and will start this afternoon, but that leaves me the morning to work on my research.

What do I know about Meadow's life before Augustus? He didn't talk about her much, but when I confronted him about his feelings toward her, he said, "She had a terrible, terrible childhood."

"What does that mean?"

He shrugged in his way. "I am obliged to keep her secrets." He touched my cheek. "You are too young to know that there are things between two people that cannot be severed. I am obliged to love her always."

I thought, *But you left her!*

What happened to their big, passionate marriage, one that neither of them is particularly over, if I'm honest? Yes, an affair, but what led to the affair? Was Augustus just an incorrigible womanizer and Meadow finally had enough, or was there something about that particular connection that broke them?

I rub my forehead, pausing in my mental spiral. I don't need to know about the failure of the marriage, at least not today. That's a personal question, one that my heart wants to understand, and maybe not at all necessary for the story I'm trying to find about Meadow. For that, I need to start with her childhood.

What made her childhood so terrible? I wonder if it was as terrible as mine, although honestly I know I got mostly lucky, considering. I had some really good foster parents and the bad ones were never violent, rather than actively cruel. Still, I know I'm a little unfinished. Augustus was my dream lover because he loved touching so much. Rubbing my head or my feet or my hands almost absently, pulling my leg to cross over his as we sat side by side, touching me always in sleep, his hand on my back, or his body pressed against my side. I'd never been with anyone who loved it as much as I did, who never got tired of touching.

I miss it a lot already.

Focus. Meadow's childhood, not mine.

I have to start with the earliest known facts about her: she started her food career at a pirate-themed restaurant for kids and tourists called the Buccaneer. It's on the beach along Highway 101, and before I head out there—thus wasting Uber fare I really can't afford to spend—I call to find out if Trudy, Meadow's old boss, is still working there.

"Dude, no way. She's like a hundred years old."

"Do you know if she still lives around here?"

"I don't, but hold on."

I hear a muffled yell and then someone else picks up. "How can I help you?"

"I'm looking for Trudy Nickels," I repeat.

"What do you want with her?"

The truth is often the best policy. "I'm writing a dissertation on Meadow Beauvais and I'd like to talk to Trudy about the early days."

"Ah. She loves talking about her girl. Let me call and make sure she'd be down with it."

"No worries. Thank you so much." He takes my phone number, and in less than five minutes, he calls me back.

"Got a pen?" He gives me a phone number, and I scribble it quickly. "She lives downtown."

———— ❧⁓❧ ————

The house is a little square box on a small lot planted by someone who loves and understands plants. It's a very hot location, with bright sun burning down, but the beds are tidy with blooming flowers I don't know the name of, and little statues peek from the foliage.

On the concrete square in front of the door, I take a minute to wipe my face and shake out my sweaty hair, then knock.

A woman opens it. She's nearly six feet tall, with surprisingly beautiful silver hair and an apple-shaped body clothed in easy-wear pastel separates, a sleeveless blouse and capri pants. Her age is hard to calculate—her face is extremely wrinkled, but her movements are brisk. Well into her seventies, if I had to guess. "You must be Norah," she says.

"Yes. Are you Trudy?"

"Come on in." She leads the way and I step inside gingerly. The heavy odor of cigarettes hangs in the curtains and walls, and the ceiling overhead is yellowed with tar. "Can I get you a glass of tea?"

"Sure. That would be great." I stand in the middle of the small living room holding my notebook. An orange cat wanders out and winds around my ankles. I bend over to stroke him, pleased when he purrs.

"Sit down, sit down," Trudy says when she returns from the kitchen. "I hope you like mint tea. I grow it myself."

I take a sip, discovering a reviving, bright brew. "Mmm. It's great."

She settles in a recliner, clearly her favorite chair. Paperbacks and sudoku digests are neatly stacked on the side table, and she tucks a coaster under each of our glasses. "Probably not much use, but I always have to try."

"Of course."

"Now, what can I help you with, dear?"

"I'm writing about Meadow Beauvais and her influence on the foodie movement—"

"Bah. I hate that word, *foodie*. What the hell does it even mean?"

I grin. "You're right. It's silly."

"But go on. Sorry. That's how you get when you get old, set in your ways. You want to know about Tina?"

"Tina?"

"Oh, that's her real name. Meadow was something she came up with along the way."

"Of course." I smile, feeling a piece drop into place. I write down *TINA* in capital letters. "Do you remember her maiden name?"

"Ah, it was a really long time ago."

"No worries. She was very young when she started working for you, right?"

"Yeah. She said she was eighteen, but I thought it was younger, even though she had a little girl of her own."

"Rory, right?"

Trudy squints. "Maybe. I honestly don't remember. Pretty little thing, as pretty as her mother."

"Did she ever talk about the baby's dad?"

"No, no. She never talked about her life before. I got the impression she came from one of the farm towns in the Central Valley. She had that roughness, you know."

"Really," I comment, surprised. "She's so polished now, you'd never guess."

"You know her, then? Why aren't you talking to her directly?"

"I am," I say, trying to make it sound obvious. "I'm just trying to create a fuller picture."

She stares at me for a long moment. Her eyes are almost colorless. "Are you doing an exposé or something, because of this whole business with Augustus?"

"No!" I touch my heart. "I swear."

"So if I call her and ask her, she'd say it was okay to talk to you?"

I take a breath and lie, gambling that she won't do it. "Yes, please." I gesture to her phone sitting on the arm of the chair. "Go ahead."

She settles back. "I never liked him, you know, Augustus. Men that charming are always trouble."

"They were married a long time."

"They were. And then he let her down like he did everybody. You just can't trust that kind of big"—she struggles for the description she wants—"magnetic presence."

"Maybe it's worth it?"

"I reckon, but some women are just more vulnerable than others."

"You think Meadow was more vulnerable?" I can't quite hide the surprise in my voice. "She's so strong. So sure of herself."

"Well, she's over fifty years old, and she's made a name for herself, found her place in the world. She wasn't always like that."

I take a sip of tea. "What was she like when she first came to you?"

"When she first came to the Buccaneer, she was about as broken as girls get. She was so haunted, and skinny, and rough around the edges, like I said. Didn't know how to set a table properly or hold a fork, things like that."

A memory of my own surfaces, my first job in a restaurant, where I had to be shown how to lay out a place setting, and learn what all the utensils were. It shamed me, but a lot of us, new employees to the restaurant world, didn't know when we first arrived.

Trudy settles her body more fully in the chair. The cat leaps up into her lap. "She was jumpy and anxious to please, which made her a good employee, you know. She has a gift for food, knowing what will taste good, what goes together, and she could work fourteen hours a day without blinking."

"What about Rory?"

"Who?"

"The baby."

"I didn't see her a whole lot. Tina was good to her, kept her clean, but I got the feeling that she didn't really . . ." She frowns.

"Want her?"

"Not that exactly, just that the baby was more like a pet or something. Like she could board her if she was busy."

A thread of sorrow winds through my heart. Poor Rory. I think of her with her own two girls, how loving she is. We didn't have any kind of relationship—my choice, because I didn't think it would be right to get involved with her daughters—but I heard stories about her, about Maya, about the family. Rory always seemed to get short shrift from Meadow, but Augustus was very present in her life and in the lives of her children.

"Did you know Maya?"

"Sure. She's had a bit of trouble herself, from what I hear."

"Yeah, unfortunately, I think she has." I tap my pen backward on the paper, and realize what I'm doing, then stop. "Did you know Meadow when Maya went to live with them?"

"Yeah. We stayed pretty tight through all of that. Up until after they got married, as I recall, and even then, we'd get together for breakfast, or she had me up to the house on the hill, though I got to where I didn't like it much."

"Why?"

"I just didn't belong, really. They were a lot of fancy people, all a lot younger than me, and it was just . . . not really that much fun after a while."

It occurs to me that she's much freer with detail than I expected. Despite her threat to call Meadow, she's speaking more like a disappointed mother than anything else. "Do you still spend time together?"

"Hell no. She's got no time for an old boss. We haven't really had much contact in a long time, probably since she divorced Augustus."

I draw a spiral in my notebook, letting ideas rise. With a deliberate shift in my body language, I lean back on the sofa. "Tell me about Maya. Do you remember?"

"Well, when her mother died, it was a big scandal. Poor kid was left in the apartment when the mom OD'd, and she couldn't work the lock to get out. She was stuck there for three days, until somebody heard her yelling and finally got her out." She shook her head. "Can you imagine?"

I have never heard this fact. For a moment, I hate Augustus with a fury that fogs my vision. "Where was Augustus?"

"Married to Meadow. Just up and left that wife when he got tired of her, like he did with Meadow twenty years later."

"That's horrible." I can't resist this personal thread. "What happened when Augustus left Meadow, do you know? They seemed to have such a good marriage."

She nods, coughs for a minute or two, then: "He was a womanizer. That's what they do, womanize. It's like asking why a snake bites."

It feels facile, but maybe it's true.

"Augustus left his first wife for Meadow, after all. How can you trust a man who does that?"

I can't think of a reply.

"Meadow favored Maya over her own daughter. She said she didn't, but you could see it in the way she talked to them, the way she talked *about* them." Her mouth twists. "I think she felt guilty for breaking up the marriage."

We've wandered off track, and although the things I'm learning are great, I also want to get back to the main idea. "You have no idea where she came from? Or what her life was like?"

"Sorry." She strokes her cat.

I chew my lip a little, wondering if Rory knows anything. If she'd talk to me.

"Thanks for your time," I say, closing the notebook. "I don't really have anything else."

"You're welcome, dear. Come back anytime."

I stand, gathering my things. "I might take you up on that."

Chapter Nineteen
Meadow

"What if we head over to Peaches and Pork this morning?" I say to Maya over breakfast. She's devouring her eggs and toast and the grapefruit sections I dusted with turbinado sugar.

She dabs her mouth with one of the dozens of cloth napkins that populate the kitchen linen closet. Linens I bought, long ago. Her hair is pulled sharply back from her face, emphasizing her high cheekbones and the uptilt of her eyes. It's a face I could stare at all day, as beautiful as a sunrise or a flower or a new puppy. "And do what?"

"Just take a look at things. The books, the way it runs. I'll call Kara and ask her to meet us there, so she can walk us through everything."

She opens her mouth, then sighs, her hands on her thighs. "I don't want this," she says, urgently. "I keep telling you. I don't have any skill to run a restaurant and I need to focus on myself right now."

"I get that." I pause, pressing my lips together. "Maybe you just sell it, and that's fine, too. It's just that it's a pretty big legacy and you actually did inherit."

"I don't know why he did this!" she cries, but even as she grows angry, she keeps eating the grapefruit sections.

Feeding people is my love language, and just now, it makes me feel like the mom of the year. She's very thin, never so thin as she was when she first came to us after her mother died, but her wrists and elbows are prominent, and I can see her collarbone quite clearly. Her body is no doubt healing from all the trauma, the poisons she's been pouring into herself for such a long time.

In my head, I hear Augustus say she *is the granddaughter and the daughter of women who died of alcoholism.*

"We've always known this was the plan—the restaurant and house to you, the farm and all that entails to Rory."

She ducks her head. "Maybe I never thought he would die."

A wave of electric sorrow moves through my body, burning my heart, my gut, my toes. "He loved you and he was devastated by everything that happened. He felt like he let you down."

Her face goes hard. "Funny, because I feel like he did, too. At least we agree on something." She forks up the last grapefruit piece and pushes the plate away. "It just doesn't make any sense that he'd leave me the restaurant if he meant for it to continue. What was he even thinking?"

"I don't think he intended for it to be a punishment."

She looks up at me. "How can you still be so fucking loyal to him? How can you defend someone who hurt you so badly?"

It stings. "I'm not loyal to him. I'm loyal to you. I want you to have what's yours."

She drops her head into her palms, and I see her knuckles whiten as she squeezes her hair, a habit she's had since childhood. She sits with her eyes closed tight for long moments, then sighs. "I know. Thank you."

"So you want to go over there? Check things out, start trying to decide what's next? At the very least, the crew wants to get back to work."

"Why can't *you* do this?"

"No," I say. "Not this time."

"Really?" She huffs like a teenager, swings herself off the barstool, then stands there, hands on her hips. "You keep saying you want to help and I'm asking for help and now you won't do the single thing I've asked."

I resist her plea to escape the acknowledgment of her father's death. "You need to go to the restaurant. I can't do this for you."

She looks toward the salon. Light cascades through the patio doors, washing one side of her face and body with golden light. She gnaws her lip. "Meadow."

"Maya?"

She turns toward me. "I need you to go home."

"Now?"

"No, not this minute or anything. I don't want you staying here. Living here. I need to be by myself while I start this next part of my life."

An ache starts up—I don't want to leave her unprotected. I don't want to leave the house I love so much, either. Which one has more pull? It makes me ashamed of myself that I should feel such a materialistic ping, but it would be nearly impossible to say how much I loved this place. It was the center of my world for twenty years.

It's not really about the house, of course. Maya senses the core of my conflict. "I know you don't trust me, and I don't really trust myself, actually, but I need to figure it out, okay?"

"Of course." I rub the dishcloth in my hand over the tiles on the counter. "I just . . . don't want you to feel lonely or lost. You're not alone, okay? Your sister is right in town, and I'm forty minutes away, anytime. Ever."

She rounds the island and gathers me into a hug. "I know, Meadow. I love you and I appreciate everything you're doing."

"But."

"Yeah." She steps away. "If I'm going to stay sober, I have to learn how to stand on my own two feet."

"All right. I'll clear out. And you don't have to go to Peaches today if you'd rather leave it a little longer."

"No, I'll go. I'm sure Kara's getting really anxious. We need to make a few decisions, for sure."

⸻ ⎯⎯⎯⎯ ⸻

We meet at Peaches and Pork an hour later. Kara is there with the books, which are not difficult for a woman who ran a winery to read.

"What the hell?" Maya exclaims. "He's in hock up to his ears."

Kara and I exchange a glance. "Have you looked to see what you owe on the house?"

Maya sighs. "No. You think it will be this bad on that, too?"

"No idea, babe," Kara says.

Maya pulls out her phone and makes a note to herself. "I need to get all the paperwork together on the house and the restaurant and see if I can set up a meeting with a banker." To Kara she says, "Can you get me a name? He must have been working with someone in particular."

"Definitely. I'll email you."

Kara wants to know if they can open anytime soon, which will mean finding a new head chef, a problem that's been looming a long time. Augustus was possessive of his kitchen and menus and no matter how we—mainly Kara and I—nagged him, he was reluctant to hire and train a backup. He didn't want to be replaceable.

Which I understand on so many levels.

Maya says, "You know, I'm going to leave those decisions in your hands. If you need to consult with Meadow, or there are things you need me for, that's great, but you've been running the place for a long time, and you're going to do it better than I will."

Kara presses her hands together in namaste. "Thanks, Maya. That means a lot to me."

Maya takes the time to look at everything, at the barstools starting to fray along the seams, not overtly, but enough to tell their age; at the linens and glassware; at the public toilets and private ones. "It's all so dated."

"It is." Standing with her in the dining room, I continue, "It wouldn't take that much to freshen it up, though. New dining chairs, some paint, different window treatments."

"Glassware, flatware, all of it," she adds, then looks over her shoulder. "God, that stinks." We're standing near the bar, and it smells sour and beery and sharply of tequila.

"Is it bothering you, the smell of alcohol?"

"A little." She touches her belly. "It's making me kind of nauseous."

"C'mon, let's go back to the kitchen. Sorry. I just didn't think about it."

"It's not your job," she says, and pushes open the swinging door to the kitchen.

"I know."

She holds up a finger and dashes toward the employee toilet. Is she going to be sick?

She is. I hear her throwing up in the tiny room. When she emerges, her face is damp, but her color is back. "That was weird," she comments, and rubs a spot beneath her ribs. "Do you think I've completely wrecked my liver? My stomach really doesn't feel right."

"You might have done some damage," I say gently, "but the liver is a very resilient organ. It will heal."

"I hope so." Her mouth twists. "Let's get the rest of this over with. I can still smell the booze from the other room."

We go to the office, which is too small for all three of us, so Maya goes in first and sits in the chair, while I slide in front of the desk and Kara leans on the threshold. Maya just sits there, her hands in her lap, and moves her head to look at things. She looks pale around the lips, as if she's still sick to her stomach. "Are you okay?" I ask.

She shrugs. "He's really very present here, isn't he?" Her eyes catch on something on the shelf and she reaches for it, bringing down a framed photo. "Look at you two!"

It's a photo of us when we got back together, the second time. We're on a beach somewhere, with a strong breeze blowing my skirt and hair, tousling Augustus's curls. He's laughing, his arm around me, and I'm looking up at him like he hung the moon. I remember the day so clearly, the clams we ate, the things we talked about—our big dreams for our lives together, the ambition we shared to make something of ourselves.

"God, we were young," I say. "I'm surprised he still has it."

Kara says, "He's always had that photo in his office." She claps her hand on my shoulder. "He loved you best, always."

Loved you best. The trouble is, I wanted to be the only.

The second time we got together, it was eight months after I broke up with him over his marital status. It had not been an easy stretch of time for me. I was devastated and lonely, and all the more despairing because it really felt like we were soul mates, like we were meant to be together, and it was impossible that we weren't. If I was honest with myself, I'd expected him to leave Shanti and come to me, and he hadn't.

My life was a treadmill of work, Rory, bed, work, Rory, bed. It seemed like it might always be that way, and as much as I loved my daughter, if I was honest, I also resented her and the way she tied me down. There were days that everything she wanted felt like an imposition—a drink of water or her hair brushed or even just attention. I wasn't proud of it, and I worked hard not to show it, but I'm sure she sensed it. Kids are wiser than we give them credit for.

It wasn't that I wanted to date. I didn't even want coffee with another guy. I had rooms at the farm, and flung myself into learning the business, the cycles of planting and harvest, and figuring out ways to key into the burgeoning organic movement. In some ways that farm saved me. I grew to love the colors and flavors, loved learning how to pair herbs and spices with the brightness of radishes or the earthiness of beets. My skin grew tan from being outside in the sun all day, and Rory turned into a puppy of a child, happy and well tended, loved by everyone at the farm. At least I'd done that much for her.

But an Augustus-size hole had been blown in my life and I only lived around the edges of it. I ached for him, if not constantly, often enough that it *felt* like constantly. At night, I dreamed of his shining eyes and skillful hands and low laughter. After a fleeting season of happiness, I felt I would never be happy again.

In August, the regional restaurant association held an outdoor food fair. The owner of what was then Henderson Farms, a widow who had been grooming me to be her successor, let me set up our booth and sell however I wished. I loved it. To show off our harvest, I made up recipes and discovered that I had a gift for it, showcasing all my heirloom pets, golden beets and red cipollini onions and exquisite herbs that had been forgotten, like borage and clary sage. Rory stayed with a friend at the farm, and I had a ball talking to customers all day at the booth, showing off our produce, offering samples of my recipes, creating a network.

It was late on the second day when a lull in traffic allowed me to find a bottle of water and take a deep, long drink. It was hot, even in the shade of the whispering eucalyptus trees. I felt wilted, and looked forward to a nice cool shower at the motel I'd booked for myself.

When I set the bottle down, I turned back and there was Augustus. His black hair was a bit too long, unruly around his face and neck, and he wore a turquoise chef's blouse that brought out all the reddish notes in his brown skin.

I froze. Every single cell in my body surged toward him, but I stood my ground. "Can I help you?"

He carried a fistful of flowers, blues and pinks and whites, and offered them to me. "I saw you setting up yesterday."

I pulled my hands behind me, taking a step back. "Not doing this."

His gaze touched my face, lingered on my mouth, washed over my breasts, thrown into uplift by my posture. I crossed my arms in front, but I could feel the heat in my ears, along my neck.

"I miss you," he said.

I barked out a bitter little laugh. "Too bad about that pesky wife."

He looked down, his long black lashes sweeping across cheekbones in a softness that was so childlike and appealing I had to look away. "You know it isn't a good marriage."

"I *don't* know that, Augustus. Men say whatever they want."

"Fair enough." He glanced away, then back, as if to emphasize how straight and therefore honest his gaze was. "It is not a good marriage, I promise you that, but more what I want to say is that I have never felt the way I feel about you. I can't sleep for missing you." He settled the flowers on the table between us. "I love you and I think you love me. Life is not always tidy, but we don't have to suffer in every possible way."

The words stirred me, I won't lie. But more I was stirred by the sinews in his exquisitely beautiful hands, by the hollow of his throat and the tiny ruby earring he wore in his left ear. Just standing there, looking at him, I felt weak and lost and acutely lonely. "I'm so mad at you!" I picked up the flowers and flung them at him. They hit his slim belly and fell to the ground.

He picked them up and set them back on the table. "After everything closes, I will have a beer at a little café called Jorge's, down on State Street. It's private and quiet, even now. Perhaps we could at least just end it properly. What is it they say?" He gave me that half grin that showed just the smallest flash of white teeth, the glisten of lower lip. "Closure?"

I shook my head. "Just go, Augustus."

He left behind a fragrant spell that worked its way into my body, spreading like alchemical ink through my veins, staining every molecule with desire. My mind and my body were at war.

My body won. I walked to the bar.

He was waiting, but he had not thought I would come. As I entered, he caught my eye and stood, waiting for me to cross the room, and when I halted in front of him, I saw tears in his eyes. He bent to take my face in his hands and kissed me until both of us were dizzy. We went back to his hotel room and engaged with the bodies we each had so missed. I kissed every inch of his skin, forehead and throat and belly and thighs and the arches of his feet. We fucked like we would die the next day, our skin sweaty and slippery in the hot summer night, and then we licked the salt away, starved for every drop of taste we had missed. He buried his face in my neck, his hands hard on my back. "I can't bear to lose you again," he murmured. "I have been out of my mind."

That very night, I started my campaign, realizing I had one thing on my side: I could be hard to get. "You're going to have to leave Shanti," I said. "I love you, but it's wrong for us to be together like this."

He slid over me again, kissing me, his hands in my hair. "I will leave her. Just give me some time."

Chapter Twenty
Maya

As I leave Meadow and Kara at Peaches and Pork, I feel splintery. The smell of the booze in the bar gave me a sense of despair, maybe some PTSD over the wine barrels I split open like I was Paul Bunyan. Now that I'm sober, I can objectively see how wasteful and foolish it was to destroy that vintage. It cost me a fortune. Everything, really. I lost the winery and the house on the land, and it was still not really enough to balance out the damages, the loans we'd carried trying to get to that tipping point, the prestige the label lost.

So much damage from one act of fury. Now Josh has the land and the winery, and I have only what my father left me.

For the first time, it crosses my mind that his death gave me an escape. Where would I have gone, what would I have, if he hadn't left me the house and the restaurant?

How could I have shattered my whole life like that?

Out in the sunshine, I pause and take a few breaths, letting the feelings rise and bring whatever they want to bring. I see myself on hundreds—thousands—of nights in bars across the world, a quiet, devoted drinker imbibing the best wine the bar had. I told myself I wasn't a drunk because if the wine was terrible, I didn't drink it. I never started on bottles of vodka or shots of tequila. I loved a good craft beer, but it was always wine that called me. *Good* wine.

I felt myself to be sophisticated and hip. I knew everything there was to know about the fruit of the vine, and I found my people in those dark rooms, others like me who found solace in the flow of wine blotting out discomfort, sorrow, pain.

How many days, weeks, months—years—did I waste that way? So many. Time I will never get back. This sense of loss layers into the tangle of PTSD and unfelt emotions I've stuffed down over and over, and now have no way to shove back down again. I long for obliteration, something to kill that pain. It seems wildly unfair that I am no longer allowed the drug of peace.

Better to feel, my counselor said, over and over. Since there is no alternative, I stand there in the sun and stop trying to shove the pain away. I let it be whatever it wants to be, let memories spin around my mind. My father, in that picture on his desk, was the age he was when he left me. Seeing his face from that time staggered me, an entirely visceral reaction in my body, not my head. I felt it in my chest and belly, stabbing me so hard that I almost doubled over.

I close my eyes, feel the sunshine, let the memory rise.

He came to me in the bedroom in the apartment we lived in with my mother, Shanti, who was deadly silent in the other room. Never a good sign. He said, "Maya-mine, I need to talk to you."

I knew it was bad, so I just sat there.

"I'm not going to live here anymore, but you're still going to come visit me all the time, and you're going to be part of my world forever, okay? And you're going to have a sister. Rory."

"Rory is going to be my sister?" This was excellent news. I loved Rory. We'd played together sometimes. "I've always wanted a sister."

He stroked my hair. "I know, baby." He had tears in his eyes. It terrified me.

"Are you crying?"

"Only because I'm going to miss you so much."

"Why can't I go with you?"

Actual tears spilled down his face, into his beard. They nearly stopped my heart. "Because your mommy needs you, baby."

My big-eyed mother, who rarely spoke, only drank and smoked. The thought of being alone with her all the time made my body hurt. I bent my head and started to cry myself. "It's not fair."

He held me and we cried together, and all I wanted was to stay right there in the moment and never move forward.

But of course, eventually he stood and kissed my head and walked out.

Walked out.

On the beach outside his restaurant almost thirty years later, I want to go back in time and grab that little girl, protect her from the awful things that were about to befall her.

I want to shake my dad until he sees the truth. How could he have left me with my mother? For any reason? What was he thinking? My mother was so unstable even before he left that it was not a big jump to realize she couldn't take care of me, and I was not equipped to take care of myself.

Furious to the point of shaking, I drive to the Brewed Bean even though it's too early for work, and park in the tiny lot that belongs to employees. In the car, I bend over and press my forehead against the wheel to get myself together. I need this job and I need to do it well to keep it. Everything else will wait. Meadow, my dad, my anger, which seems to be bottomless. I start thinking I see an end to it, and something else rises through the gloom and fires it up again.

You are not alone.

I take out my phone and tell Siri to call Rory. She picks up instantly. "Hey!"

"Hey."

"You sound a little depressed or something."

In the safe space created by my sister, my emotions spill out as tears. "Yeah. Maybe. I was just at the restaurant with Meadow and it was *hard*. Dad's just so present there. I'm mad at him for dying before I could really talk to him, before we could work things out, and I'm *really* mad that I didn't get to tell him how mad I am. And it was one thing to be mad at him when he was still in the world," I say, finding a weird sense of calm as truth emerges, "but it really sucks now that he's dead."

"I know. I miss him so much."

I watch a woman stride by the opening to the street with a dog on a leash, both of them tall and athletic. "Do you remember when you guys started living together?"

She's quiet for a minute. "Honestly, no. I remember him being there, and other things, like the wedding, I remember really well, and when you came to Belle l'Été."

"I remember that, too." A tarry pit of emotions bubbles in my gut. "Ugh. I have to go get something to eat and get to work, but I'll talk to you soon."

"Why don't you come over and have lunch with me? Nothing fancy, but I've got tuna."

Air blows through my hot, tangled emotions. "Yeah. Okay. I'll be there in a minute."

"Good. I'll make some sweet tea."

We discovered sweet tea on a family trip to Galveston as kids, and I've never found a soft drink I liked better. "I love you."

"I know."

"I'm sorry I'm so mad at him. I know you didn't have issues, but I—"

"You had good reasons to be angry," she says. "If I think about him leaving you with Shanti like that, it makes my skin hurt."

I bow my head. "Me too."

When my mother died, I was locked in the apartment with her. The deadbolt opened with a key, and I couldn't find it, not anywhere. I thought it might be in her pockets, but I would rather have crawled through a basement of spiders than touch her deadness. By the time I found her, she was dusky purple, a color I still can't bear, and her tongue stuck out of her mouth. At least she'd had the grace to die in her bed, so I just closed her bedroom door and waited.

It was okay for the first day. Well, not okay, but I had milk and cereal and the TV. I crawled up on the couch and tried to open windows, but they wouldn't budge, so whenever I heard anyone in the hallway, I stood by the door and yelled. "Help! Help! I can't get out!"

No one stopped, not for almost four full days, not that I really registered the time. I knew it was a long time, days in a row. A woman bringing groceries up the stairs finally heard me, and fetched the super, and the two of them opened the door to find me half-crazed with terror and hunger. They called my dad.

Meadow and my dad picked me up, and they were kind, touching me, hugging me. My dad held me close, crying hard, and I was so exhausted I just laid my head on his shoulder. "I'm so sorry," he said over and over. "I'm so sorry. My baby girl."

When we got to the house—which by then was Belle l'Été—Rory was asleep. Meadow fed me peanut butter and jelly sandwiches and ran a warm bath in her bedroom. I'd been in the house only three times, and the splendor staggered me. I couldn't speak for looking around at the painted tiles in the bath alcove, the plentiful soft towels stacked on the shelves, the clean floors, and the fresh soap.

In the bathtub, reaction set in. I started to shake from head to toe. Meadow sang to me, gently washing my crusty skin, my tangled hair. They tucked me into the bed between them, giving me their body warmth, and I finally fell asleep, and slept through the entire next day and night, until the morning, when I opened my eyes to see blue eyes staring down at me. "You're awake!" Rory cried. "Now we can go swimming!"

"Rory," Meadow said, coming into the room with an armful of towels. "Did you wake her?"

"No! I promise! I was just waiting and she woke up herself."

"Well, give her some room, honey. Are you hungry, Maya?"

I was aware of emptiness throughout my entire body. "Yes."

"Let's get you fed, then. C'mon, Rory, you too."

I have no memory of whether there was a funeral for my mom.

From that day to this, Rory has been my truest friend. It takes only a minute to drive to her house, and I love that she's so close again. The Shanti winery is almost ninety miles up the coast, so I'd fallen out of the habit of regular, close contact with my family. I drove down every few months, did my duty visits, then hurried back to my wine. Booze is a demanding, jealous, exhausting lover.

Right now, I walk up to the open screen door, and Nemo comes trotting out of the kitchen to say hello. "Hey, sweetie pie," I say, bending over to kiss his soft nose. "I missed you, too."

Rory trails behind him, her red hair scraped into a messy bun, her slim legs in lululemon tights. Like Meadow, she's sensationally busty, but unlike her mother, she tends to drape herself in loose T-shirts. This one says ALL THE COOL KIDS ARE READING. "Hi," she says, hugging me. "You look wiped out. Come sit down."

I follow her to the dining table. It's scattered with Micron pens and little square cards filled with particular patterns. "Zentangle, huh?"

"It's really soothing." She places a big icy glass of tea in front of me. "Maybe you'd like it."

"Maybe," I say, by which I mean *doubtful*. I take a deep gulp of tea. "Oh my God, this is perfect," I gasp. "So sweet!"

"I got you, babe."

"Thanks." I examine her face and can see the hollowness under her eyes. "How are you doing?"

She sits down opposite me and picks up her pen. The square in front of her has little dots arranged in rows, and she begins to connect them mindfully. "Not that great. I know you guys were at war, but I saw him almost every day, and the world is really empty without him."

Neither Meadow nor Rory seems to hold any anger at him, and for a moment that tension shimmers in my spine. "Weren't you ever mad at him, all his infidelities, letting our family down?"

She raises her head, and I see her working through ways to answer. "I don't know. I mean, I was heartbroken when they broke up, but my relationship stayed strong. It didn't change, really."

I look down. Pick up one of the pens, aware of some rumbling, distant truth.

"But weren't you mad that he betrayed Meadow?"

"Yes, of course I was. But . . ." She pauses. One shoulder lifts as she draws a perfect oval on the square. "I mean, who knows what goes on in a marriage?"

I'm silent.

She pushes little squares of paper over the table toward me, along with a coffee table–size book of patterns. "You should try it."

I open the book.

"The first pages have the starter patterns," she says. "Just look for one that appeals to you."

"Can we eat while we do this? I have to be at work at one."

"Yeah. I'm hungry, too." She touches her stomach. "I keep forgetting to eat, which is not really my MO. I just can't seem to feel anything except grief. It's like this constant roar in my head." She braces her forehead on her palms, hiding her face, but I see the tears.

"Oh, Rory-Bear." I round the table and put my arms around her. She falls sideways into me, and makes real noise as she cries. It feels good to be the comforter instead of the comforted, and I let her cry as long as she wants, which is a pretty long time. I wish I could feel something other than anger. I wish I could grieve like this, but there's nothing, except a wish to help my sister feel better.

Finally, her tears shudder and slow, and she sits up, grabbing a cloth napkin from the table to wipe her eyes. "Thank you."

"Let me get lunch. Is it tuna? In the fridge?"

"Yes. The blue bowl. Bread is on the counter. Plates in—"

"I remember." I open the cupboard by the sink and take out two plates, hand painted in a cheery pattern of flowers, and carry everything back to the table. "Do you want some tea?"

She looks at my glass. "Sure. What the hell."

I grin. "That's the spirit."

We eat tuna sandwiches with dill pickles, and potato chips, and sweet tea, and talk about nothing much. The flowers Rory is going to plant, the pleasure I've found in the new job, Polly's progress at swim lessons. As we sit with our plates in front of us, finishing our tea, she asks, "Have the police been out to talk to you?"

"No. Why? Should they?" I lean forward and plant my elbows on the table. "Did they come talk to you?"

"Yes. Both of us."

"But about what?"

"Dad's death."

"I thought it was a heart attack."

"I thought so, too, but they asked where we were and the last time we saw him, all those kinds of things, and they still haven't released the body."

"That's weird." I frown, looking over her shoulder to the garden I can see through the open door. "So, what, like somebody killed him?"

She lifts her shoulders. "That seems a little dramatic."

"Not like they would want for suspects," I say dryly, and she has the grace to smile.

"Not you."

"Airtight alibi," I say, and glance at the clock. "Damn. I have to go right now." I kiss her head. "Thanks for lunch and the company."

"You too. It really helped."

"Good."

"Do you want to come to dinner tonight?"

"Um . . ." I pause. "Honestly, no. I asked Meadow to go home for real today, and she's going to, so maybe I'd just like to be on my own."

"Okay." She sounds uncertain.

I take a breath. "Look, I can't promise you that I will never relapse, but I swear I'm doing everything I can to stay sober, and you don't need to babysit me. I have a program and a sponsor and lots of support"— not strictly true, all of it, but I'm working on it—"so you don't have to hold up the tent, okay?"

"I'm sorry. You just keep telling me and I'll keep trying. It's only because I love you, you know."

"I love you, too, sis. Thank you."

"Call me anytime."

As I'm heading down the sidewalk, I'm thinking about when to call my sponsor today, and maybe I'll do it when I walk on the beach. I also need to fit in a meeting at some point.

What I notice is how much lighter my step is, how much less fury is in my lungs. Whatever else might have happened, I'm very lucky that I landed my sister.

Chapter Twenty-One
Norah

It's hot when I leave Trudy, the sun a high burning ball that makes the sidewalks sizzle, and even flies are too tired to do more than buzz up lethargically when I pass. I long for the pool at Belle l'Été, for my cozy room under the oleander bushes, but of course I can't go back there right now. I have to find refuge. I head for the library. It's air-conditioned and no one will hurry me.

And books are always a source of comfort. Bookstore, library, even a bookmobile, I'm happy.

One of the great pieces of luck in my life was landing in a foster home filled with books when I was seven. I mean, *overflowing* with books. They were stacked on shelves, as books are meant to be, or so I learned, in the living room and in the bedrooms, and stacked on a shelf by the stairs that led to the basement. In the kitchen, cookbooks lined the top of the fridge, a place I'd only ever seen boxes of cereal, and filled up one whole counter.

It wasn't the nicest house in the world. It smelled of dogs and the cigarettes my foster mom Susan smoked, and she loved reading so much she didn't spend all that much time cleaning, although the army of children she cared for did a lot of it. We had chores, ordinary kinds of chores, like teaming up to do the dishes after meals, and taking turns vacuuming and cleaning bathrooms and watering the garden, not like some places I lived later, where kids were treated like slaves.

Susan and Joseph were good foster parents. I lived there for almost six years, from age seven until I was thirteen, and in that time we ranged between five and seven kids, three who were born to the family, the rest fosters Susan took in because she'd been orphaned at nine and hated it. She loved kids, and cooking and growing vegetables, but mostly she loved reading. Reading while she stood at the counter, smoking and waiting for water to boil for spaghetti. Reading in her chair after dinner while everyone else watched TV on a console in the living room. Reading in the bathtub and reading in bed. She read a bit of everything, from mysteries to biographies and everything in between, but her true love was romances of every variety, the subscription books that arrived every month and the fat paperbacks she picked up at the used bookstore for a quarter or a dollar each.

She took us to the library once a month, the whole gang, whoever was living there at the time, and let us check out whatever we wanted. No limits on how many or what subject—well, one time Billy Orly wanted to check out a book on a true-crime murder, and she didn't let him have it, and I'm just as glad; we all were.

Not everyone loved it as much as me. Sometimes, kids would just slump in the shared areas and give irritated looks at the rest of us.

But I was in heaven. I'd always liked reading, but with full permission from Susan, I became a readaholic, big-time. I tore through a book a day, gulping down everything that swept into my realm, from the Baby-Sitters Club and *The Yearling* to *Charlotte's Web* and the Goosebumps books. When I was nine Susan gave me the first two Harry Potter books for Christmas, and I was desperately in love with the world. We read them together, and she took me to a Harry Potter event at a bookstore in downtown Pittsburgh when I was eleven. I don't have many possessions I carry around, given the number of times I've had to move, but I own and protect the entire Harry Potter collection. It's one of my most treasured belongings.

In the air-conditioned library, I wander down the stacks of children's books and find Harry Potter and sit on the floor in the aisle and open it, feeling Susan all around me. I never called her *mom* or *mother*—her "real" kids never liked that—but she was the only mother figure I had, and I loved her.

When I was twelve, she was diagnosed with breast cancer, and it moved fast. By my next birthday, she was too sick for foster kids or even reading. By the time they found me a new home, she was gone.

I press my forehead against the shelf, feeling a swell of longing and loss, which seems weird so many years later, but it rises up like this periodically, out of the blue. I don't often wonder about my biological mother, or dwell on the years I spent in less-than-stellar homes, but I think of Susan all the time. Bringing the book to my nose, I fancy I catch a little wisp of cigarettes, and close my eyes, bring up a tattered memory of a wiry woman in a blue T-shirt watering zucchini. She would have liked Meadow, I think. All of us motherless daughters.

I frown. But is Meadow motherless? Why do I think that?

Holding the book in my lap, I let the thought rise. Why did I draw this conclusion, even without realizing it?

The main reason is simple: What girl leaves her mother when she has a new baby daughter?

Chapter Twenty-Two
Maya

The next morning, I'm scrambling eggs in the kitchen that is finally all mine, when the police stop by. "Hold on!" I call to the knock. They've come to the back, pulling around into the driveway, so I can see them through the window. It's not unusual, given the swoop of the driveway. Two cops in uniforms, one tall man with short black hair, and a woman who is slight but wiry, her hair pulled back into a sleek, no-nonsense bun.

I pour the eggs onto the plate and dash over to the door. My stomach is growling and annoyed, and I want to get my food in there. "Can I help you?"

"Maya Beauvais?"

"Yes."

"Can we come in and talk with you about your father?"

For a moment, I don't respond, giving myself a beat of time. Why are they here? "Is there something wrong?"

"Mostly routine."

Mostly. Huh. "I need to eat the breakfast I just made, so if you can talk while I eat, sure."

They follow me into the room. Sunlight pours through the banks of windows facing southwest, gilding the Spanish tiles of the floor and illuminating the golden wood. The man whistles. "Some place you've got here."

I slide behind the counter, pick up my fork. I wish my hair weren't still wet. "What can I help you with?"

The woman says, "I'm Detective Love, and this is my partner, Detective Vaca."

"I don't know how much help I'll be. We'd barely spoken in years."

"Why were you estranged?" she asks. In her hand is a small notebook, and she has a tiny pen to go with it. So cute. I should find one for Rory to use in her Zentangle habit.

I take a bite of cheesy eggs, and they're so delicious I almost moan. It's like my taste buds have been dead for years and I can taste every molecule of everything. I swallow. "He was a player. He deserted my mother, and then he broke Meadow's heart, and I'd just had it."

"Maybe he broke your heart, too, huh?" she asks. She has bright black eyes that reflect light like a mirror.

"Sure." I take another bite, lift a shoulder. "I mean, I was in my twenties by the time he fucked up his marriage, so it wasn't like I was some little kid. I was just . . . over it."

"Did you have a good relationship with him as a child?"

"I did." This is the hard part of it all. When he wasn't awful, he was wonderful. "I always knew he loved me, and he was fun to be around. When he was around. Mostly, he worked."

She inclines her head. "Didn't he abandon you with your mother— your biological mother—when he met Meadow?"

I meet her probing gaze, feeling anger snap and crackle along the bones of my spine. "*Abandoned* is a pretty strong word," I say. "She was my mother and he left her."

"But when she died you were trapped in the apartment for several days, isn't that right?"

I hate it when this comes up. It's so intensely, painfully personal, and yet it was all over the news of the time. Carefully, I place my fork on the plate and press my hands to my thighs. More flame edges along my ribs. "What does that have to do with anything?"

"Just seems like a crappy thing to happen."

"It was. But even if I'd somehow harbored revenge fantasies about killing my dad over that, I was in rehab the night he died."

"Your dad paid for the rehab, is that correct?"

"Yes, I think he and Meadow paid together. Again, what difference does that make?"

"We're just trying to get a feeling for what was going on in his life when he died."

I incline my head. "So he didn't die of a heart attack?"

"Maybe not."

"So what killed him, then?"

"We don't know enough to say yet. We do want to rule out poison."

I choke on toast crumbs. *"Poison?"* I frown. "Really?"

"It's a possibility."

"Can't you test for that?"

"Some things. Not all of them," Vaca says. "Doesn't your stepmother make herbal concoctions at her farm?"

I roll my eyes. "Meadow didn't poison him, trust me. She loved him."

"But they've been divorced a long time. Were there still feelings between them?"

A warning rushes up my spine. What are they digging for here? I temper my reply. "Not *feelings* feelings. They were like siblings."

"Hmm. More than that," Vaca says.

"No," I say dismissively. "It wasn't that kind of relationship. He had some new girlfriend. Have you talked to her?"

"Norah Rivera," he says. "We'd love to, but we can't find her. She lived here when he died, but your stepmother kicked her out and we haven't been able to locate her."

"Meadow kicked her out?" I draw my brows down. "Why would she do that?"

"She said she wanted the house to be ready for your return."

"Ah." I lift my chin. That makes sense.

"Who inherits all this?" Vaca asks, spinning his finger in a circle. "The house, the restaurant?"

I sigh, cross my arms. "Me."

"Nobody else gets any of it?"

"Not as far as I know. He didn't have a wife, and Rory really, really didn't want it. She was very clear about the house coming to me."

"Why?"

"Well, for one thing, she has a house in Santa Barbara that she's worked her ass off on, and they love it. As for the restaurant, she never, ever wanted to be part of the restaurant business."

"Not fair that one daughter should get everything and the other nothing, though. Is it?"

"It's not nothing," I say. "She inherits all of her mother's property. And honestly, my dad didn't do the fair thing. He did whatever the fuck he wanted, all of his life. Why should it be any different now?"

"That's Meadow Sweet Farms? In . . ." Vaca flips through his notes.

"Ojai," I supply.

The woman nods, but Vaca inclines his head. "If you hear from Norah, we would really like to speak with her."

I lift my shoulders. "I wouldn't know her. We've never met."

"All right." He holds up a business card and sets it down on the counter. "If you think of anything that might be helpful, give us a call."

"Sure."

The Brewed Bean is fairly busy when I first arrive, and it's pleasurable to lose myself in physical activity, making espressos and lattes, delivering sandwiches, running dishes back to the kitchen. It's a small staff, just me and the prep cook in the back, and whoever is upstairs roasting beans.

I can smell them, and the scent layers over the top of brewing espressos with a heady depth that makes me remember I once read that the smell of coffee has healing properties. It's so thick here that I wonder if it can also make you high. When things slow down, I run upstairs to see what they're doing, but the room is empty.

By three, it has cleared out, only four or five tables. At one of them is a dark-haired woman I've seen here before, and at another a pair of businessmen talking over something that needs a lot of spreadsheets to explain, and in the prime corner, his back to the wall, his face toward the view of street and palm trees and ocean, is Ayaz. He was here when I arrived, and gave me a simple lift of the chin in acknowledgment, but has nursed the same cup of tea for two hours. I keep expecting that he'll leave, but he's writing on yellow legal tablets with a fountain pen. Quickly, slowly. Pause. I find myself looking at his lovely hands far too much.

Mind your own business.

Maybe it's just waking up after being so constantly soaked in the poison of alcohol, but my body has been asking for attention, food and sleep, and now this, too. I want to feel hands on me. I want kissing and friendly engagement. Nothing deep or connected. Just sex.

The idea of poison makes me think about the detectives. Did someone poison my father? The idea seems absurd, and I can't believe they're taking it seriously. He had enemies, for sure, but did anyone hate him enough to kill him?

It's hard to believe.

Across the room, Ayaz focuses on his tablet. From the corner of my eye, I admire the way light highlights his profile, and the pleasure it gives me is a warning that while the need for sex is pretty ordinary and addressable, maybe not with him. It feels like it could be too much, like I might want more.

The dark-haired woman, the one who's been working on her computer, scribbling notes and nodding to herself, brings her ceramic cup to the counter. Her focus is impressive, and I've tried to leave her alone. Up close, she's remarkably beautiful, with enormous dark eyes and shiny hair and poreless skin. "Can I get another cup, please? The Tiger Blend, with cream."

"Sure." I rinse the cup and pick up another, filling it from the pot on the counter. "You're working pretty hard over there."

"Oh. Yeah." She glances over her shoulder almost guiltily. "Research, mostly."

"Cool." I set the cup on the counter. "Anything else?"

"No, thanks."

"There're some day-old pastries going for half price."

She hesitates. "Yeah?"

"Apple fritter," I say, "two dollars."

"Done." She digs the bills from her jeans pocket and smooths them out on the glass.

I fetch the pastry from the case and plate it. "Enjoy."

"Definitely," she says, raising the plate.

In the lull, I rinse a bar towel in hot water and come around the counter to wipe the tables and counters thoroughly, spraying them all with a lemony cleaner that probably isn't organic but smells like it.

I'm not sure what happens, but I swing around to spray a table behind me, and my foot catches on a chair or a table leg or something, and I'm falling before I realize what's going on. The spray bottle is in my left hand, and instinctively, I'm idiotically protecting it as I go down.

Which means that my right hand takes the full brunt of my fall, my palm landing half on the metal round of a table base, half on the floor. Pain rockets through my wrist, and before I even fully register what's happened, I know the rest of my day is going to be quite a bit different from what I imagined.

Then the slow motion stops. I slam into the ground, crumpling under the force of my fall. The spray bottle goes flying, and my feet knock over a chair. People leap to my aid—the woman with the shiny hair, Ayaz crouching, another customer who's been sitting at the counter. He's a long-haired surfer in board shorts and bright pink flip-flops, and he's first to my side. His hands are on my shoulders. "Dude, are you okay?"

I'm both very embarrassed and in a lot of pain. I sit up, holding my arm close to my chest. "I'm all right."

"Sure?" the woman says gently. "That looked like a pretty hard fall."

"I'm good." My face is flaming. "Can you help me up?"

She's strong, and hauls me to my feet with my left hand.

Ayaz calmly says, "May I see your wrist?"

"It's really okay," I say, but tears sting my eyes. The pain is loud.

He takes my elbow and very, very gently braces my hand on his palm. Even that much pressure makes me bite back a cry, and the joint is swelling right before our eyes.

"You'll need to get that looked at," Surfer Guy says. "Kinda looks broken, I'm sorry to say."

As if to emphasize this, a pain shoots through the bone, all the way up to my elbow. "Thanks."

The dark-haired woman looks at her watch and swears. "I have to get to work in five minutes. Are you going to be okay?"

"Yes. I'll be fine. My mom lives here. Or I'll call my sister."

She touches my shoulder and I feel like she's going to say something else, but my boss comes out right then. "Holy shit, lady," Jessica says. "Did you break your arm?"

"I'm really okay," I protest.

"You really are not," Ayaz says calmly.

"You can't drive, either, can you?" Jessica says. "I just sent Randi home. If we both leave, I have to close."

I stare at my wrist and know I can't drive. "I can call my sister." Except I think her kids are getting out of school, and after the big stand over sending Meadow home, I'd feel like a total ass calling her.

"Will you allow me to drive you?" Ayaz offers. "It's not far."

I'm about to protest, but Jessica says, "Oh my God, would you, my friend? It would be such a help. I'll give you free coffee for a month."

"Unnecessary." He moves my arm back to my belly and I hold it protectively. "I'm happy to help."

Jessica says, "Let me get you the workers' comp info."

I stare after her, crumpling inside. Am I going to have to give up the job, which I've started to like and is giving some shape to my days? Where else can I go? It's not like I have a lot of skills outside the wine business. Meadow would give me work at the farm, I guess, but that makes my spine stiff with resistance.

I realize I'm totally the center of attention, and people are staring, all except the woman with dark hair, who waves as she runs out.

Jessica brings out a sheaf of papers, which she hands to me. "Just let me know what's going on. If you need a day or two, we can figure something out."

"I'm sure I can work tomorrow."

"Well, maybe just wait and see what they say." She touches my shoulder. "It's all good, dude."

Ayaz drives a battered Mercedes, at least thirty years old. It's black, and the seats have been recovered. Inside, it smells ferny, foresty. The scent eases me as I settle in. I can't do the seat belt, so he bends over me matter-of-factly and clicks it into place.

The wrist hurts like something is chewing on it, and I just hold it next to my body, hoping that will ease it or keep it from getting worse. I'm struggling not to cry. "It's nice of you to do this," I say to distract myself.

"Nonsense. You would do the same for me, I think." He starts the car and it purrs to life.

It's only a few blocks to the urgent care. As he pulls into the lot, I say, "You don't have to stay. I'll call my sister. Seriously."

"Will you allow me to walk you inside at least?" His expression is merely kind, nothing more, and I nod. I honestly feel a little dizzy and I'm grateful when he takes my elbow.

At the window, I check in and give the woman behind the desk my paperwork, then turn to sit down and realize I've left my purse—along with my phone—at the café.

"Why don't you let me sit here with you," Ayaz says, "and when they take you for your X-ray, I'll jog back and pick up the purse, and you can be done with me."

"It's not that," I say, wincing as a round of biting starts again in my wrist. "I just don't want to impose." I'm leaning my head on the wall and swivel it to look at him. "This is the second time you've rescued me."

He gives me a very small smile. "Chivalry lives."

I close my eyes against the teeth gnawing on my wrist and take a breath. "What kind of books do you write?"

"Medical thrillers. Nothing you would read, I would imagine."

"I might." A little click makes me want to look him up when I get home. Maybe I know his work. "You don't sound as if you like it very much."

He spreads his palms and brings them together. "I do. When it's moving, when I'm swimming in the depths of it, there is nothing better. I've been a writer since I was a small child, and it was always a delight, making up a story, seeing the shape of it."

"But?"

"I am in the middle of something I cannot quite bring in." He looks at me. "I don't know why."

His face is very pleasing, dark lashes over expressive eyes, his lower, full lip. I say, "Maybe you're grieving still?"

"Mmm. Perhaps. It started before she died, but it's been worse since then."

A woman in blue scrubs comes out of the double doors. "Ms. Beauvais?"

I stand.

"I'll be back with your purse," he says.

The X-ray shows a hairline fracture along the radius, which will have to be set. The nurse brings in all the things she'll need to do the job—bandages in several colors, which she offers for my selection. I choose pink for the cheeriness.

Before we start, she asks some routine medical questions, and I answer without energy until she asks, "When was your last period?"

My body goes so cold I feel I've been swamped by a winter wave. I think back—did I have one at all in rehab? That's three months. Before that? I can't remember. The last few months before rehab are a blur of anger and revenge plots and patchy blackouts. My boyfriend, Josh, was living in the guesthouse at the winery, but we were not on good terms. We might have had punishment sex, I suppose, but he was so madly in love with the Frenchwoman he'd fallen for over the long months he was marooned in Provence that I really doubted it, even if I'd goaded him.

The terrible truth is that it is unfortunately and entirely likely I had random sex with some bar connection. The thought brings a surge of self-hatred the color and texture of tar. It mixes with the pain in my arm and the fear in my gut to create a perfect storm of horror.

"I don't know," I say aloud, thinking about my nausea and unsettled tummy and intense appetite.

And cravings. The driving demand for artichokes.

"Do we need a pregnancy test?" she asks.

I pause. Nod. "Yes."

She must see something on my face, because she squeezes my uninjured hand. "One thing at a time."

Alone in the room, hurting, I suddenly wish for my father. He was always the one who took care of emergency room visits, who cheered us up when we were sick or hurt. Meadow seems like the ultimate earth mother, but she was never patient with weakness, including a flu or an injury. Rory and I laugh about it.

We were lucky to have Augustus. He would make all our favorite foods—for me it was peach cobbler, his own fabulous creation with secret ingredients I never learned. Sugary peaches and buttery crust with a tantalizing mix of spices.

My mouth waters. If I had my phone, I'd call Meadow and request that delectable dessert, even if I am a bad daughter for asking her to go away.

The nurse returns with a pregnancy test. I pee in a cup with some difficulty, and leave the specimen in the bathroom. A doctor comes in to set the wrist, which she does very gently, and then I'm lying there when Ayaz comes back in. He has the strap of my purse over his shoulder, and I see the phone sticking out. He's also carrying two soft-serve ice cream cones, one of which he hands to me. "They said it was all right."

"I am probably going to cry over this," I say, blinking tears away, "because I'm very emotional right now, but this is so very, very nice."

"You're welcome." He settles the purse next to me, and admires my pink cast. "Cheerful."

"That's what I thought."

"Are you finished? I would be happy to drive you home." He winks. "It's on my way, you know."

"I have to wait for a couple of things, but yes. I would like a ride." It's impossible to pull the phone out while I'm eating an ice cream cone, but the food is much more important.

The nurse bustles back in. "Here's a prescription for Norco," she says. "It should be all right for a few days no matter what."

"Oh, no narcotics. I'm in recovery."

She nods, a hand up. "Understood. Let me get you some good Tylenol. Is that okay?"

"Yep."

"The other," she says, with a sideways glance at Ayaz, "is a yes."

"Really."

She squeezes my hand. "Really."

A strange, wild thing moves through my body, beneath my ribs, inside my breasts. I dive deep into my belly to see if I can feel anything alive in there, but what it feels like is a glowing sun brightening the entirety of everything.

Chapter Twenty-Three
Meadow

I spend two days working with Kara on the logistics of getting Peaches and Pork up and running again, driving between Ojai and the restaurant twice, when I might have stayed at Belle l'Été, but never mind.

Kara wants to aim for reopening next Thursday, which gives us time to get everybody back to work and clean the kitchen out properly. The books themselves are in good shape, thanks to Kara, but the money is very low. I can't support it forever, but for a few weeks I can float some cash flow. Crass as it is, there should be lots of interest in the place in the aftermath of Augustus's death. Kara suggests a memorial cocktail, something made with bourbon and cherries, and I agree that it's perfect.

A visual of some festive evening in the early 2000s wafts over the screen of my memory, Augustus dressed in a well-pressed linen shirt the color of peach sorbet, eyes glittering as we toasted whatever it was, devastatingly sexy, his eyes all for me. We had so much fun with those parties. For a moment, I'm lost in the memories, the pleasure of those years.

Then I'm swamped with a sudden exhaustion. Time. So much time. So many moments of laughter and sorrow. Misunderstandings, connection, the deep tangle of two human beings in intimate concert with each other.

The weight of it all drags on me as I get in the car to drive back up to Ojai. But I just sit in the car for a moment looking out at the landscape. A thread of smoke rises from a far northern spot, and a shiver moves up my arms. It seems early for a fire, but the winter was extremely dry.

But honestly, I can't worry about one more thing. To lighten my spirits, I call Rory. "Hey, Rory-Bear," I say, using Augustus's nickname for her. "I've really got the blues over all this. Are the girls home? Can I come by and get some baby love?"

"Of course!" She sniffles. "I've had a really hard day, too."

"Oh, sweetheart. Have you? Missing your dad?"

"Ye-es." Her voice goes breathy with a sob, and my heart aches a hundred times more. I would take all her suffering if I could, bear it by myself so she wouldn't have to. "I'll be there soon, baby."

By the time I arrive, she's made fresh limeade in a glass pitcher and arranged cookies on a flowered plate, which she carries out to the back patio. The girls are building a town in the sandbox, but they leap to their feet when they see me. "Lala!" they cry, and hurtle their small bodies into my legs. "Why haven't you come to see us? Where have you been? Did you know Aunt Maya is back home?"

"I did know." I brush hair from Polly's face, kiss Emma's tiny fingers.

They both kiss me, and then Polly tugs my hand. "You need to come see our town."

"I will in a minute, okay?"

They dash back to the project. Rory stands by the table, one hand over her middle, looking winded. Her eyelids are puffy and red, making her pale-gold eyelashes disappear, and I reach out to pull her into me, hugging her hard. "I miss him, too. The world feels so quiet."

"Yes," she gasps, and tears fall on my neck. "I feel like someone unplugged something inside of me."

We rock together a long time, until I feel the tension in her body start to ease. I release her, and she sinks into a chair. I pour us both limeade, and pass her a cookie studded with M&M'S. "It does get better in time."

"I don't want it to. I'm afraid I'm going to forget things. Details, you know? Like, I can't remember the back of his hands. Why didn't I ever look at them?"

"You won't forget the important things." I take a sip of pale-green liquid, and it's as refreshing as a plunge into a deep pool. "This is really good."

"Thanks. Simple syrup cuts the sharpness of the lime." As if she's remembering she has needs, too, she lifts her own glass, and takes a vast swallow. "Oh, that's a really good one. I think I might try adding some basil."

"That would be a great mocktail."

"Ah, yeah. It would be." She drinks again and picks up her cookies, picking out a red M&M. "I don't think Maya was very comfortable with us drinking the other day. I mean, I didn't drink while she was here, but Nathan drank beer. I felt bad about it afterward."

"The world is full of booze, all the time, everywhere," I say. "Maybe it would be nice for her to have places that are alcohol-free."

"Yeah, that's what I was thinking." She nibbles her cookies. "After she was at P&P yesterday, she came over here. She's pretty freaked out."

"I know. The timing is really terrible, but the law doesn't care that she was at rehab. Either she sells it or we move forward, and it's hard to know which is which until we see what happens without Augustus at the helm."

Her cheeks are dewy and flushed, and tendrils of red-gold hair have escaped her messy bun. So beautiful, and thanks to the stabilizing, steady father figure Augustus provided, she's remarkably sane. His efforts to become the kind of father a girl needed paid off in this one.

"Can I be honest?" she asks.

"Please."

"I think it's done, the restaurant. It's been losing glory for a long time, and without Dad—" She shrugs. "I can't even imagine what's there without him."

"That's a valid point," I say, but I feel resistance in my gut. Hard resistance. "It needs updating, a fresh menu, better marketing." Emotion thickens my throat. "I can't bear for it to close. It would be like erasing him."

"I get it. But we also have to think about what's best for Maya."

"Totally agree, but she also can't go back to making wine. She needs something else to do."

"Maybe you should let her figure that out."

"I know."

She raises an eyebrow.

I drink. "I really do."

We sit in silence then, the girls chattering over where to place a road. In the distance, a dog barks. Nemo and Elvis raise their heads to see if they need to chime in. A breeze softens the day, bringing with it a scent of dryer sheets. My daughter blows her nose. A plane crosses the sky.

All of it evidence of the world relentlessly, heartlessly moving on without Augustus Beauvais.

———— ༄ ————

It isn't until I'm back at the farm, putting things away, that I find the thick packet Augustus left for Maya in my purse. It gives me a pang of guilt that I still haven't handed it over. I *must* remember to give it to her tomorrow, even if I'm not sure it's the best thing for her sobriety.

Being back at the farm leaves me restless, wandering. Lonely. I built the house when Augustus and I divorced, a consolation for the loss of Belle l'Été and my marriage. It's a lovely thing, with big open rooms and a kitchen straight out of *Martha Stewart Living* magazine, with a big island topped by an antique butcher block, and a massive range. Big multipaned windows open to views of the fields and the roses I've planted everywhere.

Augustus haunts these rooms far more than the rooms at Belle l'Été. I haven't lived there in nearly a decade, and once Norah arrived, I didn't stop by very often.

In the early years after our divorce, Augustus spent little time in this house—he'd come inside only three or four times, despite how often he drove up to talk plantings for the next season at the restaurant or to claim a pig.

When Maya went to rehab and we fell to each other for comfort, our love affair started anew. He was here nearly every day, cooking with me at the island late at night, making love to me in my enormous bed, telling me about his days. Together we put together packages for Maya, and grieved over her terrible predicament. I don't know what Norah thought was happening. It occurs to me now that she must have been lonely, waiting for him to come home to that big, empty house.

Through my open windows comes the sound of crickets, and the eternal, endless perfection of it splits me open. How many summers have crickets been singing? A million? Ten million? How can they simply offer it up every night, over and over and over?

Sitting at the island, alone except for the dogs and cats, I am swamped with a vast longing to touch Augustus one more time. Smell him. Hear his voice. How is it possible I will never see him again? That he'll never call me by one of the multiple nicknames he had for me? Meadowsweet, it was sometimes, or Knees for the fact that I'm a little knock-kneed, or Pumpkin, or Sweetmeat.

So many nicknames, for all of us, but we all only ever called him Augustus. Not even Gus, ever. I didn't call him *sweetheart* or *baby* or *honey*. Only his full name.

Which might not even have been his real name. Just as Meadow is not mine. Now that I know the truth about his childhood, our deep connection makes all the more sense. We were both lost children, and came together to make sure our girls were not lost. We might have had a lot of flaws, the two of us, but we gave our children a good childhood, so much better than the ones we'd known.

Restless, aching, I wander outside to the patio. It's very dark along the mountains, the trees and fields silent under a quarter moon. A breeze tangles around my ankles. It should be cool this time of night, but there's still heat in it, a puff of exhausted day falling to the earth. Fire season is coming, and it's something we've all learned to fear. The fires are hotter and fiercer than they ever were before, and we're all in danger of going up in flames without much warning at all.

Not today. Elvis pads out behind me and slumps on the flagstones, ears twitching for a minute before he falls asleep.

Augustus, Augustus, Augustus.

I close my eyes, leaning back, and imagine he's here. To the ghostly figure I say, "You know what I've been thinking about?"

"Tell me."

"Mondays."

"Picnics." I imagine I can feel him stretching out his long legs in the chair next to mine, kicking off his shoes to let his aching feet, destroyed after so many years standing on them, get some air. "Those were good days."

The restaurant was closed Mondays and Tuesdays. Often, he worked on Tuesdays anyway, as much of the staff did, doing maintenance tasks, experimenting with new dishes, doing paperwork, but Mondays in the summer were family day. We'd pile the girls into the car and drive to the mountains or a lake or the ocean and have picnics. Augustus packed them himself, taking great care to include strawberries for Rory and bananas for Maya, some runny cheese and a baguette for us, along with cold chicken or something fabulous from Peaches and Pork, all of which we'd wash down with a bottle of wine and lemonade for the girls. When we arrived home, we sometimes played board games or watched movies from the video store.

"Those were some of the happiest times of my life," he says, and I don't have to imagine this. He's told me many times.

"You were so good at family building," I say. "I wish we could have had more children."

The imaginary Augustus disappears in a puff. This is not a conversation he would ever have wanted to have, not again. We had it so many, many times.

Although we shared our two daughters, I had been unable to have another child. We tried for years, and although I was pregnant four times, I could not carry a baby to term. The most heartbreaking loss was at five months, but usually it was less.

Not that my grief was any less shattering.

Four times. Four losses. Each one left me more depleted than the last until he refused to try again, ever. We had a spectacular fight, and he slammed out of the house. "I can't do this, Meadow. It can't be the only thing in our lives."

It frightened me, the loneliness left in the wake of his fury. When he came in, very late, smelling of tequila, I reached for him, sliding my hand over his chest. "I'm sorry," I said.

He opened the space beside his ribs and I crawled into it, pressing my flesh into his. "I'm sorry, too." He kissed my head, and held me. "I love you. I want you to stop suffering."

I closed my eyes. "It's over. I gave it my best."

"Are you sure?"

"Yes." I pressed my cheek close to his heart, and spoke a soft truth. "I just hate that it might be all the damage that's preventing a baby. I mean, how would that be fair?"

"Oh, Pumpkin, I'm so sorry. I didn't know that's what you were thinking." He enveloped me in his embrace, and I melted into him, disappearing into his gentleness.

But I never stopped wishing for a part of him to live inside me, our mingled DNA traveling on into the future.

Chapter Twenty-Four
Maya

Ayaz brought me home and saw me settled, then reluctantly left me. Comfortable on the couch with a pot of tea at my elbow, I look out the french doors and think of my dad. This is not my first broken arm.

When I was four, I fell down the stairs from the front door of our building to the sidewalk below. It was a head-over-heels tumble, and the miracle was that I broke only my arm in two places, not my head or my back or my legs or my neck. Four-year-olds have soft bones, which saved me, and I wore a hooded jacket that protected my head from the concrete, but my full body weight landed on my arm. I remember standing on the top stair, and then my father cradling me many days or hours later. I dreamed a tiny devil creature was chopping at my arm with an axe, and I howled, trying to get him to stop.

My father held me, rocked me, sang songs in his deep baritone voice. Silly songs in French and English. He read to me. He bathed my face with cold water and filled plastic bags with ice to pile on my arm, fixed by surgery and not yet in a cast because it would keep swelling for a full week. I remember waking up with him slumped in sleep against the couch, his head on the cushion below my legs. His black curls fell over his face. One hand rested on my shin, securing me to the world so I wouldn't fly away.

This is the memory that floats back to me as I lie on the couch with my broken wrist throbbing, afraid that even an ibuprofen will send me back into the spiral of addiction. Usually, I push away those memories of his good side, but lying in the living room where he reigned so often, listening to the endless sound of the sea coming to shore over and over and over and over, I hold ice on my wrist and let my father rise. In my mind, I can hear him singing in his faint accent, his voice rumbling into my ear from his chest. I can almost feel him holding my small self, and the self I am now, and I suddenly miss him starkly.

Daddy!

I'm alone in the house, and although I've been longing for it, now I want my father or Meadow or Rory, someone to love me and take care of me when I feel so crappy. My arm hurts like that devil with his axe is back again. Now, when I need someone, I've sent Meadow back to her farm, and Rory has enough to deal with, and my dad is dead.

Dead. How is that possible? How could my big, charismatic, infuriating, charming father be dead, just like that? He's always taken up so much space in my mind and life that I feel like an earthquake has knocked everything down. Along with, you know, everything else in my entire life.

My brain offers me an image of a tall cold glass of sauvignon blanc. *That will help.*

And honestly, it would. It would ease my tension. I'd feel less anxious. It would make my wrist hurt less.

I text my sponsor. **Bad day at work. Broke my wrist. No drugs, but damn it hurts.**

Poor baby! That sounds painful. Why don't you give me a call?

Maybe later.

The gnawing animal in my wrist and the restlessness in my soul combine to create a symphony of distress. Like a coyote, I want to howl, howl out my fury and sense of loss and pain. I want to make noise about it.

It occurs to me that there's nothing stopping me. If I want to howl, I can. For a moment, I consider getting up and going to the french doors in a dramatic gesture—roaring out my pain at the moon like an abandoned wolf—but instead I stay right where I am. Resting a comforting hand on my belly, bracing my swelling wrist against my chest, I take in a massive breath and just . . . howl. Howl at the top of my voice, with all my fury and loss, and my fiery arm. I howl and howl, finding release and some strange solace. My voice sails out the open french doors and into the night.

A noise makes me sit up straight, too fast, sending agony through my arm. I grab it to my chest, and call out, "Who's there?"

"Me." A woman comes out of the kitchen. She's the woman from the café, the long-haired woman who was so kind, but I cannot figure out what she's doing here. "Sorry, I didn't mean to frighten you."

I peer at her, trying to fit the pieces together. "How . . . What . . . ?"

"I'm sorry," she says, again, coming into the room. "I just have to pour this out all at once. I heard you crying and wanted to make sure you were okay."

"Heard me?"

She holds up her hands. "Wait, let me just spill it all. It will be easier. Then you can call the cops or whatever." She's barefoot, wearing jeans and a T-shirt, her hair pulled back in a braid, and she sinks down to the ottoman in front of me. Up close, I notice again that she's remarkably beautiful, and oddly familiar. "My name is Norah Rivera. I was your dad's girlfriend, living here with him when he died."

I blink.

"Your mom kicked me out when you were getting out of rehab, and I didn't have any money or anything because I'm a student and I came out here to write about Meadow, but then I got mixed up with your dad, and—" She breaks off. "Ugh. Anyway, I'm sorry, but I snuck back in and I've been living in the room off the garage."

Her words have gone into my brain, but not one single bit of it makes sense. "I don't get it," I say.

"I know. Let me get you some more ice," she says. "And ibuprofen?"

"No," I say. "I can't."

"Sure? Is it the recovery thing? I'm pretty sure ibuprofen is okay."

"It's not recovery I'm worried about," I say. I feel high even though I've had nothing. Is it serotonin or oxytocin or some other brain response to pain? Whatever, it's strange and I can't really think straight. "Turns out I'm pregnant."

For a long moment, she stares at me. "Wow." She plucks the Ziploc out of my hands and goes to the kitchen. The ice maker in the fridge grinds out its product and she brings it back to me, competently picking up my arm by the cast and placing it on the bag on the arm of the sofa. "Is that comfortable?"

"Yes." I tug the comforter around me, and it unexpectedly releases a scent I can't name but I know belongs to my dad. Tears sting my eyes again, and it's ridiculous. I let my head fall back. "Thank you."

"How about a cup of tea? Unless Meadow got rid of it, I kept a bunch of different ones."

"I think they're still there." The ice starts to cool the cast, and thus my wrist, and the pain starts to subside. "I'd love something, anything, with lots of honey."

She lifts a finger. "I know just the thing. And how about some music, something easy? It sometimes helps me stop thinking."

The situation is completely weird, but at the moment, I don't care. It's like I rubbed a magic lamp and out came a beautiful jinn to take care of me. "Yes, please."

She bustles around, turns on music with her phone, sets the kettle to boil. I can see her through the doorway, taking down a tray, teapot, cups. Napkins from the cupboard, a small plate with cookies she scavenges from somewhere. Like Meadow, like Christy, the woman Augustus left Meadow for, she's tall. Long legged. She's also one of the most beautiful women I've ever seen in real life, and I honestly can't blame my dad for falling for her.

"How old are you?"

Smoothing the hem of her summer-weight sweater down over her hips, she comes to the door. "Thirty-one. How old are you?"

"Thirty-seven," I say with a short laugh.

"It's terrible, isn't it? I was embarrassed by how much older than me he was."

I shrug with my left shoulder, careful not to jolt the other side. "He always liked women a lot younger than him."

"I think it's more that he liked young women of a certain age," she says with a clarity that surprises me. "Meadow was only nineteen. Christy was twenty-five. At least I broke into the thirties."

I raise my good hand, palm up. "Too soon."

With a nod, she goes to the kitchen and returns with a tray of tea. "It's a very light green tea, not much caffeine, lots of lemon and orange. I'm just not sure which herbs are healthy and which are not, so I thought it safer to stick with actual tea."

"Stick with . . . ?" I ask, confused. I remember. Pregnant. "Oh. Yeah."

"When are you due?"

I give a short laugh. "No idea. I just found out, by accident."

She smiles. It's genuine, and her teeth are not at all even, which brings her beauty into the realm of manageable. Her energy soothes me. "You've had quite a day."

"Quite a year, all in all."

"I guess so." She pours tea into a mug and picks up the honey. "Tell me when." I let her go way longer than most people would, but she doesn't react at all.

When we both have mugs, she curls up in the chair catty-corner to me. Her dark braid falls over her shoulder. I say, "So, you've been hiding in that awful little room off the garage?"

"It's not awful. I cleaned it up, so it's fine. Nice window, good breeze."

"Meadow kicked you out even knowing you didn't have any money?"

"I didn't tell her that part. I mean, she doesn't owe me anything."

I sip the tea and it's mainly hot water with a faint tea flavor, sharp lemon, and a thick taste of honey. It's delicious. "She never got over him," I say by way of apology.

"He never got over her, either." She blinks hard, and I see that her eyes are too shiny. "'Love Story of the Century,' right?" She laughs a little and wipes a tear off her face.

She's referring to an article published in *People*, a two-page spread with amazing photos of the two of them at the height of their adoration of each other, which could have been any year between 1993 and 2013. I was so proud of them, felt sorry for other kids. "I cut that article out and pasted it into my journal," I say.

"It must have really been something to be their child. You and Rory both." She sips her tea, head gently inclined. "I mean, that's part of the love story, isn't it, that each of them adopted the other's child?"

"I guess so." A jagged edge of pain rips upward from my wrist and I yelp, spilling a little tea onto the couch. "Damn."

Norah materializes in front of me, taking the tea, pressing a cloth napkin to the spill. "Will you let me help you get more comfortable? I think it might be better to elevate this arm more, get it above your heart."

It hurts so much I want to moan or scream, so I nod, blinking back tears.

"Stand up for a minute and hold your arm above your shoulder. Let me set things up a little."

I do as I'm told, feeling the pinch of my jeans around my waist and the poke of an underwire in a boob. It occurs to me that I'm not going to be able to change clothes without some help, and again I feel embarrassed and sad. "You don't have to do all of this. I guess I need more help than I thought. I should call my sister or Meadow. One of them will come."

Efficiently, Norah picks up and punches the pillows on the over-stuffed couch, brushing them off and shaking out the knitted blanket. "It's pretty late. You can always call them tomorrow."

I narrow my eyes. "This feels like the setup of a bad horror movie. You're going to kill me and make off with all the silver."

She laughs. "Yep, that's me, thief of vintage shit."

"Well," I say, thinking of my dad, "if the shoe fits . . ."

Her smile flashes as the joke comes home. "He was pretty vintage, all right." She shoves the oversize ottoman in front of the corner. "Sit."

"Before I do, will you help me with my clothes?"

"Ah. Is that why you wanted your mom instead of me? I get it. Do you want me to call her?"

I shake my head. "It'll be at least an hour before she can get here, and I really need this bra off now."

"How about some silk pajamas? I bet we're close to the same size, and I have some very pretty ones."

"Sure, but first help me get this fucking torture device off my boobs."

She laughs, and comes around behind me, reaching under my shirt to unfasten the bra. "Left arm up," she says, and slides her hand under my sleeve, captures the strap, and slides it off. I bend my elbow and it's free. "Now the right, easy does it." She grabs the strap from that side and pulls the bra free. "There you go."

"Oh my God, that's better." I rub beneath my left breast with relief, and sit down on the ottoman.

"It'll take me two minutes to get the pajamas. Be right back."

And maybe it's stupid to trust my dad's last girlfriend, who has been hiding in the bowels of the house, but I don't care. The universe or my higher power or whoever it is that's running things heard my cry and sent rescue. I'll take it.

When she comes back, she's carrying the promised pajamas, turquoise with splashes of flowers, and a brush, and a blanket, and a couple of pillows. "I'm going to camp out with you if that's okay. I don't think you should be alone."

I put my discomfort aside as she helps me shed my insanely uncomfortable jeans and slide on the pajamas. She's matter-of-fact and works from behind so I'm not too exposed, which strikes me as a huge kindness. When I'm changed, she helps me settle on the couch comfortably, my arm lifted higher than my heart on banks of Ziploc bags of ice. Pillows are tucked around me. "This is a good nest," I say.

"Good." She holds up the brush. "How about if I brush your hair?"

"Oh my God." I let go of a soft sigh. "I would love that, but you can't use that brush. It will turn my head into a Brillo pad."

"Oh." She looks at the brush. "Is there a better one somewhere?"

"The wire one on the sink in the main bedroom. I assume you know the way."

"I do."

When she comes back she's carrying the wide-toothed brush I use. She stands behind the couch and starts to gently comb out the tangles I've acquired this eventful afternoon, working from the bottom up, pressing down on my scalp with a palm to keep from pulling my hair. I close my eyes. "Oh my God, that's so good."

"I love getting my hair brushed."

"Did my dad brush it for you?"

A soft pause. "Yeah."

"It's kind of his thing. He would sit behind us when we watched movies and brush our hair for ages, me and Rory and Meadow." I have a flash of Meadow's hair in my hands, flowing over a brush, glittering red gold in the sunlight. "I loved brushing their hair, too. I was jealous I didn't have the same hair as them."

"I've always wanted curly hair like yours," she says, and uses long, smooth strokes over my scalp, forehead to nape, temple to nape, over and over and over. It's hypnotic and soothing. My arm starts to ease. I close my eyes, give myself up to it.

"Do you want to watch some TV?"

The idea of extra noise ricocheting around my brain sounds awful. "Not really, but I don't mind if you do."

"Not at all. This is all about you, you know. Being comfortable and feeling better. How's the arm now?"

"It hurts, but it's not like broken glass anymore."

Music plays, something mellow and instrumental I don't recognize, and it's soothing, like a spa. "How did you meet Augustus? What was all of that about Meadow?"

"That." I hear her take a breath. "I've had a girl crush on Meadow for years. Her book, the first one, about Peaches and Pork and falling in love with your dad, and you"—she gestures toward me and I have to nod; the way Meadow wrote about me, and about Rory and our sister-hood, our connections to each other as a family in that book, is one of the more healing things that ever happened to me in my life—"really changed things for me. I felt like she reached right into my soul and *saw* me. And if she could do all of this, then maybe I had something I could do, too."

"Wow," I say. "She would probably love to know this."

"Oh, I don't think so." For a moment, she looks at her tea, moves the cup so the liquid swirls. "The thing is, I decided I wanted to write something amazing about her. I could see that she was the brains and the force behind all of it, while Augustus got most of the attention, and it irked me. I wanted her to get more, to be the guest judge on *Top Chef*, to capture all the attention."

"It's so true," I say with some sourness. "He has always been a big attention hog." The present tense shreds me and I correct it. "Was."

"Right. So I kind of hit this turning point in my life, and I was in this bookstore where I lived and saw the book, and I thought, *I should write a really brilliant article about this really brilliant woman. Show how dazzling she is, bring her into the spotlight more.*"

I sip my tea. "She would love this stuff. Are you kidding me?"

"Yeah, except for that pesky little problem of my getting tangled up with Augustus before I even had a chance to meet her. By the time he introduced me to her, she didn't really have much respect for me, or interest in anything I had to say."

I'm getting sleepy. Her voice is slightly husky and soothing. "Hmm," I say to keep her talking. "I can see that."

"I still want to write the article, but do you know there's almost nothing about her childhood?"

"Have you asked her?"

She snorts. "No. Trust me, she's not going to talk to me about anything."

"Do you know why the police are talking to everybody about his death?" I ask, out of left field. Some distant part of me wonders if it might have been Norah, that maybe she poisoned him. With some discomfort, I eye my empty teacup.

But what would she stand to gain? She loved him.

"No," she says slowly, "but I think he was sick. Like, really sick, and wasn't telling anyone."

This stirs my attention slightly. "Sick how?"

"I don't know." She lifts her shoulders. "When I first met him, he was very energetic and vigorous." She pauses, and I know she at least partly means sex, and I'm grateful she doesn't say it aloud. "But the last couple of months, he just seemed less and less himself. He didn't want to go on hikes or even really a swim. He just worked and slept, that was it."

"Did you ask him about it?"

"Yes, but he just kept saying he was getting old, that's all." She sighs. "I know he was going up to Ojai to see Meadow a lot after you went to rehab, so maybe he was just sad, but I wouldn't be surprised if the autopsy shows something was wrong with him."

I don't know what to think of this, and my eyelids are very heavy. I close them and say, "I think the police want to talk to everybody, so you're probably on the list."

I feel her take the cup out of my hand and pull the blanket up over my shoulder, and there's something I should say on the tip of my tongue, but sleep washes it right away.

Chapter Twenty-Five
Norah

When I startle awake, I can't figure out where I am. It's dark and I'm curled up in a chair beneath a blanket. It's ultra soft and smells of ginger, and when I open my eyes, the soft gloom of not quite dawn spills through the french doors.

I've been dreaming of Augustus, who said, "I'm not really dead, you see? I needed to come tell you something." I was leaning forward to hear whatever it was when I woke up with a start. For a moment, I see him sitting on the end of the couch, Maya's feet in his lap. He is watching her intently, as if he's worried. Afraid to disturb the mirage my brain has manufactured, I peer at him through narrowed eyes. He seems to be talking, but I can't make out the words.

And then Maya makes a whimpering noise and the vision vanishes in a poof. Swiftly, I get to my feet to check on her, but she settles back into sleep. I pull the blanket over her more carefully, and she nestles into the pillows of the couch, turning her face away.

Her profile slays me. That curve of cheekbone and nose is so like her father's; even her ear is shaped exactly like his. It makes me want to fall to my knees with grief.

But there's no time for that now. I had an idea last night. Before Maya wakes up, I want to get into the library Augustus used as his office at home. I hadn't thought to look there for information about Meadow. This is my chance.

Moving silently on bare feet, I pad down the hall on the main floor. I make no sound on the cold tiles. The door is closed, but not locked, and I ease it open carefully, closing it back again behind me, again without a sound. If Maya finds me, I'll tell her I'm looking for my passport.

As if I've ever had the means to go anywhere a passport would take me. But she doesn't know that.

It's dark and I pull the chain for the light on the desk, an art deco beauty I think might be pretty valuable. Lots of things like that in here, left over from the original owner. Augustus said it took them two months to get all the stuff out of the house, mostly paper, which had to be sorted because the guy was a big director and there might have been a script or notes from some of his movies. They didn't find anything valuable, but once the junk was out, they found things like this lamp, a blue pottery woman holding up the lampshade made of mica. Books, original editions, which I've reverently read, sitting right in this room, like a first edition of Virginia Woolf's *Orlando*. Odds and ends like that, all through the house.

Right now, I need to focus. I sit in his chair and suddenly smell him, that fragrance of chocolate and coriander and hints of bourbon that puff up from the padding. The scent stirs up the grief I felt looking at Maya, and for a moment I can't breathe for all I've lost, Augustus and living in this house, and ease, and comfort, and the best sex of my life.

Fiercely, I quash it down. I was also losing myself here, which I'd vowed never to do. You can only count on yourself. I let down my guard, and look what it got me: right back slinging drinks and scrambling for a place to live. I can still accomplish what I came here for, write a powerful article about Meadow Beauvais, if I only focus.

Focus.

I slide open the drawers one at a time. One has office supplies, pencils and paper clips and that kind of thing. Another has hanging files filled with what turn out to be recipes and developmental notes on various combinations of ingredients. Interesting, but not what I'm after. Another holds a bottle of bourbon, which makes me smile. He did love his Jack Daniel's. I leave it, open the rest of the drawers, one by one. It's all just the ordinary paperwork of a life until I get to the lowest drawer on the right. It's nearly empty, holding only two photo albums. The first is a wedding album, which I'm surprised to see. I would have assumed Meadow would have taken it.

But this isn't the wedding of Meadow and Augustus. It's Shanti and Augustus in the late seventies. I've never seen a photo of her before, and I'm startled to recognize I look quite a lot like her—the same very long glossy hair, long limbs. She looks biracial, with dramatic cheekbones and wide-set eyes, and her expression is deliriously happy. She wears a seventies-style hippie wedding dress, her feet bare, a circle of white flowers around her head. She is very, very young. Can't even be twenty.

Augustus looks happy, too. He hasn't yet grown a beard, but his hair is seventies-long, falling to the middle of his back in a tumble of curls. I stare a long time at the youth in his face, the unlined cheekbones, his lush mouth. Again I can see how much Maya resembles him.

I probably wasn't even born when they married, but the knowledge doesn't touch me. The photo of Shanti as a girl, not yet the addict who died, pierces me. Augustus told me her story easily. She was a waitress in the restaurant where he first cooked, and her boyfriend beat her up regularly until Augustus stepped in. They got married within six months of their first meeting.

Poor Shanti.

Focus. This trip down memory lane is also not what I'm here for.

The other album is various pictures of family life from when the girls were small, and I'm tempted to leaf through them, but it's counterproductive. This period of Meadow's life is well documented. I'm looking for her past. Carefully, I put everything back and start looking around the room. Built-in bookshelves line one wall, and drawers take up the lower half. I open one at random and it holds wrapping paper and ribbons. Another has old accounts for a restaurant I don't recognize. Most of them are empty.

What am I even looking for? Basically Meadow's full name before she changed it. I suppose she would have that paperwork, but I wonder if it would be online. I turn on the computer, a sleek desktop Augustus bought a few months ago. There's no password and it lets me right in, though the same is not true of his email. I try a couple of passes, but honestly have no idea what he'd use as a password. My own is a meaningful phrase with uPpercAsE letters in weird places. I try *Peaches&Pork* in various ways. *Meadow.* Nothing.

From the main system, I run a search for *meadow*. The circuits run through everything super fast and dozens and dozens of files come up, photos and Word documents connected to the restaurant, invoices from Meadow Sweet Organic Farms. There are old forms from the divorce, pages and pages, but I'm not about to wade through all that. It makes my stomach hurt, honestly. So personal.

And breaking into your dead lover's computer isn't personal? asks a little voice.

Point taken. But one does what one must.

I tap my toes silently against the floor, thinking. What other search words can I try?

Maybe *Tina?* It can't hurt. I type it in and hit "Return." A single file shows up on the screen, a photo. *Tina and Rory at the Buccaneer.* It shows a much younger Meadow with a redheaded toddler on her hip. She is insanely beautiful, of course, all that light-sparked red hair tumbling down her back like a medieval princess, and a figure like a Vegas showgirl, all legs and breasts and hips. She's wearing jeans and a crop top. Rory's chubby leg presses against her low-ride waistband.

A twist of jealousy wrenches my gut. All his women, Meadow, Shanti. They got to have him when he was young, before he was at risk of dying too young of an idiotic heart attack. Meadow got to be with him for twenty years!

The surge of grief is so intense I can't really stop it this time. It swells upward from my gut, burning through my lungs and throat, fills my mouth with a hunger for this thing I will never have.

I go outside to swim, in a suit, while Maya sleeps. The water is cold, just what I need. I swim back and forth, back and forth, cooling my grief. I shower away the chlorine, and by the time I pad back inside in a thick robe Augustus himself bought for me, I feel calm and focused. Maya is sitting up on the couch with a tablet in her lap, her arm propped up with a pile of pillows. Dark rings circle her eyes. "Hey," she says, and it's croaky. "I thought you might have gone."

"Do you want me to?"

"No. You can stay here if you want, but you can have one of the bedrooms upstairs. Sorry I already took the main, but there are four others. Pick one."

"You don't have to do that."

She waves with her good hand, a weariness that slices through all the bullshit. "Just stay."

"You want some tea? Coffee?"

"I looked it up and I can take ibuprofen before twenty weeks."

"Okay." I smile. "I'll get you some." I sit on the ottoman in front of her and slide the plastic bag I used for ice last night from between the cushions.

And as ideas will do sometimes, one strikes me as I stand, but I'll have to figure out how to ask. I fetch the ice and ibuprofen. "Do you want me to call your sister?"

"I can do it in a little while. She's going to freak out, I think." She sighs. "I wish I could have made decisions the way she has. Turns out it makes a big difference in your happiness."

I see my opening. "Was she born here, your sister?"

"No, I think she was born somewhere near Chico. It's some strange name, like a weather or something. Some shit town up there. Meadow left the second she could get out."

I nod, secreting the answer away. A strangely named town near Chico. That I can work with.

"Is there anything I can do for you before I take off?"

"No. Thanks, Norah. I appreciate your help."

"No problem. See you afterwhile."

Chapter Twenty-Six
Meadow

On Sunday morning, I am teased out of bed by light spilling into my bedroom from the east. In all the fuss and drama of the past couple of weeks, I forgot how much I love this place, a house I built for myself with my own money, exactly what I most wanted. It's not huge, but it's reminiscent of a house I used to see in my childhood, a farmhouse with porches and long double-hung windows. A place to be happy.

My house.

Windows line both the east and north walls of my bedroom, and gauzy linen curtains float on the breezes. The floors are wide pine planks. Elvis and the cats sleep with me in the big soft bed with more pillows than three people could reasonably use.

I sleep in pajamas these days, something that makes me feel old, but also gives me a tremendous amount of pleasure. When I was married, my sleeping attire was nightgowns designed for attractiveness, with straps and lace and all sorts of uncomfortable things, and I'm not sorry to lose them. I do wonder why the hell I spent so many years not pleasing myself in the first place, but that's a thought for another day. I pad over to the window to look out over the fields, or at least the portion I can see from here, which are the strawberries covered with netting, and the edge of the herbs. If the wind is right, I can smell a wild mix of sage or dill or whatever else is being most prolific.

This morning, the light is a deep reddish gold, and my stomach drops. Only smoke makes the air that color. I open the window wider, but I can't smell anything. I look out the windows to the north and can't see the source. Picking up my phone, I ask it to show me the fire map of California. A map with red dots comes up and I click on it. So many for so early in the season!

Zooming in, I see one large red dot to the northeast. It's almost fifty miles away in the San Rafael Mountains. I look at the haze in the sky, thinking it must be a big one. When they get going in the high mountains, it's hard to get them under control, all those ravines and cliffs and impassable forests.

We've had several big fires up near Ojai the past few years, and we all have varying levels of PTSD over that particular color of light and the scent of burning in the air. Still, this one is a long way off. The farm is safe.

I shower and dress, winding my hair into a braid to keep it off my neck in the heat, and head for the fields with a cup of coffee. It's a good practice to lay eyes on the plants regularly, see if there are bugs eating too much, or leaves going yellow or spotted. I have managers who do it full-time, but I still enjoy it. It's peaceful and centering, walking between rows of crops, hearing workers trading conversations in sibilant Spanish, water running, honeybees and slow, heavy bumblebees bouncing from plant to plant to fertilize everything. The sun on my arms is warm even so early, and I make a note—it's going to be a very hot day.

These fields, this work, went a long way toward healing the broken parts of me, at first the girlhood wounds that I carried with me, then later the wrenching grief over Augustus's betrayal, and last, when Maya fell so hard and we feared we would lose her to her addiction.

I wander through the oregano and rosemary down to the start of the garlic. It's starting to sprout scapes, the curling buds that have to be removed in order for the garlic to develop its full size, and I break one off to smell, crushing the tiny seed bulbs within to set free a robust fragrance. A dozen possible recipe ideas rush through my mind. How can anyone not like garlic? But I know people who don't.

The heirloom garlics we farm here are almost entirely Augustus's doing. He had a dozen garlic specialties, and made a particularly fabulous soup with the scapes, fresh vegetables, and Parmesan rinds. It was hearty and healthy and I suddenly wish I could ask him to prepare me a pot. I wonder if I know the recipe well enough to make it myself.

I feel myself settling into calm. So of course the first bombshell of the day arrives with a ring of my phone. "Meadow speaking," I say, adjusting my earphones.

"This is Norah Rivera," she says. "I need to let you know something."

"Norah!" Startled, I stop moving and look at the top of the ridge. "Where are you?"

"I'm here, in town, but that's not the thing."

"Uh . . . okay?"

"The reason I'm calling is Maya broke her arm at work yesterday and she is really in pain. She doesn't want to call you because she thinks she was mean to ask you to go home, but I think she needs you. You, in particular."

My stomach pitches to the bottom of a deep ravine. I make myself ask the question: "Was she drunk?"

"What? No! She just tripped over a chair leg or something at work."

"Good." I'm ashamed for jumping to conclusions, but already moving toward the house and my keys and my car. "Okay. I'll be there as soon as I can. Belle l'Été?"

"Yes."

"Norah, how did you know this?"

"It's a really long story," she says. "I just wanted you to know."

"Thank you," I say sincerely, and then: "Hey, have you talked to the police? They've been looking for you."

"They are? Why?"

"They just want to question everyone in his life, I guess, and they haven't been able to find you. Honestly, I thought you'd be back in Boston by now."

"Yeah, well, I'm not yet," she says. "Look, I have to go. I'm driving."

"Of course."

As I whistle for Elvis, my fingers setting free the green, pungent smell of rosemary, I wonder if I should pack an overnight bag. Broke her arm!

The second call comes in as I'm driving down into Santa Barbara. The robot voice on the console tells me it's the police and I answer the Bluetooth. "Hello, this is Meadow."

"This is Detective Love. Do you have a minute? We have the results of the autopsy back finally. Most of it, anyway."

My stomach, which had returned to normal, pitches again. "Yes. Please tell me."

"There are some results that are inconclusive, so we need to send some tissue out to a different lab, but we have some insight. Did you know he had cancer?"

All the veins in my body ache, all of them, all at once. I lie. "No."

"It was substantial," she says.

He hadn't been feeling well for a while. Complaining of a lack of energy, weakness, even fainting. "Is that what killed him?"

"We don't think so," she says. "It's still not clear."

To hide my exasperation, I take a breath, hold it, let it go. "Can you release the body?"

"I'm afraid not. We need these last few tests to make sure it was a natural death."

I frown. "I don't understand what you're looking for."

"Some kind of poisoning, most likely. Which doesn't mean someone murdered him; it just means *some*thing poisoned him. Especially because he worked with the public, we'd like to figure out what that was."

"Of course." In reaction, my heart threads unsteadily, as if I'm preparing for a heart attack of my own. "I understand."

"We'll keep you posted," she says, and hangs up.

Furious tears sting my eyes. He was only sixty-seven! If he'd just stayed with me, safely married, he would have stayed healthy.

If only he had stayed, he would not be dead.

Over the years, Augustus sometimes dallied with this girl or that, always someone in her early twenties (or sometimes not quite that) with long beautiful hair and lush breasts. I'm not sure, but I think it started during the years I was so desperate to get pregnant.

I looked the other way. I know how that sounds, but in the ways that mattered, our family was solid, our marital rituals still in place—Monday picnics and monthly dinner parties and tangled in sleep every night. Through those dire years when I wanted a baby so badly, I rarely wanted to have sex unless I was deliberately trying to get pregnant, so in some ways I was relieved not to have to meet all his needs. I was secure in being his wife, and the women never lasted more than a month or two.

When I gave up the dream of our child, we settled back into our previous love affair, and although I did sense his dalliances, none of them mattered. He was a big, lusty man and he liked new dishes now and then. I just didn't pay attention to them.

When he met Christy, I didn't even register her presence. She started at P&P as a bartender but worked herself up to assistant manager pretty quickly. She wasn't his type. Although she was still young, in her twenties, she was tautly athletic, with short blonde hair she wore shorn on the sides. Her tattoos, weaving around her arms and even across her chest, spelled out a life lived hard and deep. Kara had a crush on her, though she pretended she didn't.

I liked her, honestly. She was smart and tough, but also wounded. I recognized that haunted look in her eye, that aura you just can't shake. I do my best to hide mine, but it's there if you look. Shanti had it, too.

The brokenness should have tipped me off. Wounded women were catnip to Augustus. He loved the song "Angel Flying Too Close to the Ground," about a man rescuing a woman who'd fallen and needed help; he patched up her wings and sent her on her way.

He rescued us. All of us. He'd rescued me, teaching me how to love sex, how to build a family, but also how to take pride in myself and my accomplishments, how to stand up for myself and ask the world for what I wanted. Without Augustus, I could never have found the courage to buy the farm, to write the book, to do the 1,001 things I could do after he loved me.

Shanti, too, had been a rescue, the daughter of a woman who abused her until she ran away from home somewhere in Mississippi to the golden shores of California, then found a boyfriend to abuse her some more. Augustus had not been as successful healing her as he'd been with me. She couldn't kick her addictions, and someone once commented it was because she'd never examined her ghosts and traumas, but I call bullshit. Only people without the kind of wounds she and I carried think you need to live it all over again. Not everything can be forgiven. Not everything can be healed.

By the time Christy arrived, Augustus had attained a certain amount of fame with the big foodie movement; with his good looks and good humor, he was a delightful guest judge on various shows, including more than one stint on *Top Chef.* I found myself in demand as a speaker at conferences devoted to food writing, cooking, and sustainable farming, and I traveled a lot. For the first time, my star was rising higher and faster than his, but we both reveled in the attention and the way all of it fed into our fortunes.

The farm and everything related to it, the cookbooks and merchandise and the website with the blog I wrote, the recipes that we generated, overtook Peaches and Pork in the aughts. Augustus was a more famous face, and his food was highly celebrated, but it was the farm side that became most lucrative.

And it was *very* lucrative. Mostly, I was working so hard I didn't think about it a lot, but every so often, Augustus and I would sit by the pool with cocktails and ground ourselves in remembering where we'd come from.

Only he knew what that actually was for me. It wasn't part of my public story in any way. I made sure of that. If you let people into the secrets of your life, the worst of it will always be at the forefront of their minds. I wasn't about to let that happen to me.

Augustus knew, but I trusted him to keep it to himself.

One hot summer night, I came back from a long trip to Australia, a place we always said we'd visit together. I'd been invited to give a keynote on organic farming and sustainable restaurant practices. Although I'd spoken many places, going somewhere international was a first, and I was deeply excited about it. Augustus couldn't get away from the restaurant, but I wasn't about to miss the opportunity, and I went on my own.

I loved every second of it. Loved being by myself on the long flight, staying in a great hotel by myself, and after the conference, I traveled by myself to Uluru and the Great Barrier Reef. Honestly, I loved the freedom to do whatever I liked, never having to check in with anyone. I missed him, of course, but I didn't call all that often because I was content and whole in myself, something that came to me very last. One night, I sat on a balcony and listened to a wild mass of birds chattering wildly and I did try to call Augustus to share it, but he didn't answer.

I'd been gone four weeks, and couldn't wait to kiss him, tell him my stories, share all that I'd seen and learned and thought. We made love until we were sweaty and slippery, and fell back on the bed side by side to let the breezes dry our skin. We'd feasted on lobster risotto that Augustus prepared and bread I baked, and vegetables fresh off the farm. By then, the girls were both grown and gone—Rory married at twenty-three to her high school sweetheart, Nathan, and Maya exploring the world to learn viticulture.

Augustus rubbed his foot over my arch, his fingers tangled in mine. I gazed toward the starry sky, replete with love and happiness and a sense of accomplishment. "Sometimes I can't believe how lucky we are," I said. "How lucky I am."

"You've overcome so much," he said, admiration in his voice.

"Thank you." I leaned on my arm, touched his belly, growing slightly softer with time. At fifty-eight, his legs and arms were still strong and muscled, but time showed in ways. That soft belly, the skin on his neck, the white lacing through the hair on his chest and beard. I kissed his shoulder, so grateful.

"Christy quite admires you," he said, "all you survived."

"Christy?" I echoed, trying to place her.

"The bartender. You've met her."

"Have I?"

"Blonde, a tattoo of a panther on her chest. You commented about it."

"Ah." A hush moved through my body. I knew, in that moment, but I didn't allow that knowledge to surface for months. "What do you mean? What does she think I survived?"

"Just a bad childhood. I didn't tell her a lot."

"What's a lot?"

Only then did he realize how cold and still I'd gone. He turned, pulling me into his body. "Nothing. Really, nothing." He kissed me.

"Why were you even talking about me?"

In the silence that greeted this question, I had a vision of the two of them in some crappy one-bedroom apartment, naked, sharing pillow talk the way we did right now. My lungs went tight.

He said, "She had a pretty bad time, too. Like you. I thought it might help her to know that you'd also faced something like that."

"Why did she tell you her story?"

A shrug. "People tell me things. You know that. Hers is one of the worst I've heard. Which is why I talked about you."

I pulled away, sat up. "What did you tell her? How much?"

"Nothing. Nothing much, I swear. Just that you—"

Everything, I realized. "How *could* you, Augustus? You know how I feel about that."

"Meadow, love, it's nothing." He captured me with his arms and legs, our skin connecting, enlivening. He kissed me. "I'm sorry, Sweet Pumpkin. I didn't mean anything by it."

I wanted her gone after that, feeling the existential threat, the dawning recognition that the walls of our fortress had been truly breached. I tried to get her fired but she stayed on.

He was smitten. He didn't want to give her up, but he didn't really want to leave me, either. It dragged out for six months, my spinning in a whirling dervish of fury and betrayal, Augustus falling ever more deeply for a woman he could rescue, not the one who'd learned to stand on her own two feet.

He came to me on an October evening and said he wanted a divorce. It astonished me, infuriated me, all the things a scorned lover feels. But it also seemed impossible. *We* were the match, *we* were the soul mates—ask anyone. How could I still feel so completely in love and he didn't feel it at all?

How could I go on without him? What would my life even look like?

So I refused. I told him he was being an ass. "Sleep with her," I said. "Get it out of your system. We are not dismantling this empire. It would be ridiculous."

I went to bed, and in the morning, his clothes and most treasured things were gone.

It was almost the worst moment of my life.

Chapter Twenty-Seven
Norah

I hang up after talking to Meadow and tuck the phone in my pocket. The sun is hot and I can smell smoke as I walk down the hill into town. For once, my belly is full and I'm clean as I make the trip. I was fully prepared to be kicked out last night when I went upstairs to make sure Maya was all right, and instead, we connected immediately. That she has invited me to stay feels like a hand from the other side, as if Augustus is still present, helping me.

Also helping his daughter. She tried to put a stoic face on, but her agony was plain. I was glad to be able to help her get a little more comfortable. And I was not at all surprised to discover I connected with her. She's a lot like Augustus, but I recognized something of myself, too. A tough woman used to doing things herself.

A ripple of disappointment moves through me. I hate that I'm scrambling day-to-day again, trying to make sure I can eat and have a dry place to sleep. Making do with other people's scraps was the story of my childhood. I thought I'd finally left it behind. Maya's kindness is helpful, but it won't solve the bigger problem of my unstable life.

Writing something meaningful will help get me where I want to go. If I can do a powerful, feminist take on Meadow and get it published somewhere highly respectable, it will go a long way toward establishing a career in food journalism.

The librarian waves to me as I settle into my place. My first search is to examine the map around Chico, a town north of Sacramento, and see if I can find a town with a strange name up there. A weather name, Maya thought.

I work my way across the map in a clockwise method. There are a lot of small towns up and down the Sacramento River, mostly farm towns, but I don't find anything with a weather name. A sense of frustration grows as I scan around again, tension growing in my neck. What am I even looking for? A girl named Tina in a little town? How is that going to help me?

The truth is, it's the only lead I've got, and I zoom in and try again. There, right on the river is a town of twelve thousand called Thunder Bluff. I type it into Google. The first thing on the list after Wiki is "What is the crime rate in Thunder Bluff?" and it has a D.

Several of the links are about crime in the town, but when I click on the local newspaper, the crime reports are kind of random—cows wandering into a neighbor's yard, burglaries, dog complaints, a lot of domestic disturbances.

Domestic disturbances, I think. As if things that happen at home are mild, not the violent assaults and rapes and murders that happen every day in homes around the world. Why did we even start calling it "domestic violence" anyway? Why not assault and battery? Why not rape or murder or psychological terrorism? Flashes of memory blast through my brain before I can stop them. I was lucky as these things go—I suffered more neglect than violence, but that wasn't true of all the people in the houses where I lived. I saw it. I heard the stories and saw the scars.

Focus.

Thunder Bluff. Tina. Rory. I feed the information into Google, but it comes back with a strange combination of offerings, most with one or the other of the search terms crossed out.

Try again. *Birth records, Thunder Bluff.* That narrows it down a bit. I run Rory, guessing her age to be thirty-five or so, so I set the parameters with a ten-year range.

Nothing.

Chewing on my lip, I narrow my eyes at the cursor and try to think. Yearbooks? There's only one high school in town, so Meadow must have gone to school there. I try searching for yearbooks, but they're locked behind a paywall, and I'm not that desperate yet.

How old is Meadow? That's probably an easy thing to find, and it pops right up—she's fifty-three this year. It startles me—she was fourteen years younger than Augustus, which is substantial. Not as substantial as the thirty-six between us, but still a lot.

Seized with a hard yearning, I type in his name, Augustus Beauvais, and up pop hundreds of results, image upon image upon image. There are a lot of him and Meadow at various events, for stories online or in magazines. One in *Parade* catches my eye and I click on it, unprepared for a close-in photo of the two of them looking deep into each other's eyes. There's so much heat coming off the page that I instantly find myself imagining his body, strong and long limbed and not at all what I thought an old man's body would look like.

I click through more pictures of him—the guest-judge seasons on *Top Chef,* the opening of Peaches and Pork. And more. Casual shots of him walking, family pictures with the girls, a photo of the woman he briefly married after he divorced Meadow eight years ago. She has hard eyes and tattoos in lines up and down her arms. A panther tattoo covers her chest, and I touch my own cleavage, horrified to imagine covering that flesh with ink.

It was a big scandal when it happened. People talked about it in the food world, precisely because of the lore around Augustus and Meadow, the love-story-of-the-century crap. Because it is crap. They were just two people with a strong connection who fell apart in the end. It happens.

Looking at the photos, I feel his breath in my ear. I feel his mouth on my body. I feel overheated and my skin hurts and I want to do something dramatic like tear my clothes or slice marks into my forearms. Something to show that I loved him, that he mattered, that it feels like I might never be myself again.

Stop.

I force myself to shut the window down completely to erase the photos, then open a fresh window, not even really thinking of what I need to do next. A photo of dawn stretches across the top of the search engine window, and that weird little part of the brain that puts things together says, *Aurora, not Rory.*

Maya told me this morning that she's thirty-seven, so Rory must be close to the same or a little younger. I count the dates in my head and run a search in the Thunder Bluff records for "Aurora born 1985." The wheel spins and shows me a single result.

Aurora Sullivan, August 10, 1985. Mother: Betina Ann Sullivan. Father: Unknown.

Father: Unknown.

I do the math. Meadow was sixteen. The father was probably some local teen who didn't want anything to do with it. I narrow my eyes. But why have the baby? Abortion was legal and easy. Why not just abort the baby and go on with a normal life? It's hard to believe that the girl Meadow was didn't have a lot of ambition back then, too.

Doesn't add up.

I run a check of Betina Ann Sullivan's name to see what comes up. A birth record for Betina Ann Dorset comes up, 1969, in the same town. Mother: Kimberly Dorset; Father: Billy Dorset (deceased). A sense of excitement rises, that intellectual curiosity that leads to all good things in research. *Now we're getting somewhere!* I wonder what happened to Billy.

I find an obituary for William Adam Dorset, age twenty. His photo shows a good-looking guy in an army uniform. Died in Khe Sanh, Vietnam.

Ah, damn. Poor Meadow. Poor Kimberly.

Digging deeper, I look up marriage certificates for Kimberly Dorset, and one comes up for Kimberly marrying Gary Sullivan, 1978. Meadow was nine.

My eyes are getting dry staring at the screen so intently, and I force myself to sit up straight, stretch my arm, roll my neck around. From the corner of my eye, I see another line at the bottom of the screen, and scroll down to find an obituary.

For Kimberly Sullivan, killed in a car accident in 1984. My heart clutches. Meadow was only fifteen.

With a start, I notice the time—I need to be at work in an hour, and it's a good walk from here. For a long moment, I can't move, thinking that we are both orphans. Motherless daughters. It's almost laughable how drawn I am to others like me in this way.

I look at my notes and incline my head, wondering what I'm hoping to see. How can I set myself up for the next session?

Meadow changed her name from Betina Sullivan to Meadow Truelove, an improbable name but very hippie. It fit her, as Meadow Beauvais fits her now. It's impossible to even imagine her as Tina.

She has no contact with her family as far as I can see, but I need more information. Brainstorming in my notebook, I write down my next set of questions: Does her stepfather still live in Thunder Bluff? Did she have any siblings? What about yearbooks? There might be something there.

Reluctantly, I gather my things, mulling over the same central question that's been nagging me from the start of this journey.

What did Tina leave behind?

Chapter Twenty-Eight
Maya

Norah helps me shower and get dressed in easy clothes—loose sweats and a T-shirt sans bra—and braids my hair efficiently to get it out of the way and keep it from tangling.

Then she's off to work and I'm alone. I sit outside in the shade of a shaggy eucalyptus tree, watching the waves wash to shore down below. Overhead, a small bird offers a series of chirps, metallic and rhythmic. My uncast hand rests over my belly as if my palm can give me information.

Pregnant. My belly feels slightly rounded, but I've been attributing that to better health. Toward the end of my drinking, I rarely remembered to eat or even drink water, lost in the madness of endless bottles of sauvignon blanc. Endless. Sometimes in the morning I mixed it with grapefruit juice and ice to sip so my hands would stop shaking and I could function. For a while, usually until late afternoon or so, depending. By dinnertime, I was always too far gone to remember much of anything that happened.

Shame spreads beneath my skin like acid. How could I have allowed myself to fall so far? I'd been a hard drinker for a long time, a couple of decades, but so was everyone around me. We took pride in our ability to handle our booze, to drink everyone else under the table. I was nearly always the last one standing. It was a badge of honor. Josh bragged about it.

At what point does hard drinking turn into a problem? When does problem drinking turn into alcoholic drinking? I used to take quizzes about my drinking way back in college, when I'd wake up somewhere with no memory of how I ended up there. Sometimes, I was terrified by the bouts of memory loss, wondering what I'd done, where my friends were.

But we were studying viticulture. Our friends were chefs and bartenders and winemakers and brewers. All of us drank. A lot. We made jokes about a particular person being the memory keeper on a given night.

Even in that crowd, I was a little further in. My friends took turns watching out for my blackout markers and tried to steer me home before anything dangerous happened. Miraculously, nothing did, probably because I didn't have a car at the time. I also had Josh, who drank at least as much as I did, but he was a big guy, tall and broad shouldered, so he could handle more. He always had my back, and wouldn't leave me, even if we had some stupid fight.

Which happened a lot. He could be morose, while I could be angry. So angry. In daily life, as a regular student and girlfriend, I wasn't angry at all. It was only when I drank that the fury rose from some unknown source like the noxious bubbles in the cauldron of a Shakespearean witch.

After college, things evened out. Josh and I found work at a winery in Italy and studied there, and the local culture normalized our consumption. It wasn't liters every night, just an ordinary two or three glasses of wine before and through dinner, with a set point when everyone just stopped. It wasn't every night, either, which helped. I was working hard physically and slept hard, ate a lot, and was probably the healthiest I'd ever been.

From my perch beneath the eucalyptus tree, I watch a trio of surfers in wet suits carry their boards out to the line. Josh loved surfing and tried to teach me, but I have a very deep-seated terror of drowning that seems to have no basis in any trauma I can dig up. There are plenty of others with factual grounding—cockroaches and the smell of crack and people driving away from me—but not drowning. It drove him crazy.

Honestly, we drove each other crazy. The only real thing we had in common was our mutual love of sex. It was a very sexual relationship from the start. We shared vigorous appetites, and were compatible physically.

Not so much in any other realm. We didn't have the same tastes in books or movies or architecture. He liked everything to be extremely tidy, whereas I like things out where I can see them. He liked hearty foods, meats and stews and thick sauces, while I prefer vegetarian fare and fruit and sugar in every form known to man. He didn't eat sweets and judged me for my consumption. He liked crisp, tailored clothing, while I liked bohemian. He liked baroque architecture, and I loved art deco.

But you know, great sex will take you a long way. We also both loved wine, everything about it. The history and lore, the methods and the bottles, the geeky experiments and the old-school powerhouses. Our talents were as well matched as pinot noir and Syrah grapes. I have a nose so finely attuned that I've astonished old masters with my ability to sense almost anything in a wine—a variation, a particularly good vintage, a flaw.

It's painful on some level I can't even reach to know I'll never make it again.

Josh had the business sense. Together, we created a label—Shanti Wines, named for my mother in a fit of generosity that I don't understand even now—and it gave us the glue we needed when the sex started to flag. For seven years, we built the brand and the wine itself, and at last bottled the best of what we'd done. I could smell its perfection when it went into the barrels, and my instincts were proven right when the wine won a highly coveted early tasting medal, designed to help young vintners find a footing in the crowded market.

That was when Josh was stranded in Provence during the pandemic. For almost nine months, I had time to perfect my alcoholic drinking and nurse my increasing despair and unhappiness within the relationship. I was lonely and in deep denial about how bad my addiction was getting.

When Josh came home after the pandemic, we struggled to get things back on track, at least with the winery. Both of us were excited by the dazzling vintage, and prayed that it might be the thing that would carry us into the big time.

Except that we couldn't get things right between us. I wasn't even sure I wanted them to be right. I spent hours talking to Rory, who patiently said over and over, *Why don't you come home for a few weeks? You sound terrible.*

But if I went home, they would see what was happening to me. I couldn't imagine how I'd swim to the surface of my wine habit. On some far, distant level, I knew it was out of control. Some mornings, stirring to yet another doom-filled hangover, I'd swear I'd quit. By the time I showered, I'd already be so sick that I rationalized the grapefruit and wine breakfast cooler as medically necessary. I'd just take it easy the rest of the day. Cut down. Cut back.

For months. Probably years.

I move my hands over the being within me, tears stinging my eyes because I have no memory of who or when she—or he—was planted. Josh and I were not having sex since he'd declared himself in love with his French girlfriend, but that doesn't mean it was impossible. One of our hallmarks had always been furious sex when we were both drunk and angry and in hate with the other.

My sober, more thoughtful self thinks, *Why the hell did you stay in that toxic relationship, Maya?*

Why did I do any of it? Who ever makes good choices under those circumstances?

Holding my hand on the swell of my belly, I sort through those last few weeks before I took an axe to the entire vintage. They're blurry. I was mad at the entire freaking world, mad at the pandemic that trapped me in my isolation, mad at Josh for getting stranded, and lost in the sea of wine, and lonely beyond expression. I ruminated about my father leaving me, and my mother leaving me, too. Poor, pitiful Maya.

There's nothing so lonely as that lostness, that sense of falling down a hill really fast and being unable to stop or ask for help. At night, I went out, taking Ubers into a small but sophisticated town not far away to drink and party with whomever I found. I'm sure I had sex.

I mean, obviously I had sex. It's just that it could have been a fuck in a bathroom, or a roll in the hay with a local, or Josh, or anyone, really. Who knows? I rarely remembered the night before when I woke up. It was standard, not strange.

It sounds awful. The shame of it burns in my chest now, spreading out to join the sharp pricks under my skin, and I can't breathe.

Why didn't I just stop?

That's what people ask, the Muggles who don't understand. *Why not just stop? Why not just have one? Why keep doing something that makes you feel so awful?*

If only. It just doesn't work that way. Not for me. Not for the millions and millions of people who are also plagued with this addictive *thing* in a world where it's perfectly normal to drink, and keep drinking, and laugh about going overboard and even blacking out, and make Mommy-wine memes about the stresses of parenthood driving you to the bottle, and you have to explain why you don't drink rather than why you do. If people quit smoking, the world says, "Oh hey, good for you." If you quit drinking, they peer at you and say, "Why?"

I bend my face into my hands, my cast banging against my cheekbone, and let the shame escape my body through my tears. I resist crying, but my counselor insisted I allow it back into my life, and I've been trying. For long moments, I just let the hot emotions flow out of me, tears of shame and tears of regret and tears of frustration, feeling tension ease along with them.

"Hello?" says a gentle voice. "Are you all right?"

Ayaz. I keep my head bent for a moment, trying to get myself together, but it's not stopping. "I'm fine," I say.

"Hmm. Here, take this."

I peek through my fingers to see a big white handkerchief, snowy clean, and accept it. "Thanks." I wipe my face and my nose, compose myself. "Sorry."

"No, no. I am the intruder. Shall I leave you?"

His soft British voice is so soothing, I shake my head. "You can stay." I gesture to the other chair beneath the tree. "Watch the surfing with me."

"I brought ginger tea," he says, and opens an old-fashioned thermos, pouring liquid into the plastic cup. "It cures many things."

I smile. Beneath everything, I become aware that my broken wrist is starting to throb along with my heartbeat. I prop it on the arm of the chair. "Would you mind doing me a favor?"

"Not at all."

"There's a bag of melting ice in the sink. Would you dump it out and refill it?"

"Of course."

"There are cookies, too, if you like. They might be nice with the tea."

He flashes a smile, not very big, but it transforms his rather severe face into something kinder, younger.

At least the pregnancy solves this problem. We're meant to be friends only, so I don't have to engage the part of me that's vividly attracted to his gentle competence, his beautiful eyes, his deep calm. I think of him on the beach, slowly going through a tai chi sequence. I've never known anyone so calm.

The tea is warm and soothing, and the high angst of moments before slips away. A breeze dries my face, eases the heat of shame. There is nothing I can do about the past anyway, so I might as well be here now.

"Here you are," he says, returning with the ice and a bag of cookies, which he sets gently on the table between us. The ice he settles on my cast, inclining his head as he holds it there. "Is that right?"

"Yes, thank you."

He sits on the chaise sideways, facing me. He wears a wheat-colored linen shirt with the sleeves rolled up on his tanned forearms, revealing a silver bracelet carved with symbols. His elegant hands are beautiful, as I've noticed before.

"I hope it's all right that I checked on you," he says. "I worried that you were alone with a broken bone."

"You're a kind person. I appreciate it."

He only nods.

"I ended up not being alone, actually. My dad's girlfriend . . . showed up, and she was remarkably kind."

"That's good, yeah?"

"Yes." In the dappled sunshine beneath the tree, he looks like everything good and calm in the world. His eyes rest on my face without judgment. "It's not hurting so much this morning. I was having a little breakdown over . . . everything. My dad. The winery. The whole big"—I wave my hand around—"everything."

"I have had those moments," he says, lifting his face to the sunshine and closing his eyes briefly.

"It's hard to imagine."

"What is?"

"You, having a meltdown."

A smile crinkles his eyes. "Perhaps our methods are different, but the emotion is the same."

A low stirring washes through me and I realize I'm reacting to the scent of him, salty and green, layered with faint perspiration in his hair or on his skin, which seeps into my pores and slams into my heightened hormones and gives me a picture of kissing him, not lightly, but with extreme and possibly sloppy attention. A lusty heat burns my cheeks.

I take a breath, look away, focus on the horizon. After a moment, it cools. When I look back, I see that he's studying my face, my throat, and some of the same heat burns across his temples. He sees me looking, drops his gaze to his steepled fingers.

And then we just sit there in awkward, burning silence. The old me would have set aside the ginger tea, offered a hand, and taken him upstairs, living for the moment.

The me I am in this minute doesn't want to risk the friendship I feel here, and he has come to visit, so it's up to me to make it more comfortable. I pick up the bag of cookies and offer it with my good hand.

Only then do I remember that I'm braless beneath my thin T-shirt, my breasts swinging with the gesture to reveal their unbound state. It feels weirdly slutty, but why? It's perfectly normal to be braless on my own patio, when a broken arm means a bra is a massive challenge.

No. Even that is a dodge. I'm braless. So what.

Better. I lift my chin.

He takes a cookie and our eyes meet. A current of desire burns down my spine, crosses my thighs, and I give him a half smile. For once in my life, I just tell the truth. "Under different circumstances, I would be very attracted to you."

"Would be?" He takes a bite of cookie, waiting.

"Am," I correct.

His calm British politeness drops away, and he inclines his head. "Same," he says simply. "And same."

I smile naturally. "Good. I could really use a friend right now."

"So can I," he said, and brushes crumbs from his hands. "Do you play backgammon?"

"I love it, actually, and there's probably a set in the library. I'll go see."

"I can fetch it if you like."

I shake my head. "No, that's all right. I'll be right back."

Chapter Twenty-Nine
Meadow

Rory calls me as I'm arriving in town. "Can you come over today? I told the girls that their grandpa is gone." She pauses. "Dead."

"Oh, honey." Why does it seem that both children have a crisis at the same time? This happened over and over when they were young, one having trouble with a friend while the other was struggling with a subject in school. I pull the car over into the parking lot of a gym. "How are they?"

"I don't think they really get it. Maybe I'm bad at this."

"You're not bad at it. It's hard."

"I guess."

Something in her voice makes me lift my head. Rory is always the even-tempered one, the easy one. She was never much trouble, even as a teenager, blessed with that easygoing way. I have no idea where she got it.

Now, my mother-nerves are prickling. "How are you, sweetie? Did the police call you, too?"

"Yes." A pause, and I can hear the emotion in her voice. "How could he have had cancer and not said anything?"

"Maybe he didn't know," I say.

"I didn't think of that." She sounds broken. "When can you come?"

I was not always the best mother to this child, and I want to do the right thing now, but Maya's need feels more urgent. The light changes and I turn right to go up the road toward Belle l'Été. "I can come in an hour or so. I'm on my way to see your sister. Did you know she broke her arm at work yesterday?"

"What? No! Where is she? At home?"

"Yes. I'm almost there."

"I'm coming, too," she says, and there's no dissuading her when she takes that tone. "Should I get anything? Watermelon, maybe?"

"Are the girls there?"

"No. They went to day camp this morning."

"Nice. Could you possibly make some more of that limeade? It was good."

I hear laughter when I get out of the car at Belle l'Été, and follow the sound through an arched wooden gate down a flagstone path to the pool area. Maya sits with a man at the glass table in the shade of the pergola, the pair of them bent over a backgammon board. I'm struck by her ease, a body posture I don't often see, and as I round the pool to the side of the patio, I see that there's something particular about them. It takes me a moment to pull it in—they have the body language of a long-term couple, as if they belong together. A strange emotion rises in me over that, confusion and a sense of loss and jealousy.

Until he raises his head, I don't realize that he's the doctor from the horrible modern house down the road, the husband of an actress who drowned not long ago. He sees me as I see him, and he raises a hand. "Hello."

Maya looks up, and her expression is confused. "Meadow!" She stands to give me a one-armed hug, and I smell sweat and old coffee. Her eyes are tired. "What are you doing here?"

"I heard about your broken wrist." A bright pink cast covers her arm to the elbow. "What happened?"

"A work accident," she says, holding up the cast. "I swear." She lifts her chin toward the man. "Ayaz will vouch for me. He was there."

I glance at him, feeling another wave of that loss and the worry their body language gave me. Her sobriety is too new for a relationship. "I believe you. Are you okay?"

"Yeah. I'm fine, honestly." She glances at the board, then at the man, as if they were carrying on a conversation I interrupted.

I turn to him, holding out a hand, gathering details about him from his face. Weariness around his eyes, his mouth. A high, intelligent brow. "Meadow Beauvais," I say. "You're the doctor, right? I remember when you moved in eight or ten years ago, but I'm not sure we ever officially met."

"Doctor?" Maya echoes. "I thought you were a writer."

"Both," he says, standing to shake my hand respectfully. "Dr. Ayaz Kartal," he says. "Pleased to meet you."

"Did you call her?" Maya asks him, pointing to me.

"No."

"It was Norah," I say, twisting my mouth at the irony. "She thought you might want some company."

"Ah. Sit down, Meadow."

"How did Norah know?"

She glances at the man. "Long story, but you're here. Thank you."

"Perhaps I'll take my leave," he says.

"Oh, don't," Maya says, and there's a note to it that pierces me. How could they have strong feelings in only a day or two?

And yet . . . he hesitates, standing with his body half turned toward her, even as his words say he's leaving, all his energy directed toward Maya. Everything about him is urbane and well tended, his linen shirt, the expensive belt, and although I would not call him handsome, he's compelling.

"Don't worry about me," I say, taking my cue. "I'll get settled." I pause on my way into the house. "Rory is coming in a little bit, bringing some limeade. You should stay and have some, Dr. Kartal."

"I really must be going."

Maya gives me a look, but says nothing, and humming under my breath, I head into the house. From the kitchen, I pause and look through the frame of the windows to the pair of them. Maya's body language is completely open, fully trusting. He moves a little closer as she speaks, and his body faces her, his head bent down to hear what she's saying. A hand falls on her arm, and I expect them to kiss any second. Instead, he nods, straightens, and then gives a little wave.

Not good. Not good at all.

The last thing she needs is a boyfriend right now. I read somewhere that a person in recovery is supposed to be sober for a year before she has a relationship. It hasn't even been four months. As I bustle around the kitchen, my mind spins out a dozen disastrous scenarios—heartbreak and fights and even things being thrown, all ending in the same place, with Maya drunk and swaying and sick.

She really doesn't need this.

When I see that he's gone, I get my overnight bag from the car and head upstairs with it, but stop short in Maya's old room. The bed hasn't been slept in, but a suitcase is open on the floor, and I see a boho dress I know to be Norah's. Is she sleeping here now?

A few piles of books and papers are stacked on the bed. One of the books is mine, the memoir about falling in love with Augustus, starting Peaches and Pork, and turning Meadow Sweet Organic Farms into the business it now has become.

I pick it up off the stack—several other food histories of the region and a couple of cookbooks—and see that it's marked up, passages highlighted or underlined, with notes in the margins. The handwriting doesn't belong to Maya. Several are quite long, including one about Maya, when she came to live with us: *Affair brushed over. Maya's mom?? Social services?? Why didn't Augustus take M with him when he left if S so bad?*

A roll of anger and discomfort moves through my body. None of her business. Nobody's business. I chose what to tell the world. It's my story. I'm allowed to leave out what I don't want the world to know.

I sink down on the bed and flip through the notes. More of them are commentary than questions, but a long note in purple ink fills half a page at the end of chapter fourteen.

What about childhood influences? Where did Meadow come from? Who is Rory's father? And which of the stories Augustus tells is actually true? Both of them seem to have reinvented themselves whole cloth when they arrived in California. Which is something people come to California to do, I guess, but it seems like a big gap in the story. If you write a memoir, isn't it supposed to be the whole story?

Fascinating person.

Again, resistance rises in a protective wall around me. She has no right to ask those questions. It's not hers to know.

I knew she'd wanted to interview me, and that's how she met Augustus, who took her for himself before she could even talk to me once. A dark burn of anger flares in the pit of my stomach. He always did that, or tried. Took the best of everything without much thought for anyone else.

I flip back to the first note, about Maya. Maybe I've taken things, too. I mean, obviously I did. Although I broke up with Augustus when I found out he was married, I didn't resist very hard when we got back together. I didn't honestly care about Shanti or her story.

Maybe that's why the universe punished me by not allowing me to have another baby with the man I loved so much. What goes around comes around.

Except that it doesn't.

Life is as cutthroat as any jungle, and if you want anything, you have to take it. I wanted Augustus Beauvais and I took him. Then Christy wanted him and took him for herself. And then Augustus took Norah for himself, when it's plain she was here to write about me.

Anger grows, burning through my gut, up my esophagus, fueled by a million things—Augustus and the past and Christy, who took him when I would have kept him healthy and well until his nineties and then just dumped him after our marriage was destroyed, walking away without looking back when it was too late for us. Anger at Norah for digging into my privacy this way, and taking up space in this house when I told her to leave. Why won't she just go away?

And what the hell is she doing here, anyway? I toss the book aside and stomp down the stairs. Maya is still sitting outside, stacking the backgammon pieces in their spots. "What is Norah doing here?" I demand. "I kicked her out. This house is yours."

Maya glances up at me. "She's broke and stranded and she was hiding in that awful room off the garage." She finishes stacking the pieces and closes the board. "She heard me crying over my arm and came up to make sure I was okay."

"All of her stuff is in the room I've been using."

"I told her she could sleep there." She folds her arms.

"But I was sleeping in that room. You can't just—" I halt.

"It's my house, right?"

"Wait, why are you angry with me? I'm here to help you."

"I didn't ask for your help, Meadow. I really don't need to be rescued, not from anything. Or anyone."

I glance toward the beach path where the doctor disappeared. "You know he's only been a widow for six or eight months."

"I do know that, and I also know that it's none of your business. I'm a grown woman and I know how to manage my life."

"No, you don't, actually," I blurt out. "You're barely out of rehab. You have a huge number of things to decide, and the last thing you need is a boyfriend."

Her chin lifts, and a red stain flushes her tan cheeks. When she looks up at me, I see a side of her that almost never shows, furious and wounded. "Thanks for your faith, Meadow." She shakes her head. "You need to go."

"Wait." I close my eyes, reaching for a sense of calm, something blue to draw through the red fire burning through me. I draw in a breath, see it cooling my fury. "I'm sorry. I didn't mean that. I was just freaked out by Norah calling me in the first place, and then your sister called and she told the girls about Augustus, and she's upset, and then I saw that guy here, and—"

"You can't stay here," she says. "I want to be by myself."

"But Norah can stay?"

"It's not the same, *Mother*," she says with emphasis, a word she only ever uses when she's annoyed with me. "You have your own shit to deal with, and I don't have any bandwidth left for you. Norah's easy. She was good to have around when I felt like shit."

I sink onto the other lawn chair. "She was raised in foster homes, did you know that?"

Maya shakes her head, exasperated. "What difference does that make?"

"Your dad always wanted to rescue people. Women." I look toward the gleaming blue pool, framed with hand-painted tiles. "Me, your mom, Christy. Norah, too, I guess."

For a moment, she focuses on the horizon, her lips pressed together. "That's rich, since he did the opposite of rescuing me."

The truth of that thuds through the air. I nod, looking at my hands. I was, at the very least, complicit.

"Norah doesn't really seem like a lost soul, honestly."

I think of her gleaming hair, the sharpness in her eyes. "Maybe not." The handwritten notes on the pages of Norah's copy of my memoir float back to me. A warning squeezes my belly. The last thing I need right this minute is someone digging through my childhood. "Where is she?"

"At work, I guess."

"Hello!" Rory comes around the corner carrying a jug of limeade and a box of doughnuts. "I thought it might be nice to have something junky." She deposits the box on the table and kisses Maya's head. "How are you, sis?"

"Okay. Just bummed, really. I really like the job."

"You won't have to quit. It'll be okay. Trust me. Nathan said they were thrilled with how quickly you've picked up the bean science."

Maya shrugs, insulated in her mood. "Will you get me some more ice?"

"Of course. Mom, why don't you come help?"

I know I'm probably going to be the bad guy, but I stand up and follow her into the house anyway. May as well get it over with.

But Rory doesn't yell at me for meddling. She drops everything on the counter and turns to me, bending down to fling her arms around my shoulders, and bursts into tears. "I can't stand this! I miss him so much!"

I hold her, wishing for the clear, uncomplicated grief she feels for a man who loved her solidly, always, and never left her until he died.

She's the only one he never left. How have I not noticed this before?

Chapter Thirty
Maya

My entire body vibrates with emotion as I sit in the chair beneath the pergola. Clematis vines climb the posts, offering shade and food for the bees swirling from flower to flower, and I almost wish one of them would sting me so I'd have a reason to explode. My heart is racing, and sweat edges my hairline, and I'm not even sure what the emotions are, only that I don't like how congested my lungs feel, how upset my stomach is.

I jump to my feet, cradling my aching wrist close to my body so my movements won't jar it, and pace toward the boxwood at the back of the pool, along the roses planted, then down the south end of the garden, up the long end of the pool. I wish I could jump into the cool water, but of course, that would ruin the cast. Instead, I step onto the stairs at one end, up to my knees. The water is cool, and the clear turquoise color eases me. For a moment I can breathe.

What am I so mad about? Meadow being so bossy, but that's nothing new. Bossy about my love life is infuriating, but nothing to the level I'm feeling.

What else? asks the voice of my therapist. I see her in front of me, that perfectly smooth white pageboy, her bright blue eyes.

My father. Even the words bring up a sense of incandescent rage, choking off my throat to the point that I have to reach down with my left hand and bring up water to splash on myself.

He rescued everyone. All his little lovers and wives and girlfriends. Even Rory. He rescued her from a lifetime without a father, and now she's in the kitchen crying her eyes out over him, and justifiably so. She loved him. He was good to her.

He was good to me, too. My childhood, after my mother died, was enviable. I never doubted their love for me. I never doubted that he regretted leaving me with my mother. I forgave him until he wrecked our entire family so thoughtlessly.

"Maya!" Meadow calls. "Come in and have some limeade."

The very word makes me thirsty, but I'm reluctant to be in Meadow's company. She tipped her hand about her faith in my ability to stay sober, and I just don't need that in my life right now.

And yet, who do I have but Meadow and Rory?

As I'm stepping out of the pool, I suddenly remember in a rush about the baby. Or maybe it's too soon to call it a baby. Maybe it's only a pregnancy, something distant and far away to think about rationally.

But I don't feel rational. Or even the slightest bit conflicted, honestly. It makes me want to keep the news to myself a little while longer. I don't want Meadow to say again, *"The last thing you need is a boyfriend."*

As I pad into the kitchen on wet feet, however, the first thing out of my mouth is, "I have some news for you guys."

"What kind of news? Did Josh give up the name?" Rory asks, handing me an icy-cold glass of limeade.

I take a long, deep drink, and it's absolutely perfect—tart and sweet and fragrant with lime peel curled on top. "No, nothing like that." I take a breath and settle my hand over my belly. My right hand, with the cast. "I found out yesterday that I'm pregnant."

Both of them just stare at me. "Did you say 'pregnant'?" Meadow finally asks.

"Yes."

Rory reaches for my hand. "How do you feel about that?"

It's easy to tell the truth to her beautiful blue eyes. "Kind of amazing."

"You're not going to keep it?" Meadow asks.

Rory hugs me, tightly. "Don't listen to her. Just listen to you," she says softly in my ear.

"I will."

When she releases me, she asks, "Do you know how far along, due date, anything?"

"No. I mean, it was kind of a gigantic surprise. It's hard to know just from ordinary life, but I've been sick every morning for weeks. I just thought there was something wrong with my liver."

"Oh, you poor thing!" Rory says. "I was sick like that with Emma, and it was a shock because there was nothing with Polly at all. Saltines help."

I nod and look at Meadow, raising my eyebrows in question.

"I'm just worried that it's a bad time," she says.

"Or maybe it's the best time ever," I say. "Maybe it's a gift for finally getting sober."

"But it's only been a few months," she says, her mouth twisting. "I mean, aren't you worried about yourself more than a fetus? This is a delicate stretch in your sobriety."

"Mom!" Rory says. "Think about what you're saying."

"No," I say, waving a hand. "Don't think about it, just say whatever you want whenever you want because then I *really* know what you *really* feel."

"Maya," she says, "that's not fair. I'm just thinking of you."

"Are you?"

"Yes. What if Josh wants to be mixed up in the baby's life? How will that even work?"

"For one thing, the father is not Josh, since we didn't touch each other for two years. I don't know who the father is. For another, problems have solutions and I'm learning how to figure those out."

"So it's not Josh's baby?" Rory asks.

I close my eyes. One of the things that was great about rehab is that there was literally nothing I could say about my behavior while drunk that would shock anyone there. Not even a little. Often the response to what would be an embarrassing story in the outside world was that somebody would tell a story that was even worse, the "that ain't nothin'" shares, as a friend of mine called it. I wish I were there now. I wish I could say the truth and everyone would just nod, instead of giving me the slightly horrified expression I'm going to see on my sister's face in two seconds.

"I don't remember having sex with anybody, which doesn't mean anything because I can't remember a lot of things from that last couple of months." I lift a shoulder. "It doesn't matter. The baby is in my body, so it's mine."

And Rory does look mildly distressed, but it's not horrified. It's something else, something maybe *for* me, rather than against me.

Meadow hugs me wordlessly, and I feel something coming from her that's hot and sad and intense, but I'm not sure what it is. Or maybe I do know. "Rory was always only mine," she says. "I get it."

And here is the truth of Meadow, too. By virtue of her own hard road, she has a lot of compassion. She had a baby at sixteen, fathered by no one Meadow wanted to claim. She *does* know. It feels good to rest in her arms, against her soft shoulder. Something too hot drains out of me. "I'm sorry about Norah," I say. "She's just not that bad."

"Norah?" Rory pops up. "Are you kidding? She was the most normal woman Dad ever dated."

Meadow stiffens, but when she lets me go, she's found a smile to paste over her emotions. "Are you implying that I'm not normal?"

Rory raises a brow. "If the shoe fits . . ."

I make an appointment with Rory's doctor to find out more about the pregnancy, and because of the situation, she squeezes me in the next day. This satisfies both Meadow's and Rory's need for order, and I call my boss, too, to discuss my options about the job with my arm in a cast.

To my surprise, she's very relaxed about it. "Things happen," she says. "Obviously you can't work as a barista, but Nathan was telling us that you were known for your nose in the wine business. What about applying that to coffee? Maybe you'd enjoy the roasting and blending, and if you hate it, you can come back to work in the café once you're able."

Humbled, grateful, I say, "That would be great."

"Take a few days to feel better, then give me a call."

In the early evening, storms roll in, bringing gusty winds and dry lightning arcing over the ocean. I find myself in the kitchen, the Bluetooth synced to my phone and my playlist of cooking tunes, which I haven't accessed in a long time. It feels good to hear the old favorites, an upbeat mix of soul and rock, much of it taken from the years when my parents had their dinner parties right in this house and would spend the day cooking together, playing music and chopping.

The memory is a happy one, and when the Beatles sing "Ob-La-Di, Ob-La-Da," I break from chopping onions in the food processor to spin around the island myself, shimmying my hips, singing along with the music. I don't even miss wine, not tonight, and I know it's partly because of The One living inside me right now, but it's also just letting go of what was. Finding something else, like grapefruit seltzer water over ice with a twist of lime. Delicious.

Outside the rain and thunder create a seascape of tossing waves. Inside I'm simmering onions in butter very slowly, while I crush two dozen cloves of garlic. I've been dying for garlic, and this was one of my dad's best recipes—caramelized onions, a cup of garlic cloves, salt and pepper, and Parmesan cheese topped with cream. The whole room smells amazing. "What do you think, baby?" I say to my belly. "Will you like garlic?"

Struggling a little to do everything left-handed, I peel garlic and toss it into the processor, and then scrape it into the butter. The scent slams into my taste centers, filling my mouth with saliva. It makes me laugh. Maybe my appetite isn't just my body healing, but the baby, being hungry and growing, too.

Impulsively, I punch the contact for my sponsor. It goes to voice mail, which does happen sometimes, and I leave a cheery message. "Hi, Deborah. It's Maya. I'm cooking my dad's garlic soup. I'm all alone in this beautiful house and it feels like heaven. Even the weather is making me happy. Give me a call when you can. I have really interesting news!"

Just as I hang up, another call comes in. The screen says Ayaz, and I hesitate. Maybe Meadow is right—the last thing I need is the complication of a man. But didn't we get that out in the open earlier today? I could use a friend. A sober friend even more. "Hello, Ayaz," I say.

"Hello, Maya. I'm calling to see how you're feeling."

"It's modestly painful, but not constant," I say. "And I'm cooking tonight, which makes me happy."

"Ah. A good activity for such a stormy night. What are you cooking, if I may be so bold?"

"Garlic soup, with cheese biscuits." Again my mouth waters. And before I know I'm going to say it, the words come tumbling out of my mouth: "Would you like to join me?"

For a moment, he hesitates, and I feel that something between us. I hurry to excuse him. "No pressure."

"I would love to. Shall I bring something?"

"Nope. Just yourself." A great crashing boom of thunder slams the air, and we both laugh. "I wouldn't walk."

"No. I'll be there soon."

I hang up and the music comes back on, filling the room with upbeat love songs. I think of Meadow spinning around with her hair flying, and my father tipping her backward almost to the floor, kissing her neck. They were so beautiful, so passionately in love with each other. Rory and I rolled our eyes, but we both loved it. A swell of tears burns behind my eyes.

Nope. Not crying over an asshole who fractured our family without a single backward glance.

Not doing it.

But I miss him.

Chapter Thirty-One
Norah

I'm filling condiments at the bar, chitchatting with the bartender, a guy with a fabulous beard and the longest eyelashes I've ever seen. In the days before Augustus, he would have been my exact catnip, but nothing about him attracts me at all. I wonder sadly but without a lot of heat if I am broken now, if Augustus and his charming ways have ruined me for anyone else. As I wipe down salt and pepper shakers, I think about that, wondering what it was exactly that made me fall so head over heels in love with him. Why Meadow did. Why all of us do. So many of us, and by the time I got him, he was pretty freaking old.

It didn't matter. It was something about the way he turned his attention on you, completely, with a kind of laser-like focus that blocked everything else out, as if you were the only star in the entire galaxy. He gave compliments, but never smarmy ones—he paid attention, so he noticed when a color made my eyes stand out, or when I changed my nail polish or tried a new lipstick. He examined and admired every inch of my body and worshipped it, which was the sexiest thing in the world.

And other things.

He brushed my hair. He massaged my hands or my feet when we were watching a movie. He knew all my favorite foods and bought them for me with no care over whether they were elegant or gourmet or junk.

I have a weakness for crunchy CHEETOS, and he'd sometimes just bring a bag home from work. Or Cinnamon Toast Crunch. Or Cara Cara oranges. Whatever.

He read to me. *Read* to me. No one in my life had ever read to me, not anything, but when he found out I loved poetry, he read my favorites to me—Mary Oliver, Ellen Bass—and also his own favorites, love songs and manifestos from the sixties. He loved Simon and Garfunkel poetry, which he joked was way too white for him to like, and yet he did.

He whistled when he cooked, and sang in the shower with a voice that boomed out as big as his laugh. He made dolls of hollyhocks for his granddaughters and brought Rory a beer that could be purchased only in a town sixty miles away.

He was known for little presents—a single flower, a pair of earrings, a book, a pencil, a toy, a piece of candy.

"You're going to wash the silver off the top of that," the bartender—his name is Jeremy—says. "Something on your mind?"

I shake my head. What can I say? *My lover died and I miss him.* But that just makes everybody uncomfortable, and it's not like he could do anything to make it better. I just have to long for Augustus until I don't. Maybe I always will. As someone said, grief is a thing you have to carry.

The door swings open and we both glance up. Two cops in plain clothes come in. "Norah Rivera?"

"Yes. How can I help you?"

"You're a hard woman to track down," the woman says. "I'm Detective Love and this is Detective Vaca."

"Is this about Augustus?"

"It is. Can we sit down somewhere?"

"Is that okay?" I ask Jeremy.

"Sure." He shrugs. "I'm not the boss."

I lead them over to a booth in the corner. "Maya Beauvais told me you'd want to talk to me."

"Is there some reason you didn't come in on your own?"

"I don't have a car, and I've got a job, and I only found out yesterday that you wanted to talk to me."

"Fair enough." She flips her notebook. "You've been living with Augustus for nine months, is that right?"

"Yeah. I came out here in September, and didn't leave."

"Whirlwind romance?"

I nod.

"He was a lot older than you."

"Yes." I deliver a level gaze at her. "Did you ever meet him?"

"Can't say that I did. I don't really run in those circles."

"Circles?"

"Celebrities. The beautiful people."

I let myself smile a little, gesturing toward the bar. "Me either."

"How was your relationship with Mr. Beauvais when he died?"

"Good, I would say."

"And his mental state?"

I turn a fork upside down on the table. "He was worried about his daughter in rehab, pretty worried about the restaurant, too." I take a breath, add the truth. "His health was not great."

"The restaurant was in trouble?"

I nod. "Not really my realm, but yes, I think everyone kind of knows that."

The guy leans forward. "What kind of relationship do you have with his family? His ex-wives, his kids?"

"Not much. I'm friendly with Rory, and I know both Maya and Meadow, but only socially, really. Maya is letting me stay at Belle l'Été."

"That's the house Augustus owned?"

"Yes." It strikes me as something they'd already know, so they're leading up to something. "Is there something in particular you think I might know? I've only had this job a couple of days and I need it."

Vaca lifts his chin. "If you knew someone poisoned him, who would you finger?"

I blink. "Poisoned?"

"It's still inconclusive, but the evidence is pointing that direction."

I know a lot about poison as a method of murder thanks to a class on Agatha Christie I took as an undergrad. "Fairly hard to pinpoint, isn't it?"

His eyes narrow. "Did you poison him?"

I meet his gaze. "He was the best thing that ever happened to me, Detective. Why would I kill him?"

"Did you know he was sleeping with the bartender at Peaches and Pork that night?"

I feel an electric shock jolt my nerves, setting them abuzz. "No, that's not right."

"I'm afraid it is," he says. There's a slight, aggressive satisfaction in his pronouncement. "He was also sleeping with Meadow, fairly regularly by the look of it." He settles a grainy photo of the two of them engaged in a passionate embrace. Her shirt is pulled off her shoulder, which Augustus is kissing. "Were you aware?"

"No." I swallow, and it takes everything I have to keep my voice even. "But I did suspect. They spent a lot of time together after Maya went to rehab."

"Do you think Meadow could have poisoned him?"

I meet his eyes again. "No," I say distinctly. "She loved him like he was the sun and moon and stars."

"How does she feel about you?"

Out of the corner of my eye, I see my boss come into the room, and I stand up. "How do you think she feels? Sorry, I have to get back to work."

<hr/>

Dinner is slow, and as the newbie, I'm the first to be cut. It has taken all that I've got to keep a professional face up during service, so I'm not disappointed.

The good news is that my tips are excellent and I have some money in my pocket as I head out, trying to decide what to do with myself. It's not quite seven thirty, and I don't really want to return to Belle l'Été yet. For one thing, I'm reeling from the bombshells the detectives dropped on me, and for another, I really need that room and I don't want to get on Maya's nerves.

Instead of wallowing, I head back to the library to do more research. It's already closed, so I carry my laptop to one of the patio restaurants along State Street. The Sunday crowds are remarkably thin, and I doubt anybody is going to care if I nurse a beer for a couple of hours. I had a good meal at work but order some tapas to go with it, Marcona almonds and little roasted peppers and olives. Augustus would have ordered the pulpo, octopus, but I can't bring myself to eat something that's smart enough to free itself from an aquarium, which I saw in a video somewhere.

Girls walk by in tiny dresses and tinier shorts, and boys follow in groups. It's warm and clouds are gathering over the ocean, but no one has said a word about it raining. Even if it does, I'm sheltered beneath a canvas roof and will be fine.

When the server delivers my plate, I fire up the laptop. The man next to me is talking quietly and repetitively to himself, but he's easy enough to ignore.

Did someone kill Augustus? It seems so wildly unlikely. Even his enemies loved him in some way. Only Maya managed to keep up her walls against him, and she's off the hook.

Still. Poisoned? The possibility rolls around in my gut.

On the computer, I call up the raft of images of him I find on Google. So many of them. So many with Meadow.

A visual of Augustus kissing Meadow's shoulder blasts across my vision. It feels like my ribs are breaking, collapsing around my heart, and I press both palms to the middle of my chest. I was jealous of Meadow, honestly, but it never really crossed my mind that he'd actually cheat on me. We were so together, so enmeshed.

So in love.

The sense of betrayal is painful, a burning rock in the pit of my stomach, but I also feel a keen sense of embarrassment. Did I think I was the only person he'd never cheat on, even though it was always his signature?

Honestly, yes. I was about as young as he could go—or so I thought. The bartender was even younger. Maybe not even twenty-five, which if I read it on Twitter would seem creepy and disgusting, but seems perfectly natural for Augustus. People who don't know him probably think he's a predator. You can't think that if you know him. After all, I flung myself on the altar of his attention within twenty minutes of our meeting.

Tears blur my ability to read the screen in front of me, and I can't remember what I was going to look up, anyway. Instead, I type in his name, Augustus Beauvais, and click on images. They show up, so many.

Did you know he was sleeping with Meadow?

If it had been only that revelation, I might not feel this way, partly because I did already suspect, and partly because she holds—held—a powerful position in his life. They had a remarkable connection, and maybe I wouldn't have minded so much if it had just been Meadow.

But the bartender! She was so young she couldn't really walk very well in high heels, and her collarbones and wrists showed beneath the white shirt of the uniform. She had great tits and long glossy hair and a sharp intelligence that was learning itself. I recognized myself in her the first time we met, but it never crossed my mind, not for a single second, that Augustus would fuck her.

I click through the photos, tears flowing down the back of my throat. The thing is, we weren't having that much sex those last couple of months. He was tired. He didn't feel well. He dragged home from Ojai or the restaurant and collapsed into bed, his hand over my belly as I read. I tried not to mind, tried to tell myself that he was worried about Maya and he had a lot of business trouble, and it wasn't personal.

Turns out, it *was* personal. He wasn't fucking me, but he had plenty of fucks to give Meadow and the bartender, whose name I can't remember.

It's humiliating. It stings in exactly the same place as those times I had to leave a foster home for some specious reason—but usually because I ran afoul of one of the other kids. It stings the same way losing an internship to another privileged white boy stung and sent me on my way here.

It stings because I knew better. I know better.

The only person I can count on is myself. It's me who will drag me out of this hand-to-mouth life and into the one I want.

And Meadow Beauvais is my ticket—I can just feel it.

Chapter Thirty-Two
Meadow

Rory glumly watches them play with Barbies. "It's like they don't get it at all. I thought they'd be so upset."

I rub her shoulder, aching for her. "They'll understand more over time, but it just doesn't make sense to them now. What's death? What does that even mean?" I brush her hair away from her face, tuck a lock behind her ear. "Why don't you sit down and let me make some dinner?"

"That's okay. You don't have to cook for me."

I push her a little, and she sinks heavily. "I don't have to. I want to."

"I was just going to make spaghetti, nothing fancy. I even have bakery garlic bread. It's pretty much the only thing the girls will reliably eat."

As she talks, I fill a glass with ice and some of the tea I find in a pitcher in the fridge. As I set it down, she says, "Kind of a shocker about Maya being pregnant."

I let go of a sound that's not exactly a laugh. "That's an understatement."

"It's exciting, though, to have something happy in the middle of all the sadness."

"Yeah." I wash my hands thoroughly and choose an onion from the mesh bowl on the counter. "I guess." My gut twists again. "I just don't want it to threaten her sobriety."

"You made that pretty clear," she says.

I glance up. "You don't think it's dangerous?"

She sighs, leaning on her elbow. "I don't know. Having a baby was one of the best things that ever happened to me. I loved it. Maybe she will, too."

My own experience was slightly different. I spent the entire nine months terrified, trying to hide my expanding belly. All Rory knows about her sperm donor is that he was someone I didn't love and don't think mattered. "It was harder for me."

"I know, Mom," she says. "I hope you know that I'm grateful."

"Oh, baby!" I rest my palms on the counter, pausing so that she knows I mean it with my whole heart. "You changed my life in the best possible ways. I'm grateful to *you*."

She blinks, my blue-eyed daughter, and I see the shimmer over her irises. "You don't say that very often."

"I know. I'm sorry about that." I score the papery outer layer of a yellow onion. "But one has nothing to do with the other. Your sister has a very serious alcohol use disorder, and she needs to heal."

"Yeah," Rory says. "She does." Her expression grows pointed. "Look, I know you're struggling as much as I am with Dad's death, but you can't funnel all your emotions into running Maya's life."

My hands freeze and I gape at her. "Is that what you think I'm doing?"

"Maybe." She inclines her head. "From the outside, it kinda looks that way."

"When I got there this morning, she was playing backgammon with that doctor who lives a few doors down, the one with the wife who drowned."

"Oooh," she says. "Backgammon! What's next? Chess?"

"It's not the game." I start to dice the onion, fiercely. "He's a widower and she's newly sober and they're both in a vulnerable place. I don't want Maya to get hurt. Again."

"Okay, Mom," she says, standing. "You really need to get the focus back on yourself. You can't save her." She shoos me away from her counter. I relinquish the knife, wiping my hands on a paper towel, a hole opening in my heart.

"I'd like to cook," I say.

"I know. I'm just agitated and this will calm me down. Do you want a glass of wine?"

"No." I'm not sure, just this minute, if I'll ever have another in my life. The specter of Maya, wine soaked, like a strange version of *Carrie*, haunts me.

Rory says, "You can pour me one, if you will. Bottle on the door in the fridge."

The small task is one I can do. The wineglasses are on the sideboard, and I pour a measure into one of them. "It's a bit early, isn't it?"

"It's three p.m., already six in New York," she says without missing a beat. She takes a long swallow of the cold wine, and sighs. "That helps."

I watch her drink it down. When I was a child, the women around me never drank, ever. Not my mother, not any of her friends, not teachers or anyone else. I'm sure they must have sometimes, but I didn't see it. I knew about "cocktail hour," when people drank cocktails and looked sophisticated, from books and movies, but that was not the reality in my blue-collar world.

When did women start drinking so openly, so *heavily*?

How much drinking is too much? Where is the line? I really have no idea where a person falls over the edge, and that raises my anxiety, too. Have we all been drinking too much, all their lives?

"Listen," Rory says. "You can't save Maya from her own choices, not with the baby, not with a man, not with her alcoholism. You just have to love her and show up for her."

I sink down on a barstool. From the first moment I saw Maya, with her unbrushed hair and wary eyes, I was caught in the desire to protect her, and perhaps by extension the boy her father had been, and later, the children I wished we'd had. "How do we keep her safe?"

She shakes her head, pointing with her knife to the girls playing outside the back door. "We can't even keep those two completely safe."

"Mostly, we can."

"Not really. Believe me, I run the scenarios constantly. What if a killer bee flies in from Mexico? What if one of them falls down the stairs and breaks her neck? What if somebody snatches one of them?"

I press a hand over my belly. "God forbid."

"I know." She leans on one hip, facing me. "You need to find your life, Mom, instead of trying to run the world for everybody else. Now that Dad's gone, you really need something to give your focus to."

"We've been divorced for eight years. I was hardly living for him."

She nods in a way that makes me feel patronized.

"What? You think I was?"

"I don't want to upset you."

"I'm a grown woman. I can handle it."

"Well, you spent a lot of time together even if you were divorced. The farm, the restaurant. Didn't you see him almost every day?"

"So? We had a lot of business interests in common."

"I'm pretty sure he was up at Meadow Sweet a lot more than he was down here in recent months."

A memory rises, of his mouth kissing a line down the side of my neck to my shoulder. I shake it off. "How do you know that?"

"He told me." She pours olive oil in a heavy skillet and drops the onions into it. "He said you were pretty wrecked over Maya, and he wanted to help you through it."

I open the plastic container of basil, take it out, and rinse it. "That part is true to a degree. But he was also having a hard time about it."

She gives a sharp, humorless laugh. "Of course."

"What's on your mind, Rory? Get it out."

"Nothing. It's the same story as always—Maya, Maya, Maya. Maya needs rescue. Maya needs nurturing to recover from another injury— her mom or getting left or bombing out of college or whatever."

"She didn't bomb out of college."

"Only because you both ran to her rescue! Bailed her out of jail, right? Pulled strings to keep her from getting expelled?"

I look away. It's true. She wrecked a car while drunk, and walked away without a scratch, but she was arrested and charged. We bailed her out with cash and lawyers. Another time, she and Josh had such a knock-down, drag-out fight in their on-campus room that they were both nearly expelled. Only the intervention of Augustus, who was on TV a lot through that period, and a generous donation to the scholar-ship fund kept them in school.

At the time, I really thought it was the influence of Josh that was causing her to drink too much. He was a hard-core partier, and the two of them drank a lot together. He was not a good influence.

After the fight, they settled in and got through the rest of college, then headed off to travel the world and work vineyards and learn more about techniques for making wine, and she entered what seemed to be from a distance one of the better stretches of her life.

I look over my shoulder for little ears. Polly and Emma are absorbed in their game. "I did do all of that, but I was honestly just trying to help her. She's wounded, Rory, in ways you are not. Children are not equal. You know that."

"Whatever." She slams a pot into the sink and begins to run water into it. "I don't want to talk about it anymore. I wanted to talk about you, not Maya."

"We did talk about me."

"Not enough." She turns the water off. "I need you to promise me that you're going to let her do whatever she wants with that baby and you're just going to support her."

"Okay!" I lift my hands, palm out. "I promise."

"And really, you need to back off with her sobriety. Go to Al-Anon, get some tools."

"How do you know about Al-Anon?"

She takes a breath, lets it go. "I started going to meetings when she went to rehab. She asked me to. But I don't want you to go to the same meetings as me."

A flush burns up my neck. "What's with you two? When did you start to dislike me so much?"

"No one dislikes you. Well, neither of us, anyway. You're just meddling a lot."

I stare at her, embarrassed and wounded. Neither of them knows one thing about what I survived to get to this moment, to be the kind of woman I wished I'd had in my own life.

"Well, I guess I'll stop right now." I pick up my bag and toss my hair back over my shoulders. "Girls, come give me a kiss. I'm going home."

"Mom!" Rory says. "You don't have to leave!"

I hug the little bodies, smelling sweet sweat in their hair. "Be good."

"We will! Love you, Lala."

"See you soon," I say, and kiss Rory's cheek.

"Mom!"

I raise a hand, shaking my head. "Not now."

Chapter Thirty-Three
Maya

The smell of rain blows in through the open patio doors, but nothing is actually hitting the ground. *Virga.* The word comes to me from a long-lost science class. An undertone of smoke blows in with the non-rain. I go upstairs and look north and south and east, but the clouds are too low to see the fire.

Cosmo chases behind me, up the stairs, trying to attack my ankles. I grab him and kiss him, burying my face in his soft, thick fur. "You're a little wild man, aren't you?" He licks my nose, then takes an experimental nip. Tears spring to my eyes and I hold him away from me. "Ouch. No nose-biting!"

He barks and I set him down. He tumbles down the stairs behind me, and I grab him again when I hear Ayaz knock. I open the door. "Did you see fire anywhere from your place? It smells pretty close."

"No. Perhaps it's just the cloud cover, trapping the smoke lower to the ground."

"That makes sense." I step back. "Come in."

He passes me, turning his body toward mine, not away. He's not tall, almost exactly my height, and our eyes meet, his dark and kindly. "It smells divine."

I smile, closing the door, and put the puppy down again. "Divine," I repeat.

"What?"

"It's not really a word I'd ever use."

"Why not?"

"It's just not in my lexicon. I think it might be more of a British word than an American one."

"Perhaps." The puppy sniffs around his feet, tail wagging, then sits and looks up with a bid for attention. When Ayaz doesn't notice, Cosmo yips, and Ayaz chuckles, kneeling to scrub his knuckles along the puppy's back, then around his ears. "My apologies. You're clearly the most important being in this room."

It makes me like him more.

He stands by the island, looking around. "It's lovely. Twenties?"

"I think so. Old Hollywood, anyway. A director built it and lived here the rest of his life." Cosmo snuffles along the edge of the counter, finds some invisible tidbit and slurps it up, then waddles over to his bed and collapses with a sigh. I lift the lid on the pot simmering on the stove, give the soup a stir, and turn back. "Meadow says it was a hoarder's paradise when they got in here, but that meant they could buy it for a price they could afford."

He nods, touches the tiles. "Handmade."

"Yes. For a couple of decades, my parents made some serious bank." I lean on the counter. "I think my mom is still doing well, but Peaches and Pork is on its way out, I'm afraid."

He nods, settling on one of the stools. "Will it be sold now that your father is dead?"

"I don't know. That's one of the things I have to decide, actually. He left it to me, so I have to figure it out."

"The house and the restaurant both, hmm? That's a big responsibility."

"Tell me about it." I look around the kitchen, at the tiled alcove for the stove, the windows opening to fresh breezes from the Pacific. "I love the house, honestly, but taxes and upkeep are enormous."

"I'm facing the same choices. My wife was very wealthy, so it was nothing for her."

"Did she leave it to you? The house?"

He nods. "California is a community property state."

"So there should be money to keep it up, too."

"I suppose." His weariness feels akin to mine, and as if to emphasize, he wipes his face with his hands. "I feel I'm wasting time, doing nothing, not making choices."

"I so get that. I have no idea what I'm going to do. None." I think of the baby and it feels more pointed, but not yet so urgent I have to decide right now. "One thing I do know is that I am not going to run a restaurant." I stir the soup and fragrance surrounds my head. "It's ready," I say.

"What can I do to help?"

"Take the bread to the table." I gesture to the breadboard. I've already set the table with fresh linens, a summer tablecloth printed with big dahlias, woven green placemats, soft pink napkins as light as clouds. The linens are all Meadow. Why did she leave them behind? To remind my father that she'd made a beautiful home?

I ladle soup into bowls, but am hobbled by the cast, so Ayaz carries them one at a time. I open the fridge and point to the pitcher of limeade my sister made. "Would you like ice?"

"No, thank you."

It's easy to be with him, to move around the space without bumping, as if we know the path of the other's feet already. When we sit at the round table in the breakfast nook, the windows open to the view of lightning crackling across the horizon, I feel as calm and happy as I have in—

A long time. Forever.

I raise my glass. "Cheers."

"Cheers." He sips and raises his eyebrows. "Excellent. Did you make this?"

"No, my sister. She's been working on her alcohol-free game, and this is the top of the heap so far."

"It tastes very like a fresh lime soda I used to buy from a vendor in London."

"Is that where you grew up?"

"Partly. Partly in Turkey, though we left when I was seven, so I remember very little. The smell of roses, and the river that ran through the city. The call to prayer."

"That's very evocative." I taste the soup, garlic sprinkled with Parmesan, layered with parsley, and I have to pause and close my eyes. My father is in the room, in my head and my heart, sitting at the table with us. I think suddenly that this baby will be his grandchild and he will never see it, and my heart cracks.

I keep my eyes closed until the highest peak of emotion passes, but still a tear leaks out, and I have to wipe it away.

"Are you all right?" he asks.

"Yes." I take a breath. "I'm sorry. I was planning to be completely normal for once, but I guess I'm just going to be a wreck whenever you're around." I shake my head. "Or maybe I'm just a wreck all around at the moment."

"Understandably," he says smoothly. "And I rather think becoming emotional over this soup is perfectly appropriate. I'm ready to wipe a tear away myself."

I laugh. "Thank you."

Our eyes meet and hold, and it isn't my imagination that there's something strong and . . . true . . . between us. Maybe it's friendship. Maybe it's finding someone else in the same boat. Or maybe it's something more. The radar in my body says that whatever it is, right now it's okay.

The moment stretches, but it's never awkward. I simply arrive at a place where I ask, "What kind of medicine do you practice?"

"*Did* practice," he answers. "Nothing very exciting, I'm afraid. Geriatric medicine, but I haven't done the boards in America."

"Really? How long have you been here?"

"Almost six years." His smile is self-deprecating. "It was all a whirl at first, the excitement of the move and being with a celebrity and all the luxury." He raises a brow. "I found I was as easily swept into it as anyone."

I nod.

"I was writing on the side in London, and had been modestly successful, so I thought I'd just keep doing that in America, but"—he shrugs—"a year passed and then another and another."

"I get it." I tear bread from the loaf and dip it in the soup without thinking, then wonder if he'll think I'm rude. Instead, he follows suit, nodding. "Do you miss it?"

"Medicine?"

"Yes."

"I do, but I didn't realize how much until I was with you at the A&E. The smells, the sound of the machines, the people who need help." He lifts a shoulder. "Medicine has meaning. Deep meaning. Science is reliable, and powerful."

"Will you go back to it?"

His expression lightens. "Until yesterday I would have said no. But today, I think the answer is yes."

I cross my pink-casted arm over my chest and grin. "Because of my arm? That's so cool."

He laughs a little, and hair falls on his forehead. "It is."

The electricity between us is not friendship, and I realize that I'm not entirely playing fair. "I found out something else yesterday," I say, stirring my soup, sprinkling a little more Parmesan on top. "I've been so worried that I'd damaged my liver, the way I've been getting sick and all of that. Turns out . . ." I pause.

"You're pregnant?"

"Yes. Did you know?"

"I suspected." His gaze sharpens. "How do you feel about that?"

I take a moment, let it fill me, all the gold light and promise and hope. "So lucky."

His smile this time is dazzling, showing teeth and the creases by his eyes. "I'm so glad." He raises his glass again. "Congratulations."

"Thank you." I clink the glass. "I have to see a doctor tomorrow to see how things are and all that, but"—emotion rises through my heart—"it feels like a miracle."

"And the father?"

My therapist said I didn't have to tell anybody anything I didn't want to tell, that my life and my path were mine to share or not share. For a moment, I weigh the possibilities. I could play it off and just claim Josh, or I can tell him the truth.

But I really, really like him, and the potential for something deep is blooming between us. He's not a vintner or a dude or any of the kinds of men I've been with in the past. He's a physician and a writer who grew up in a Muslim family; even if he hasn't said if he's religious, it must have influenced his views of the world to some degree.

Tell the truth.

Honesty is the cornerstone of all I am now. I have to own myself and my life, so I take a breath and speak it. "I don't know who the father is. It's kind of a blur, that whole period."

The light in his eyes dims the faintest amount, and I'm instantly defensive, casting away any thought of connection I had. "People don't go to rehab for slightly misbehaving," I say sharply.

He reaches for my hand and captures it. "I know."

"But you're judging me." I pull my hand away.

"You're right," he admits, and there's the slightest roll of his childhood accent amid the British. "I apologize."

I duck my head. A flush burns up my chest to my cheekbones, and I wish I could snap my fingers and disappear. I wish I could be back in rehab, where somebody would say, *Oh, that's nothing. Let me tell you . . .*

"Maya," he says softly. "I am so sorry. Please don't banish me, all right?"

I laugh. "Banish you?"

To my surprise, he rounds the table and kneels by the chair, taking my free hand. "Forgive me. I am sometimes at the mercy of a patriarchal society that judges women very harshly."

I look at him, narrowing my eyes. "Did you actually just say that?"

"I did."

Everything in me surges toward him. It's that clean and that simple, and I bend in to kiss the sad mouth that's so close, smelling pine and hope. For a split second before our lips meet, I'm afraid he'll be appalled and push me away, but quite the opposite happens. Our mouths lock and he stands, pulling me with him so our bodies are pressing tightly together. My arms wrap around his torso, his around my shoulders and waist, and we fit like Russian dolls. His head tilts and mine tilts the other way and we dive into kissing like it will end climate change. The low-level restlessness I've been feeling, that longing for sex, for connection, for skin-to-skin nourishment, rises in a wild current in my body, setting all the circuits to on, my skin rustling to life.

He makes a noise and pulls me harder into him, his hands traveling over my back, down to my ass. I follow suit, tugging his shirt out the back of his pants so that I can touch his skin, and at the feeling of bare flesh, hot and smooth, I make a noise myself. I want to tear his clothes off, bite him, ride him like a bronco.

I break away and look up. "Is this okay? Do you think . . ."

"Very okay," he says, and his hand is under my skirt, on the back of my thighs. "I think yes."

"Let's go upstairs."

The balcony doors are open and we shed our clothes in the breeze. It feels inevitable, obvious, the only possible thing that could happen. We fall together in fierce, almost bruising intensity at first. Lightning crackles and explodes outside the windows as two bodies give each other the meal they've been so starved for.

And then we begin again, taking our time, exploring nooks and crannies, kissing and kissing and kissing and finally falling asleep naked beneath the covers, tangled in the most natural possible way.

As I'm drifting off, I think, *Is it possible to fall in love at first sight?*

Chapter Thirty-Four
Norah

A man is in the kitchen when I come down the next morning. He's making espresso with a machine I've never once used. "Wow, that smells amazing."

"Hello." He looks up and I realize he's the guy from the coffee shop the other day. He frowns slightly. "I recognize you from the Brewed Bean, don't I?"

"Yeah. I used to live here. Or, well, I do live here for the moment. Maya's letting me stay."

He nods, focus returning to the nozzle dripping extreme coffee into a cup. He's already made one, with frothed milk in a big mug, which I assume is for Maya. I look for her and spy her by the pool in the soft, cool air of morning, wearing a lime-green T-shirt dress and no shoes. She looks content. Cosmo is leashed beside her so he won't fall in the pool.

I look back to the guy, who also has that just-laid easiness about him, his feet bare as he carries the coffee across the tiles to the door and settles one by Maya's left elbow. The connection between them is practically visible, shining with iridescent exuberance between them, around them.

It makes me painfully, embarrassingly jealous. For the space of an entire minute, I stand by the island and stare at them, wishing for Augustus, or for the Augustus I first knew, not the one who betrayed me, betrayed everyone, all of us.

And yet.

I still miss him, the bastard.

With more vigor than is actually required, I grind beans for the french press, and set water to boil in the kettle. While I wait for it, I lean on the counter and think about the tasks of the day. I was in too much of a state last night to get any more work done, so today I'll hole up in the bedroom I've slept in the past two nights, which I think must have been Maya's at one time, and continue my research into Meadow's life.

"Norah, please join us," Maya calls over her shoulder. "It's beautiful out here this morning."

When my coffee is finished, I carry it out to the patio a little shyly. It's not like I've been included in much of anything, and it's a relief to be around people close to my age. I think the guy, who introduces himself as Ayaz, is a little older, but not as old as Meadow and Augustus and all the people I've been surrounded with.

It's nothing. We just drink coffee in the sunshine, commenting on the edge of pink in the smoke-tinged air and the high level of the surf and what to make for breakfast.

It's nothing and it's everything, because it's the first time I've really been able to breathe for nearly two weeks.

So it seems like the least I can do is make breakfast. It's simple enough, scrambled eggs with cheese and toast, but we all devour it hungrily. We're finishing up, swinging our legs from the barstools, when Meadow shows up. At the first sight of her, I know something is not quite right—she's slightly unkempt, her hair left out of a braid to tumble over her arms and shoulders, her face showing every single minute of her life on earth, her jeans damp on the hems. She's always a bit bohemian, but this morning she looks like she slept in her clothes.

She's brought Maya flowers and some kind of tea and hurries away in only a couple of minutes, looking ravaged and a little broken.

"Is she okay?" I ask as Maya comes back in the room.

"I don't know. She didn't look particularly good, did she?"

I shake my head, looking the direction she went. "No."

"She's trying to keep it together for everybody else, but probably out of all of us, she's the one who will miss him the most." She looks at me. "No offense."

"Yeah." I carry my dishes to the sink and rinse them before putting them in the dishwasher. "I'm going to work in my room for the day if that's okay."

"You don't have to go up there. Take my dad's office. It's a lot more comfortable. I have to go to the doctor in a little bit, so I won't be around to bother you."

"Okay. Thanks."

———— ⸙ ————

I shower in the main bathroom on the second floor, which I've never used. It boasts handmade tiles, and from the shower, a person can look through a window out over the Pacific, which feels deliciously decadent.

In Augustus's office, I open the blinds to let the light in. It's always been so dark in here, with heavy cherry furnishings and a Turkish carpet in hues of red and blue. Just opening the blinds changes the entire aspect. Light splashes over the bookcases and the desk, and as much as I admire all the cherrywood, if this were my room, I'd paint everything white, bring in some area rugs in beachy shades, exchange the old leather couch for something midcentury in turquoise or yellow.

Comforted by my flight of fantasy, I open Augustus's computer and pause. What am I looking for? What detail is going to unlock Meadow's life? What brought her here?

Obviously, she was looking to start a new life after the birth of her daughter, and I have to admire her for taking a chance and striking out in the world, leaving a strangling little town without opportunities to start fresh.

But it feels like I'm missing something. What happened to her stepdad? Did she just run away? It's possible he'd talk to me if I can track him down.

A good place to start. I run his name, Gary Sullivan, but the first time, there are hundreds of results. I narrow it to Thunder Bluff, and the marriage notice from the local paper shows up.

So does an obituary, which kills my idea for getting him to talk. He's been dead a long time, about thirty-five years, since 1987. It's short and sweet, just the notice of his death, nothing more.

Flipping back through my notes, I look for the dates Meadow started working at the Buccaneer. I don't have the exact date, but I flip back farther in my notebook and find the date of her marriage to Augustus, which is 1991, four years later. Augustus and Meadow had two rounds of their affair—the first one that she broke off when she found out he was married to Shanti, and the second when he left Shanti (and Maya) for Meadow. When did she first arrive in the area?

I listen for Maya outside the office, and creep to the door to see if I can spy her. She's sitting on the side of the pool, her feet in the water, talking on the phone to someone. Gently, I close the heavy door and dial Trudy, Meadow's boss at the Buccaneer. She answers with a scratchy voice. "Hello."

"Hi, Trudy. This is Norah Rivera, the woman you spoke with a couple of days ago about Tina Sullivan."

"You found her last name! Good for you."

"Yes. I was wondering if you remember the exact year she started at the Buccaneer?"

She lets go of a heavy sigh. "Let's see. I was still with my ex-husband at the time, and I kicked him out on Fourth of July, 1988, so before that—'87 somewhere, I'd guess."

"That's great, thanks."

"You're welcome. You should come by and pick up some zucchini this week. I'm going to have enough to feed the whole of Estonia."

I laugh at the colorful hyperbole. "I'll try."

Okay, so maybe she left when her stepfather died. Nothing much to keep her in the town, with both her mom and stepdad dead. Presumably the baby's father wanted nothing to do with Rory or he never knew, and maybe best to let sleeping dogs lie at this point, considering how wealthy Meadow has become.

Tapping my finger on the glass, I peer out the window toward the horizon, thinking. Thinking. What else?

So often with research, you don't know what you don't know. I have to just keep looking at things, reading.

I start with the yearbooks from Thunder Bluff High School, which I find online at a paid service. I pay the fee and call up the years Tina was there, or I think she was there. I check my dates again, and she was born in '69, so she must have started high school around '83 or '84. I hit the jackpot in '83, where a classic black-and-white photo shows freshman Tina Sullivan. She's not fallen prey to the horrific bangs of the period, and she's already beautiful. Luminous, really, with wide eyes and long hair. It pierces me to see her so young. Rory looks quite like her.

In '84/'85, she was a cheerleader. It surprises me to see her on the squad, with a tiny skirt and a sweater that shows off her curves. She's a knockout, and somebody liked shooting her photo—there are over a dozen of her, all credited to the same L. Newton. She's manning a bake sale with her hair pulled back in a very long ponytail, and staring dolefully out of a window, and in midair in a jump. The photographer already has a flair, and the pictures give me a strong visual of who she was.

I write the name down and look him up in the class photos. Leslie Newton is not the nerd I was expecting, but a sturdy youth with black hair, a strong jaw, and penetrating eyes. I run a check for other photos of him, and two show up—one of him on a debate team trip, hair longer than in the class photo, and another with a girlfriend, head to head. The caption is telling. **Lovebirds Leslie Newton and Tina Sullivan share a moment.**

Is this Rory's dad? The timing would be right.

Except . . . how did she have the parchment-white Rory with a boy so dark?

I click through to the next year, '85/'86. There's a class photo of Tina, but only that photo. She looks almost exactly the same, so it was taken before she was pregnant, or she hid it very well. I look for photos by or of L. Newton and there's nothing, which stumps me until I realize he was a senior the year before. He probably headed off to college.

Or to work. His photos are so good I hope he found a way to continue.

I pause and stretch my shoulders, and realize I need to pee. Padding out of the room, carrying my coffee cup, I realize I feel as good as I have in months, as if things are on the right keel at last. I stick the cup in the Keurig and drop a fresh pod in, feeling the same guilt I always feel, which isn't enough to stop me using such a radically perfect machine. At least Augustus ordered compostable pods.

While it brews, I duck into the bathroom on this level, and when I come back, Maya is standing in front of the fridge, chewing her lip. When she sees me, she straightens and closes the door. "I don't know what I'm looking for," she says, and rubs her arms. "I'm so restless today."

"If you think of anything, let me know." I stir cream into the coffee, and wait for a minute. "Maya, I am so grateful for this, I can't even tell you."

"Oh please. You're like my voodoo to keep Meadow in her own house."

"Ah. Ulterior motive. Still, it's really nice." I take a tiny sip of coffee. "It just seems like she's worried about you."

"I know, but you know how mothers get on your nerves."

There's that ordinary thing, that something a person says that makes you know that you're not like everybody else. "I never knew my mom."

Her eyes are suddenly shiny. "I'm sorry. I didn't mean—"

"How could you know?" I shake my head. "I grew up in foster homes."

"That's right. I think Meadow said that yesterday."

I narrow my eyes. "Why? I mean, why was she talking about me?"

"Her theory is that my dad needed to rescue people. Women." She moves her jaw, back and forth, tension and unspoken words in her mouth. "You, Meadow, that crazy woman Christy who broke up their marriage and then took off." She shrugs a little. "Meadow said you'd grown up in foster care."

It makes me feel weirdly revealed. "I didn't really need anybody to rescue me, though. I rescued myself a long time ago."

"That's what I told her. You don't seem like a person in need of rescue."

"Meadow, either, really, at least not now." I think of all I've been digging into. "Do you know anything about her childhood? Rory's dad, any of that?"

"Nothing. It's always been completely off-limits." She glances at the clock. "I have to go to the doctor. I'll see you later."

"I have a shift at four, so probably a lot later. Or at least I hope so. I'd like to make some money."

"Okay. Lock up when you go."

"Thanks." There's something about the tilt of her head that makes me say impulsively, "Do you want company? I don't want to be weird but I'm happy to go along."

She seems very young when she twists her mouth and nods. "If you wouldn't mind?"

"Not at all. Let me turn off the computer."

Chapter Thirty-Five
Meadow

Unable to sleep, I tie on my shoes and go to the fields. The smell of smoke is in the air, thick and threatening, but I can't see any fire glow anywhere close by. When I went to bed, it had still been burning fiercely in the barely accessible high forests. A long way from here, even if it doesn't smell like it.

Still, it adds a layer to my restlessness. Elvis and I putter outside beneath the cloudy skies. A hush covers the night, and it adds to the sense of expectation, of worry. What's coming?

I walk the rows of the herb garden, taking refuge. It's been my habit since I was a girl, growing things in a hot, baked patch of ground behind the small house we lived in. My mom loved flowers and taught me how to plant seeds and water them, how to thin them to give each one room to grow. It turned out I had a flair for it, or maybe we just learn easily when we're young. I loved everything about that patch of life in the middle of the dry, hot stretch of yards all around us. We grew corn because I thought it would be cool, and it was amazing to harvest it at the end of the summer and peel it and cook it and eat it with butter.

And we grew herbs. They thrived in all that sun. Parsley, sage, rosemary, and thyme, like the song. Dill and chives, which bloomed in wild purple profusion in the spring. She grew a large crop of traditional medicinals, as well, and used some for mild illnesses, like chamomile for trouble sleeping, and mint for stomachaches. Raspberry leaf tea for pregnant women.

Brushing my fingers along the tops of the plants in my own garden, decades later, I wonder how a woman who was so nurturing could have loved a man so selfish. Her life had been hard before my stepfather arrived in it, and his income alone made our lives better. He drove a truck, long haul up and down the West Coast, and made good money. He was also not home a lot, which gave us plenty of space without him.

The first time he raped me, I was fourteen. My mother had been dead for barely a month, killed when a boy in a big truck ran a red light out of confusion. He wasn't drunk or high. He was sixteen years old and had only had his license for a few months, and he was devastated. He hadn't even been speeding. It was just a brutal accident, his truck crushing her little car and killing her on impact.

She'd always been a buffering presence in that house, but after she died, there was no place to hide, nowhere to escape. I'd always kept my distance from him, always aware that he watched me too closely, that he made jokes about my breasts or my bottom. He came too close, crowded me in the kitchen or the hallways, rubbing past me very slowly. I don't know if my mother knew. I like to think she didn't, that he was slick and made sure she didn't realize.

Once my mother was gone, I locked my door at night and spent as much time as I could away from the house, spending the night with friends, anything I could think of. I had no relatives anywhere else, and because my parents were married when my mom died, I was stuck with him.

And I didn't tell anybody I was afraid of him, either. It seemed like I must be doing something wrong for him to treat me like that.

That first time, that's what he said, that I was asking for it. It was summer and I was washing dishes in shorts and a T-shirt, sweating like a pig. I was alone, listening to the radio and dancing along a little, imagining the day I might have my own home, my own kitchen. I loved it when he went on the road, loved having my world to myself.

I wasn't expecting him until the following day when he banged into the house, smelling of beer. I knew right away I was in big trouble. I dropped the dishrag in the water and headed for my room, where I had a chair I could latch under the door handle, but he caught me before I made it to the hallway. "If you wouldn't dress like a slut," he said, "I wouldn't have to treat you like one." He flung me on the floor. I fought him as hard as I could, kicking and biting and scrambling away twice, once after he got my shirt off and I was running for the door. He grabbed me by my hair and flung me back down on the carpet.

He raped me, and after, when I was crying so hard I had the hiccups, he hauled me to my feet and told me to go take a shower.

I didn't tell anybody. Who was there to tell?

My life narrowed into a tiny circle of horror. I went to school and acted like a normal person. I had friends and I did homework, and if my grades were slipping, so what. I was only headed for the local diner or grocery store and everybody knew it. People like us didn't get out of Thunder Bluff.

I ran away. The first time, he found me within a day, hitchhiking. He beat me so badly that I didn't go to school for two weeks. The second time, one of his buddies picked me up in a town down the highway. The punishment that time was imaginative and painful and made it not worth another attempt. I feared if I told anyone, the retaliation would be even worse.

A person can get used to anything. After a while, I just let it happen, left my body while he used it and went mentally out to the garden

I grew outside our tiny house. I grew vegetables and flowers and herbs, learning everything I could about all of them. Strawberries loved garlic, and cucumbers wanted to climb, and a tincture of rosemary could help memory problems.

I just had to get out of school and find a way out. I just bided my time. And then I got pregnant.

Pregnant. As the scent of rosemary rises from the herbs beneath my fingers, I think of Maya's baby. Who will be the blood grandchild of Augustus. Who might look like him, or be like him or have his big laugh. Standing knee deep in herbs I've grown, my heart lifts at the possibility, and I realize I've been thinking about this all wrong. For the first time in weeks, I feel something like hope.

In the morning, I've still barely slept, but I have to talk to Kara at Peaches and Pork to see where we are on the Thursday opening, and I've already left a message to find out about Augustus. They can't keep him indefinitely.

First, I have an herbal blend of tea for pregnant women that I made for both of Rory's pregnancies, and I'm taking some to Maya to show I support her decision to have the baby. I've also cut an armload of flowers from my kitchen garden as an offering for my ambivalence yesterday.

Two cars are in the driveway, and I don't recognize the second one, a slightly battered Mercedes. For a moment outside my car, I hesitate, wondering if I should come back another time. But Norah's probably here, too, and therefore I won't be intruding. Buoyed by good intentions, I carry my gifts to the back door. Voices float out the french doors to the patio, more than two, I think, and I cross the grass to go in that way, singing out, "Hello! Is anybody home?"

"Meadow!" Maya says, coming out the door. She's wearing a little green T-shirt dress that shows off the tan on her legs and arms and clings to her still-too-thin body. "What are you doing here?"

"That particular phrase makes me feel very unwelcome," I say with a jokey tone. "I'm not staying. I just brought you a couple of things."

Behind her in the kitchen are the doctor from down the road and the impossible Norah, wearing shorts that make her legs look a hundred miles long. She raises a hand toward me, and I have no idea how to respond. "Flowers from my garden," I say to Maya, who takes them and bends her head to smell them. "Some artichokes I saw at a farm stand on the way down here and"—I hold up a baggie—"some tea for your special problem."

"Problem?" she echoes with narrowed eyes.

I glance at the other two and move so that her body blocks the gesture I make over my own abdomen.

"Ah." She smiles. "Thank you."

The sun falls on her, coaxing red highlights from her dark hair, pointing out the freckles across her nose. All at once, I see all the ages she has been: the small, aloof girl I first met, the child who brushed my hair; the weary, hungry girl who came to us after her mother's death; the vigorous eight-year-old who made forts and bossed her sister around; the fourteen-year-old who already had substance issues I didn't take seriously enough. Love like an ocean fills me, moves through me, uncontainable, inexpressibly huge. I have loved her just this much since the very first moment we met, as if we were on our hundredth life together, as if she had been born to me in another dimension.

"A tablespoon steeped in hot water for five minutes," I say. "You can add as much honey as you like."

She hugs me. "Thank you, this was very sweet. I love you, you know."

"I know. I love you, too," I say, and close my eyes and smell her hair and am so grateful that she's alive and here in the world that I almost swoon with it. To avoid showing any of that, I pull away, pat her shoulder. "Call me when you get back, okay?"

"Yes. I promise."

I wave to the others. "I have to meet Kara," I say, and don my sunglasses. Shoulders straight, I leave her. To her own choices, her own friends, her own everything, even if it breaks my heart.

Chapter Thirty-Six

Maya

The doctor's office is filled with well-tended women at various stages of pregnancy, and I halt just inside the door so fast that I can feel Norah screeching to a stop behind me. I turn around and head back into the white-painted hallway, sweat breaking on my neck. "This is a mistake."

"Which part?" Norah asks. "The baby or the office?"

I look through the sidelight window beside the door. "Look at those women." I think of them in perfectly furnished homes, with husbands waiting at night to see what the doctor said. They're all wearing yoga pants that cling to their toned bodies and T-shirts that tuck around the baby bump for utmost adorability. A roar fills my ears. "I can't go in there."

"Okay," she says, and there's nothing pro or con or über-patient about the word. It's just a word of agreement. "Is there somewhere else you'd feel more comfortable?"

My heart is beating a little too fast, and that noise is still filling my ears, but . . . "Rory will be so disappointed in me if I don't keep this appointment. It will seem like before, when I was always unreliable."

She nods. Her braid is like silk falling over a tanned shoulder as she peers into the room. "I could just go in and wait in the room and you can stay out here if you want."

The alternative gives me space to breathe, as if I'm in a cage, but one with an open door. A woman about my age comes out, her very round belly pushing ahead of her. She looks tired and her face is spotted with red blotches. "Hi," she says.

"Not far away for you, huh?" Norah asks.

"Maybe today," she replies wearily, holding up crossed fingers.

"Good luck," I manage. She waddles down the hall, her hand on her lower back. "I guess I can go in."

I'm still jumpy and uncomfortable, but it's uneventful. Norah reads on her phone and I leaf through a magazine about expectant mothers, and the reality of everything starts to hit home. I'm *pregnant*. That will end in a *baby*. In between will be a growing belly. Waddling.

By the time the nurse calls my name, I've worked myself into a state of anxiety, high enough that my hands are shaking, and right on the edges of my eyelashes are tears ready to spill at the slightest provocation.

But I also have to show up for this. I know how important it is to tell the truth, too. I had a long talk with Deborah after Ayaz left, and while she gently chided me about getting involved with anyone so early in sobriety, she focused mainly on the pregnancy news. With her I could say the things I'm terrified about—how long I've been pregnant, how long I might have been drinking, how that might affect the baby.

I spill it all to the doctor, a woman in her fifties with short, no-nonsense hair colored bright red. I like her immediately, and that makes it easier to tell the truth. Which she seems to take in stride. "Well, let's see where you are before we worry too much about the rest. What did you do to your arm?"

I make a face. "I tripped on a chair leg. I'm a barista at the moment."

"Ah." There's something about her face that makes me wonder if she thinks I was drunk when I did it. Which might have been true a while ago, but isn't today.

Don't project. I suddenly wish I'd brought Rory with me. Why didn't I? "My friend is in the waiting room. Can I have her come in?"

"Sure." She walks to the door and murmurs to someone outside, then comes back in. She examines me inside and out, then rolls over an ultrasound machine. "We will get a better idea of the age of the fetus this way."

A knock sounds at the door and Norah sticks her head around. "You rang?"

I smile, and reach for her with my left hand. "Yes. Thank you."

It is completely natural to hold her hand, which she covers with both of hers. "You're okay."

I nod and ask the doctor, "Can you tell how old the baby is without the information on my period?"

"Happens all the time." She squirts cold gel on my belly and rubs the wand over the spot. I see gray shapes, coming together, moving apart, and then—

"Oh my God! I see her. Him. Her?" A head shape, a back. *Hands.* That feeling of light and astonishment moves through me again, filling the marrow of my bones, the cells of my heart. "Oh my God," I whisper again.

Norah squeezes my hand, and I look up at her. "Crazy, right?"

"Yeah." She blinks hard and I know it's miraculous for her, too.

"Do you want to know the sex?"

"Um. I don't know. No. Not today."

"Okay." She runs the wand around the edges, across the body parts. "I'm guessing you're about eighteen or nineteen weeks, so you were impregnated about four months ago. How does that sync up with your alcohol use?"

Terror fills my throat. "I went to rehab ninety-seven days ago."

She nods and I can't read her face. "So you might have been three or four weeks pregnant by then." She hands me tissues and I wipe my belly. Does it look like it might be getting a little bowed? Maybe. My heart squeezes. "I'm going to be as straightforward as I can so you can make good decisions."

"Okay."

"How stable is your sobriety?"

Emotion swells through me. "Pretty good. Today," I say honestly. "One day at a time, and I really want to be sober, so . . ."

"Do you have a good support system?"

"Yes. My mom and my sister." I squeeze Norah's hand. "My friends."

"Good." She pauses. "The ultrasound is most accurate before fourteen weeks, but I'm pretty sure this is a fetus at nineteen weeks. Since you went into rehab ninety-seven days ago, the window for your drinking continues until about three weeks postconception, and that, unfortunately, is right on the line. At three weeks, a lot of things start happening, and alcohol can interfere."

A thud hits my heart. "How will I know?"

"You won't, not until the baby is born."

"And what kind of problems will she face if she does have it?"

"It's a spectrum, and it's different from child to child, but it's not insurmountable as long as you stay sober. There are many programs to help you and your baby."

As long as I stay sober. I look at her, the joy of this whole beautiful gift sliding out of my body, pooling in glittery puddles on the floor. Behind it is the shame of my life, the things I've done. "Is your recommendation to abort?"

"No!" Something must show on my face, because she takes my hand. "No! Not at all." Her face is calm. "There is a chance of some problems, but there's also a chance the baby will be perfectly healthy.

There are never any promises, and a lot will depend on what you do from here forward. What do you *want*?"

"I want the baby," I say, clearly. "Girl or boy, I don't care."

"Good. In that case, congratulations. If you want to choose me, I'll see you in about a month."

Tears are pouring from my eyes, making my nose run. "When am I due, then?"

She glances at her tablet. "Right around Thanksgiving."

"Thank you."

When she's gone, I look up at Norah. "I'm having a baby!"

She hugs me. Her hair smells of Herbal Essences. "Congratulations, Maya. You're going to be a wonderful mother."

"I hope so."

Norah wants to go to the library, so I drop her there and then head over to Rory's house. She's waiting for me, sending texts every twenty minutes. Meadow's car is out front, of course—I don't know why I would have expected anything else. She was so vulnerable this morning that I resolve not to get irritable or weird with her.

Nemo trots out and licks my hand, then leads me to the front door. I rub his silky-soft head as I knock, and then Rory is there. "Why are you knocking? Come in here right now!"

Her hair is down and she's wearing a printed sleeveless sundress that makes her look about twenty, and I can see what Meadow must have been like as a young woman, all softness and curves and smooth skin. "Nemo!" she cries when he stands in front of her. "Go in the backyard with the girls!"

With a doleful look at Elvis, sitting as always at Meadow's feet, he obeys. The drama makes me laugh, and I catch the big dog at the door, bending over to kiss his nose and head. "I still love you."

He slurps my nose, mollified, and jumps down to the patio, shaded heavily this time of day. Again I smell smoke. "That fire is still burning?"

"Uncontained," Meadow says. "Over fifty thousand acres."

"There's not going to be anything left of California," I say. "Do you have any more of that limeade? It's so good."

"Yes! I just made some. Sit! Tell us what the doctor said."

Meadow is nibbling a cookie, all the way around the outside, which she has done as long as I can remember. Blue circles show through the fine skin beneath her eyes, and the marionette lines around her mouth are pronounced. I touch her arm. "You okay?"

"Yes! Fine." She injects energy into the words, but it doesn't touch her eyes.

"Well, you are going to be a grandmother again, around Thanksgiving."

Rory claps excitedly. "Oooh, perfect! I can't wait. Girl or boy?"

"I don't know yet. I wasn't sure I wanted to know."

"I get that," she says, and brings me a tall glass of pale-green limeade over ice. "Nathan was dying to know, so we did, but I think it's fun to keep the surprise."

Meadow takes my hand. "And the alcohol at the beginning?"

"She said that it could affect the baby, but there's no way to know until it's born."

"Are you prepared to deal with that, a baby who might be deformed or handicapped?" Meadow asks.

The words fall into the world cruelly. *Deformed. Handicapped.* I gape at her, but before I can say anything, Rory tsks. "Mother! Stop! You're being so negative about everything. This is a happy accident. Act like it." She scowls. "Not to mention the hurtful words you chose."

"I'm just worried. I mean, God forbid, but what if you start drinking again, like—"

She has the grace to halt, but I fill in the rest with a sharp twist of bitterness. "Like my mom?" I give her a tight smile. "Maybe you can swoop in and rescue this baby like you did with me, and all will be well."

"That's not what I meant." She ducks her head, and I see that she's struggling, but enough is enough. "I just want you to be okay. You didn't even want to take care of a puppy—a baby is a lot more than that. And you don't have a job—"

"I do, actually."

"You won't be able to support a baby on that."

All the shame that was trying to crowd in back at the doctor's office now rises up from the swamp where it lives and fills my cells with sneering doom. I look at my hands, at the pink cast, and my fingernails. I think of the empty future and have no idea how I will live in it. I think of my mother, lying on a bed with purple lips, and squeeze my eyes tight.

Rory says, "Mom, can you give us a minute?"

She gets up, shaking her head. "Everything I say is wrong. I'm just going to head home today, get some rest."

"Just have lunch. Let's toast the new little one."

"I'm not in the mood for toasting." She kisses my head, then Rory's cheek, and heads out.

When the front door slams, I look at Rory. "What the actual hell?"

"I'm worried about her." She sits down. "Please don't take any of it personally. You're doing great, and I have every faith that you'll continue to do well." She covers my hands. "The universe is giving you a brilliant fresh start."

The voice of my lingering shame points out all the "truths." "People do relapse."

"I know. And if you do, we'll deal with it." She bends to get me to look her in the eye. "You're not alone, Maya, okay? I'm here for you, and Nathan, and even Meadow, although she's losing her mind at the moment."

"I need to figure out how to set boundaries with her. She's making me feel like a loser."

"Maybe you should. I think it'll get better once everything is settled with Dad and the restaurant and she can get on with her healing." She blinks and swipes two fingers over her cheek. "All of us can."

"Yeah."

"Let's eat. Oh, and I bought you something." She passes me a present. "Open it!"

It's so very Rory that she wrapped an impromptu gift. I rip the paper off and find a package of Micron pens, a ribbon-tied stack of square thick paper, and a Zentangle book. "Hey, this is great! Thank you."

"It's very peaceful," she says. "Meditation without having to concentrate so hard."

The front door opens again, and Meadow slams into the kitchen. She holds her phone aloft. "They released his body."

"What?" Rory says.

"The coroner," Meadow clarifies. "They released Augustus's body to the crematorium. They found no evidence of foul play and think he must have just had heart failure, maybe due to the cancer." She stands there a minute, staring at us, her finger below her nose.

Rory falls into Meadow's arms. "Finally."

I stand, and Meadow holds out her other arm toward me. For a minute, I think I will hug them both, and then I realize it's not at all what I want. I'm mad at Meadow, and mad at my dad, and there are so many emotions slamming around my body that I just shake my head. "I've got to go."

Rory snags me as I go by, yanking me into the huddle by the back of my shirt. I fall into their bodies, so familiar, and am surrounded by their scents, which mean home and comfort and all the things I really need right now, but I feel strangled by everything else, shame and anger and loss.

"I'm sorry," I gasp, pulling away. "I have to go." I head to my car and pull up all the meetings listed online. There's one that started ten minutes ago just a few blocks away, and I drive there directly, hardly breathing until I sit down in the featureless room. A speaker with a french twist and a cashmere sweater is telling her story.

I lean back and listen, my hand over my abdomen.

Chapter Thirty-Seven
Norah

In the library, I go back to work on tracking down details of Meadow's teen years. I feel like I'm missing something, right out of the corner of my eye.

It hits me as I look at the yearbook photos again: all this is entirely ordinary history. Why hide it? It makes a nice little Horatio Alger story—the girl from the sticks coming to town and making good. She has made good. I think of the way she looked this morning, a little wild. A little lost.

Wiggling my foot under the table, I go back through my notes. Mom. Dad. Stepdad. High school. Mom dead. Boyfriend. Baby Rory.

What about the boyfriend? I can't find an obituary for him, or anything more in the yearbooks. But it's a small town with a small newspaper. Maybe something will be there in the grad pages. I look through the notices but don't see anything with his name. I keep scrolling through the headlines of the spring, then the summer, looking for . . . I have no idea what. A fire on a farm out in the boonies started a grass fire that hit the ridge and burned for two weeks. A flurry of burglaries. In the fall, the dullest of days—harvest festival, local mayoral election.

What am I looking for?

I go back through my notes one more time. Rory was born August 10, 1985. Meadow showed up at the Buccaneer just a few months later. I look at the numbers and realize Meadow was pregnant with Rory when she was a cheerleader, while her big romance was going on. But again, how did she have Rory, who has skin so white it's transparent, with a guy who has skin the color of tree bark?

Whoever the father was, Meadow walked a hard road.

For a moment, I have to sit with the ache of recognition, the ways life let her down—war taking her father, her mother dead too young, her chances for happy teenage years ruined by a baby.

And then she found Augustus, who loved her and lifted her up and gave her a sense of herself and what she could do. He took in her daughter (*and left his own behind, don't forget,* says a little voice in my head) and loved her for twenty years, until the marriage broke up over yet another affair.

As I scroll restlessly through the newspaper headlines from Thunder Bluff thirty years ago, I think about Augustus and Meadow and the affairs he had, over and over and over. Am I trying to make sense of Meadow's life, or my own?

Maybe it's both. Maybe if I can figure out her story, I can make sense of my completely out-of-character passion for him. I fell so completely, so entirely in love with him, a man more than thirty years my senior. Why?

The good things surface. His beautiful forearms and hands that first day. The way he looked at me, as if there were never a woman on the planet he'd rather look at more.

He probably looked at all of us that way. It's humiliating to realize, but if I'm honest with myself, I know it's true. And however much I might miss him, Meadow is suffering a thousand times more.

A headline catches my attention.

Local Man Dead, Girl Missing

Monday afternoon, police found Gary Sullivan, 47, dead in his home at 72 Oleander Street after a neighbor reported a bad odor. Sullivan appeared to have been dead for more than a week, and while there is no evidence of violence, an autopsy will be performed. Police are searching for the deceased's stepdaughter, Tina Sullivan, 17, and her 1-year-old daughter, who have not been seen. The young woman lost her mother two years ago in a car accident and had been despondent since. She was employed as a waitress at Pie of the Day, and her boss said she's been worried since the girl failed to show up for a shift last Monday. Anyone with information about the death or disappearance is urged to contact police immediately.

No evidence of violence.

As I sit at the table of the library with my laptop, a sense of cold moves through me. In the stacks are two girls whispering and giggling, and a man has fallen asleep in the corner, his coat thrown over his head. My cursor blinks at me.

No evidence of violence.

Carefully, I scan every page of the paper for several weeks, but there's nothing until almost three weeks later, a small article, that says only that Gary Sullivan, forty-seven, had been buried at Law Cemetery. He was found dead in his home, but no foul play was discovered. He appeared to have died of a heart attack.

My skin goes cold. *A heart attack.*

The detectives asked me if I thought Meadow could have poisoned him, and I said no, emphatically, but now I search for "poisons that mimic heart attacks." A list of several show up, including thallium, the classic Agatha Christie poison, as well as monkshood and oleander.

My heart is pounding as if it is afraid it will be next, but my phone alarm rings, reminding me that it's time to get to work. Reluctantly, I close everything down.

Wondering, wondering, wondering. Could Meadow have poisoned her stepfather, and then Augustus?

How in the world can I find out . . . and what am I going to do with the information even if it's true? I don't want Meadow to go to prison. Maybe I don't even want her daughters to have this information. It would be too painful for them.

So what, then?

I have no idea.

Chapter Thirty-Eight
Meadow

The coroner released the body to the crematorium. Before anyone else gets involved, I want some time alone with him. In the hot July afternoon, I drive through the streets of the city, my nerves on the outside of my body. The world looks impossibly beautiful, a girl on skates being pulled by her dog, the ocean sparkling blue in the sunshine, the sky a hot, dry blue. In the distance, a plume of smoke rises over the mountains.

The facility is pink stucco, and as I get out of the car, a pair of parakeets flash green through the trees. They've become part of the landscape here, escaped pets that found each other and bred in the mild climate. They make me think of Australia and all the bright birds that live there. Augustus and I always said we would go see them, go on a long vacation there and see kangaroos and lorikeets and Uluru.

We never made the time. Instead, I did it on my own. That was when he took up with Christy. Maybe as a punishment to me. Maybe just bad timing. I will never know.

A skinny man in jeans and a white shirt greets me. He warns me that Augustus has not been made up or dressed, and I might find that difficult. I brush his concerns away. I don't want the pretty version. I've seen that.

In a cold room, he leaves me with the open drawer holding the body of the man I have loved most of my life, for thirty years now. His lips are a grayish blue, and his skin is bled to a dull yellow, but it's still his face. His thick hair, his beard. I touch his hair, running my fingers through the curls, and they feel the same. My walls crumble, and I am flooded with a hundred memories, a thousand. Waking up to find him sleeping beside me, that beautiful hair scattered over the pillow; watching him toss a Frisbee to the girls, over and over, until they learned it; offering me a taste of whatever he was cooking; wiggling his eyebrows at me across the table over an inside joke.

When he came back to me the third time, I thought we would finally heal the rift between us. Our connection was less sexual and more comforting. He crawled into my bed to hold me, and talk. He brought me presents, a scarf he thought matched my hair, a pen with peacock colors on the barrel, an embroidered tablecloth and matching napkins. He spent so much time with me over the months Maya was in rehab that I started to feel bad for Norah. He spent entire nights with me.

"Why did you have to go?" I whisper.

A wild force moves through my body, making it feel like my heart is exploding, my lungs turning inside out, all the blood inside me boiling and burning with something so huge I don't know how to even begin to feel it. I lift my chin to the ceiling and scream.

The poor attendant finds me on the floor beside the drawer, and helps me up, gives me water, helps me outside.

What I hadn't realized is that my grief would devour me. I can't stop the flow of tears, the hiccups and sobs. I drive anyway. I drive and drive and drive, around the streets where our love played out its story, by the first little house where we lived, through the parkway where the fair was held, up to the bluff by Belle l'Été, but I don't stop because I see Maya's car. She made clear her wish to be alone, even if I'd like to hug her and weep with her and share some of this pain.

I drive without realizing it to Peaches and Pork. It looks sad in the bright afternoon sunlight, the paint worn away by sea breezes and salt, the parking area cracked, the landscaping going seedy. It sums up the truth: his time has passed away. Augustus Beauvais is no more.

Kara's car is parked by the kitchen door, which is propped open to the breeze, but I don't go inside. I walk on the sidewalk around the restaurant to the beach in front of it, and over the burning sand to the cool stretch flattened by pounding surf. Around me, families play and kids build sandcastles and a pair of youths in wet suits swim out to the wilds.

I wade into the water, up to my knees, up to my hips. The tide sucks at my calves and I wade deeper, to my waist, letting the cold seep into my waistband. Wind lifts my hair and I close my eyes, tilting my face to the sun. Grief like a wild animal crawls through my body, slamming itself into my belly, my heart. I can barely breathe.

Augustus stands with me, not at all ghostly. "Glorious, isn't it?"

"What is?"

He gestures with one big hand. "Everything. The world, the sea. Children." He smiles at me. "You. Life."

"I can't," I say. "Not without you. I just don't know how to be in the world without you."

"You do." As if he's unreeling a film, I see myself leaving the house in Thunder Bluff, locking the door behind me as if that would contain the secret there, and hitching my daughter on my hip, and walking to the highway. "You know how to do everything you need to do."

"Not without you."

He brushes hair from my face, his thumb lingering on my jaw. "You were always the better of us."

I laugh slightly. "That's true."

"You can't leave them, all those girls. Rory and Maya, Polly and Emma." He pauses, his dark eyes kind. "Norah. She loves you, you know. It wasn't me she came for."

The sea knocks me, and I stumble sideways, and the vision or the ghost or whatever it was is gone. I'm alone in the ocean with water up to my waist. I could keep wading toward the horizon and disappear, all my sins forgotten, my grief a thing I can drown along with my joy.

Instead I have a sudden vision of the future, of another grandchild, a boy like Augustus, with his black curls and snapping eyes, laughing on my lap. For one long moment, I stand there, buffeted by waves; then I turn and walk back to shore, and back to Peaches and Pork, into the kitchen where Augustus died.

Kara is counting dishes, and turns when I come in.

"Let's figure out how to save this place, shall we?"

She grins. "Now you're talking."

Another figure comes in the back door. It's Norah, whose beauty never ceases to astonish me. Today her long hair is loose on her shoulders, and her big eyes are earnest. "Meadow, can I talk to you?" She glances at Kara, waves with one hand. "It's kind of important."

"How did you know where to find me?"

She looks bewildered. "Um. I don't know. I just came here first."

I slap my wet jeans. "Okay. Let's step outside."

Chapter Thirty-Nine
Maya

The cleaners are just leaving when I get back, and the entire house feels scoured and fresh. The cushions are plumped up, the floors clean, the counters spotless.

It doesn't help. The meeting didn't help. Nothing is helping this roiling restlessness that moves through my body, as powerful as the waves washing over my feet, opposites moving back and forth. I want to drink. I don't want to drink. I love Meadow. I hate her. I miss my father. I'm glad he's dead. I want to stay sober. I miss alcohol desperately.

In an effort to calm myself, I walk from room to room around the circle Rory and I chased each other through—kitchen, living room, salon, dining room, kitchen. I run my hand over the counter, over the back of a chair, over the table. I stop. The dining table is an antique, solid wood, dinged and banged up. It can seat ten easily, although it's been a long time. A linen runner, embroidered with turquoise and yellow, is freshly straightened. A gorgeous glass vase with dried plants sits in the middle.

In memory, I hear the music they loved to play and the laughter of guests. I see myself and Rory, stealing desserts the size of graham crackers, and beers and appetizers, and running outside with them. I see Meadow bending down to kiss my dad, her hand on his shoulder.

How long since anyone was here? It seems so bloody sad that it all ended over something so stupid. Aloud, I ask, "Why did you wreck our family, Dad? Why, why, why? I will never understand."

We've never had that conversation because I was too furious to talk to him. He seemed like a fool, chasing a woman no older than me, breaking Meadow's heart into a million pieces, destroying the future we'd been trained to envision: all of us and all our children and grandchildren, a circle and an empire, a bastion of safety against the dangerous world.

After the big cataclysm, after Meadow moved up to Ojai and her farm, and they hired lawyers to split everything properly, Christy left. It was only six months in, not even time for them to get divorced. She said she'd never meant to cause so much trouble, that she was too young to really settle down like that, and she was sorry, but . . . off she went.

By then, the damage had been done. My dad lived alone here at Belle l'Été. Meadow lived in Ojai, and built a farmhouse there that was both elegant and easy, not as large as this one, but also not right on the ocean.

I severed the relationship with my father when he told me he'd left Meadow. I didn't revive it again, not in all the years since. He tried. He wrote me letters, and called me on the phone and even sometimes drove out to where I worked, and then to the winery to surprise me into talking to him. The last time was only six or eight months ago. He drove up to Shanti Wines and found me in the fields. He strode between the vines in the boots he always wore and jeans, and a heathered long-sleeved T-shirt that showed he was as fit as ever.

I shook my head when I saw him. "I don't want to talk to you."

"I'm worried about you," he said plainly.

"Whatever." I tossed the weeds I'd just pulled into a bag at my feet. "You don't get to do that."

"You're drinking too much."

"I'm a vintner. It goes with the job."

He shook his head. "No. It's gone beyond that."

The words were like tiny arrows shooting through my conscience. I did know. I drank all the time, and I'd known for a long time that there was a big problem here. I looked at him. Pointed at him. "Pot." Pointed at myself. "Kettle."

He rested his hands on his hips, looked out toward the horizon, where blue mountains rose in showy beauty against a pale-blue sky. "I drink a lot," he said. "But it's not the same for me as it is for you. You're like your mom, Maya."

"Oh hey, thanks." I turned my body away from him.

"It will kill you if you don't stop. It killed her." He pauses. "It killed my mother, too."

I looked back at him, walls of anger safely holding him at bay. "And?"

"You need to go to rehab."

I snorted. "Not happening." I walked down the row, carrying the bag with me. "Bye, Augustus."

"Maya!" he called. "I drove all the way here."

I turned, still walking backward, which a person in need of rehab might have trouble doing, by the way, and shrugged. "Too bad, so sad."

He didn't move. For the tiniest moment, I almost relented. He was still my father, still the man who cooked my favorite pie and made me dolls out of flowers, and read me books until I fell asleep.

But I shook my head and kept walking.

Thinking of it now, I am so furious I can't even think. He left me. *Again.* This time, it's for good, and there's nothing I can do to fix that. I'm furious with him, furious with myself, devastated that he will never meet his grandchild, that our perfect family life was destroyed by his selfish, selfish impulses.

Stomping to the garage, I take three delivery boxes from beside the recycling bin and stomp back into the house, into his office. I yank open drawers and start throwing stuff into the boxes—some for Meadow to look at, some for trash.

In the lower right-hand drawer is a photo album I've never seen, and I pull it out. Laying it flat on the desk, I open it.

And there is my mother. Not Meadow. Shanti. I have only one photo of her, and all this time Augustus had this whole album of their wedding. My knees go weak and I sink into his chair, which lets go of a poof of air that smells of him. Something in me breaks.

Memories of my mother are of her terribly thin and despondent. I never liked to be left alone with her, and my father took me with him a lot. She wasn't abusive, but I might as well have been with a plant. She never ate, so she never fed me. She didn't shower, so she didn't bathe me. She was wan and thin and pale and never spoke, as if I were a ghost.

In these photos, she's happy, carefree, young. So very young. Her eyes are bright and her skin healthy. My dad is young, too, and less self-aware, his body posture sometimes awkward.

I think about what Meadow said, that he rescued women. Shanti was a runaway with drug issues when he found her and took her in, and they fell in love. I actually don't know how long they were together, how long her addictions held sway in their lives. I have no memory of her sober.

Why did I name the winery after an addict?

The question slides into my mind sideways, and once it's there I have trouble dislodging it. What twisted thing was in my mind when I came up with that? What weird curse did I bring down on my own head?

I look at her young, pretty face. Why did she get so lost? Why didn't anyone help her? Why didn't my *father* help her? The thought brings up another surge of powerful emotions, and it's so much I just want it to stop. I want to stop feeling. Stop the pain of it.

Stinging, I put the album back in the drawer and open the other side. I halt.

All the drawer holds is a bottle of bourbon. I pull it out, planning to carry it to the kitchen and pour it down the sink, but instead, I place it on the desk and turn away, get up, leave the room.

Start my pacing once more.

I walk to the french doors. Clouds are blowing in from the west, and the wind cools things down. A buzzing restlessness burns up and down my spine, a sense of loss and longing and hope and—"Argh!" I say aloud, and walk back into the office.

The bourbon sits in the middle of the desk and I grab it, carry it to the kitchen. Open the lid. Lift it, ready to pour it down the sink, but the smell suddenly snares me. I bring it to my nose and inhale, closing my eyes as memories flood through my brain. My dad's chest, rumbling with his laughter as I rested against him, the sharp voice of his reprimands, the way he got down on the floor to play Barbies with Rory and me. How proud I was of him when he was on television, how great he looked when he made jokes on-screen.

Without even thinking, I lift the bottle to my lips and drink. It tastes so good, and the heat slides down my throat like a magic elixir.

Tears are rolling down my face, and I don't know if they're for my dad or for myself, for all the time I've wasted, all the things I've lost. I stand in his kitchen, tasting the booze in my throat, and feel the relief of giving in, finally. I was never going to get sober, not really. I was just stopping for a while to get everybody off my case. I take another long swallow and let the tears come, wild and hot.

"I can't do it!" I cry aloud. "I just don't know how. I don't know how to be this new person."

And as if I conjured him, there's my dad. Not at all ghostly, not strange, just himself. "You do know," he says. "Pour it out."

Instead, I lift it to my lips, drink. Close my eyes as it burns down my throat, welcoming the edge of peace that seeps in. I bang it down. "Why did you leave me? Why did you leave my mother? And Meadow? Why couldn't you just stay? Why did you rescue all of them and not me?"

He puts his hand over mine and together we pour the bottle down the sink. I watch it go, feeling lightheaded and lost. "I did," he says.

And I suddenly remember. Sitting on the concrete stoop of the winery, soaked with wine and shivering, I waited for Meadow.

But when a car arrived, it was my father who stepped out of it. He gathered me up and carried me back to his truck and covered me with a blanket. "I'm so sorry, Maya," he said in the dark.

Now, in the kitchen of the home he's left me, I watch the bourbon glug down the sink. "I miss you," I cry. "I'm so sorry."

And that's all there is to say. I bend over and let myself grieve him, grieve the time I lost not speaking to him. I let go of all the things he should have been, and allow myself to love the things he was. As he loved me, as they've all loved me, my beautiful, beloved family, loved me when I was drunk or sober.

They still love me. And the knowledge blooms, full and whole: we are still a family.

My father couldn't wreck what was built to last. Whatever form our family takes, it's still a bulwark against the winds of the world. It's still mine.

I pull my phone from my pocket and dial a number. When Rory picks up, I say, "I've had a little relapse, and I need to go to a meeting right now. Can you come get me?"

"Yes. Yes. I'll be right there."

Standing there, waiting for her, I think of my young self, waiting for someone to get me out of that apartment. Waiting to be rescued.

But what I see now is that I didn't just wait. I tried to open a window and stood by the door and screamed whenever I heard someone in the hallway. I yelled until someone finally heard me and broke down the door and let me out. I couldn't manage the door, but I could use my voice.

I can do this.

I press my hand over my belly. "I'm so sorry, baby. That won't happen again, I promise."

And I know it won't.

I just know.

Chapter Forty
Norah

I wait for Meadow on a bench in the shade of a monster-size tree, my knee wiggling with my nervousness. I'm not exactly sure what I want to say.

When she comes out the back door, she's wearing a plain skirt that doesn't seem like her style and a pair of flip-flops, her hair pulled out of her face in a ponytail. She looks like she's getting down to work and I feel bad. "I hope I didn't interrupt anything too important," I say, standing.

She waves me back down. "Sit. I'm too tired to stand." She flops on the bench and leans forward, her face in her hands for a long minute. "They released his body, did you hear?"

"No!" My heart squeezes, hard. "What did the autopsy say?"

"Inconclusive." She sighs and sits up. "What can I do for you, Norah?"

And I realize I have no idea where to start. "Um. This is kind of hard. But . . ." I take a breath. "I've wanted to write a feminist piece about you for at least two years, and I came here to interview you, give the world a story that would show that you, not Augustus, were the impetus behind the Peaches and Pork empire."

She just looks at me. Her face is bare of makeup so I can see her freckles, and her lashes are as light as her hair. Her lips are pale. Her expression is weary. "And? I don't really have time for this right now."

"I did some research. On you, on your life. I, um, talked to your first boss, Trudy, and she knew your . . . original . . . name."

Her attention is more taut now, her back straighter as her eyes narrow. "That's none of your business. My story belongs to me. Only to me."

"Except that now I know it. Maybe not all of it, but most."

She waits.

"I know that you grew up in Thunder Bluff, that your mom died when you were fourteen, that you got pregnant there, and Rory was a year old when you disappeared."

"So what?"

"I think you poisoned him."

"Don't be ridiculous. They just did an autopsy and found nothing."

"I actually meant your stepfather. They found him dead in your house and you had disappeared."

A hush falls between us. She looks down, then back at me. "And what if I did? Are you going to write that into an article and get famous while I go to prison?"

"No," I say. I'm not even surprised. "I'm not going to write the story at all. I don't think you deserve that."

She closes her eyes, and her fingers are tightly woven together. "You grew up in foster homes. I don't know what it was like for you."

I frown, wondering what she's getting at. "It wasn't great, but it was mostly okay."

She nods, looking at her hands, then back at me. "You're not broken. He usually chose broken women, so that's what I kept seeing when I looked at you. But you're strong. Whole. Maybe that's what he needed, in the end."

I blink. It would be disastrous to weep right this second. I say nothing.

Meadow sighs and looks toward the sea. I see that she's struggling to contain her emotions. "My stepfather raped me repeatedly for two years, even when I was pregnant."

I swallow. "I'm so sorry."

Another long silence falls and I feel something in her shift. She turns to face me. "Augustus was sick," she says at last. "Really sick. Leukemia. He probably only had three months left and it would have been brutal and long and you would have suffered, too. All of us would have."

The knowledge of what she is implying moves like an electric eel through my body, stunning me. "What are you talking about? You killed Augustus?"

She takes a breath. "It wasn't like that."

Chapter Forty-One
Meadow

Oleander is a flowering plant that used to grow in wild profusion all over California. At our house in Thunder Bluff, the entire backyard was framed by hedges of it, red and pink, that bloomed in careless abandon for decades. They're beautiful, but also deadly—touching the leaves can cause dermatitis, and eating a flower will kill you. People dismissed them as a nuisance plant, and ranchers railed over the periodic poisonings. Now the plants are dying, thanks to a parasite, leaving gaping holes wherever they were, and people mourn them.

A hearty crop of oleander still lives at the back of the old bunkhouse at the farm, protected by some unknown confluence of things—they've never been attacked, so the flowers provide a splash of color against the old wood, so picturesque I've seen dozens of workers and visitors stop to snap a photo.

When I was young, my mother taught me to make a tincture of almost anything. In my sixteen-year-old desperation, I made a tincture of oleander from brandy steeped and refreshed for two months. I wore rubber gloves, and threw the used plants away carefully in a dumpster where nothing would eat it by mistake, not that many creatures can bear the bitter taste. I wasn't sure how much it would take, but in the end, my tincture proved to be quick and deadly.

This season, I worked stealthily, cutting leaves and flowers only under cover of night, like an old folk witch. Augustus watched as I pressed the plants into a dark blue mason jar and covered it with vodka, his dark eyes taking in the process at every step. The fresh cuttings, the vodka, the shaking and stirring of the material.

In the end, I extracted a small bottle's worth with an eyedropper, taking care to dispose of the rest like the toxin it was, as if it were turpentine or gasoline. I wrapped the small bottle in a length of linen and tucked it in my pocket for the trip down the hill.

We'd agreed on a Friday night, after everyone had gone home. He opened the side door of the restaurant to me so the cameras wouldn't pick up my arrival, and when I came in, we embraced for a long time without speaking. "Are you sure?" I whispered.

"Yes."

We ate the meal he'd prepared, all his favorites and mine—pork chops with caramelized peaches, fresh peas, and bread I'd made the night before for this very celebration, spread with herbed butter. We drank wine, and ate a decadent upside-down cake that had been one of the first things he'd ever made. He took off my blouse and kissed my breasts reverently, and I touched his body, every inch, kissing him gratefully. Touching his hair.

I left him in the kitchen, well into his cups already. "Another bottle of wine," I said, swallowing my tears. "Then in the last bit, drink the whole thing."

"Will you stay?"

I closed my eyes. "I can't."

And so he called a young thing, all aflutter to be summoned, I'm sure, so he wouldn't be alone when he died. I don't even mind.

He did what he had to do. As we all must.

Chapter Forty-Two
Norah

I listen to her story, and as I hear it, the pieces fall into place. Augustus's exhaustion and weakness those last couple of months. His inability to make love, his soul-deep weariness. "I have to go," I say to Meadow.

"Are you going to tell the others?"

I pause. "No. It's what he wanted."

She nods. Exhausted by the day and my emotions, I call an Uber to go up the hill to Belle l'Été.

No one is home. I walk in and turn on the lights in the kitchen. An empty bottle of bourbon is turned over in the sink, Jack Daniel's, and with a sudden clutch of fear, I rush into the office, where I saw a bottle in his desk. It's gone.

Did Maya drink it? Why didn't I think about taking it out of here when I first saw it?

I text her. Are you ok? I saw the bottle.

At a meeting. All is well.

I send a happy emoji and sink back down in Augustus's chair. He had cancer. It makes sense. He was so exhausted all the time, and it was getting worse. And if he'd lived, I am sure I would have ended up caring for him.

I wouldn't have minded. I wish he'd known that.

Restless, weepy, lost, I wander out to the patio. The air is still and warm, and smoke makes the sunset deep pink and orange. A lone surfer is silhouetted against the shimmery light, and I shoot a picture with my phone, then another, and another. It's quiet. Some bird I can't see is singing, a pretty sound like a recorder.

Without thinking, I strip off my clothes and dive into the pool, gasping a little at the cool water on my body, then surfacing to breathe. I kick into laps, letting the day and the revelations slide away. It's only me, in the water, in this house I love so much, swimming in the dusk.

A year ago, I was sweltering through a Boston summer, unsure of my prospects, breaking up with a guy I should never have allowed into my life. On a whim, I'd written to Meadow to ask if I could interview her. Instead, I reached Augustus, and he invited me to come to California.

When I've worked out the tense exhaustion in my muscles, I turn over and look up at the sky, watching stars emerge.

I will never see Augustus again. The knowledge is a purple ball of sadness in my gut.

But I also know I wouldn't trade the time with him, not for anything. For all his philandering, he was sincere. He sincerely adored me and I felt that. He held me in high regard. He loved my hair and my body, but he also loved my wit and our long conversations over longer meals. I made him feel young and vigorous, and he made me feel valued beyond measure.

Most of all, he gave me tenderness, which I'd never in all my life known from anyone. The tenderness of brushing my hair and rubbing my feet and listening, very intently, when I talked about . . . anything. Everything.

He loved me and I am better for knowing him.

For loving him.

Chapter Forty-Three
Maya

My father left me a letter, which Meadow brings to me two days after they released his body. She apologizes for holding on to it, but I get that she was protecting me.

When she brings it, I'm sitting in the living room to avoid the bright, hot sun of midday, and Cosmo is asleep, his soft paws folded on the arch of my right foot, and even when I wiggle my toes, he doesn't move. We've been working on swimming lessons every morning, and he adores it, but it also wears him out. A tired puppy, Meadow always says, is a good puppy.

"Knock knock," she calls from the patio doors. "Is this a good time?"

"Sure." Our relationship has been strained since her meltdown at Rory's house, but I'm trying to give her space to be herself. Deborah coached me on letting other people be who they are, and it's hard but I can have boundaries but also give her room to figure things out.

This morning, she's dressed in work clothes—jeans and a V-neck T-shirt and bright yellow tennis shoes—and her hair is tightly braided away from her face. The circles under her eyes are still deep, but I know this time it's more about the fire, which swept west and all too close to Ojai last night. "The farm okay?" I ask.

She drops into a chair. "The wind shifted," she says with a sigh, and rubs her face. "It never came over the ridge, and with a little luck, it's finally under control."

"Good."

"I brought you something. I picked it up after your dad died, but I kept forgetting to give it to you."

"Forgetting?" I echo.

She hands me a thick envelope. "I wanted to make sure you were okay before I gave it to you." I start to speak and she holds up a palm. "Let me finish."

I look at my dad's handwriting, elegant, almost calligraphic, and wait.

"I went to an Al-Anon meeting this morning," she says, and claps her hands together. "I . . . guess I have a lot of things to work out myself, and I don't want to make things worse for you."

Something like relief spreads through my lungs, soft and light. "What did you think?"

"I liked it, oddly enough. I thought it would be a bunch of sad people in a sad little room telling sad little stories, but it wasn't." She looks at me with her cornflower eyes, the light hitting them just right so that she looks like a seer. "It was a relief, honestly. I could . . . I don't know. Let down my guard."

I blink tears away. "Yeah. I know what you mean."

"I know I'm still going to screw up and say the wrong thing and make you mad, but I'm trying, okay? I'm going to do what I need to do to heal, too."

"Thank you, Meadow."

"Anyway. Your dad left you the letter and I just wanted to make sure you had it. Do you want me to stay while you read it?"

"No. I think I need to be alone."

"Okay." She stands. "I'll be at the restaurant if you need me, but otherwise, I'm just going to let you be until you call. Is that right?"

"It's perfect."

She kisses my head. "I love you, Maya. More than I can possibly say."

I grasp her hand and squeeze. "I love you, too."

For a long time after she leaves, I sit where I am, washed by the breeze coming in through the open doors. The sea rolls in and out, and some bird is singing his heart out in the bushes. A plane drones over. I turn the envelope over and loosen the flap. A single sheet of paper is contained within, and I pull it out. A photo falls out, a faded black and white of a boy sitting on porch steps with a smiling woman.

Dear Maya,

I am not so much a writer, but there is much on my mind tonight. I am gravely ill, which I have known for a little while, but they tell me it is very bad and I will not be walking among the living for much longer, and I cannot even be sure I will be well enough to speak with you when you get out.

You will be very angry with me, I fear, but the thing I want to spare you is being forced to sit in a hospital room, day after day, with your dying father wasting away while people say kind things you know are not true. I can't bear it for myself, but I especially cannot bear it for you.

Instead, I will take steps to see to a cleaner exit, which will not surprise you, I think. If I were a dog, I would go now into the forest and die on my own. It is the best I can do for you.

I think of you every hour, wondering what you are feeling, who you speak with, what you might be saying, learning in that place. If I try to put myself in your shoes, to answer your questions, I struggle, and I don't know what to say. Or perhaps I don't know how to say it right. I have not always been so good with words, with English and proper speech.

But nothing has ever been so important as this. I have loved many people in my life, but know this, Maya. You are and always have been the most important person in my life. My love for you is unlike any other feeling I have known. I don't know how to tell you that I mean that, and I know you don't trust me, but believe this. I want to set you free, so that you can soar like the powerful bird you were meant to be.

How do I free you, Maya-mine? I could apologize all day long, for a million things I have done wrong. Believe me, when they tell you to get your affairs in order, your life suddenly becomes a thing you can see at a distance, as if it belongs to someone else. I cannot change the past, and I could spend every hour from now until the moment of my death atoning for my sins and it would make no difference.

I ask myself what would make a difference to you. You stopped speaking to me when I left Meadow, but that was a thing between Meadow and myself, and nothing to do with you. That doesn't mean I wasn't a ridiculous old man, because it was the most foolish thing I ever did, but it was hardly a thing against you. Marriage is complicated, and none so much as ours.

Or maybe it does have to do with you. I don't know. There is not time for all of it, for me to number my transgressions one by one, though I would if I thought it would free you.

I have let you down in so many ways. I wish I could return to the day I left you with your mother, alone and untended. It was the worst sin of my life, to abandon you that way, and I will spend centuries in purgatory atoning. I would still leave her. I should have left her before I did, and perhaps she would have fallen far enough to find help, but I just kept hoping I could help her. Save her, I suppose. She was a good person, Maya. Kind and lost. She loved you the best she could, but her illness devoured her, as it devoured my mother, as it nearly devoured you. I could not save her, but I should not have left you with her.

I return to that afternoon over and over in my mind. Over and over, I see your eyes begging me to stay. I see your little hands on my wrist. I hear your voice.

I abandoned you, Maya. It was the worst thing I ever did, and I cannot say any words that will make that better. I tried to atone afterward. I hope we gave you a good child-hood, Meadow and I. You seemed happy. We loved you so much, and our family, our funny blended family, was so beautiful. I hope you had a childhood worth living. I think you did, finally.

The worst thing I ever did was leave you that day. The best thing I ever did was love you. I don't know how to say it more clearly than that. You are my daughter, my flesh and blood, my heart and soul, and I want you to live a good life. I want you to love people without reservation. I want you to have children and name one after me and tell them about me. I want you to dance. I want you to cry. I want you to be fully in every minute and really live it. Will you do that for me, Maya? Please live and be happy and remember me. Wherever I am, I am thinking of you. I am part of you and you are part of me, always and forever. Be happy, my sweet girl. Be well.

Forgive me if you can,
Papa

Chapter Forty-Four
Maya

It's a bright October morning when we gather on the beach below Belle l'Été. There are only five of us here, all barefoot as we carry the ashes down to the sea. Meadow, dressed in a flowing gossamer dress, her hair loose, leads. She carries the urn in two hands. Behind her is Rory, wearing shorts and a white peasant blouse with a flower wreath in her hair. Then Norah, in a turquoise T-shirt dress that lights up her skin and hair. She lives with me now, and is working on a dissertation about women in the organic-food movement, tracing their influence on the modern restaurant world. Meadow is included, but she isn't the whole story. They've become friendly, Meadow and Norah. Not besties, never that, but mutually admiring. Kara walks beside them.

I bring up the rear along with the dogs, Nemo and Elvis and little Cosmo, whom I've adopted after all. He's an exuberant ball of fluff who makes me laugh every single day.

Meadow has taken over Peaches and Pork, sinking some of her considerable fortune into reviving the tired decor and menu. At first, it didn't seem as if Kara would stay—she was so broken up over the loss of Augustus that she couldn't see her way forward into the new version, but when Meadow suggested they switch the name to Pork and Peaches, she laughed heartily and committed to the new vision.

As I walk into the water, my belly sways, full of a baby who is vigorous and healthy by all measures we can use now. I've stayed sober after the relapse incident. The doctor was dismayed, but thanked me for my honesty. All we can do now is wait.

I am not currently working. It turned out that Augustus had paid off the house with a loan he took out on Peaches and Pork, not the other way around, and in a letter he left with Meadow, he explained how to deal with every possible problem in the house. He left me a file of tradespeople's numbers on his computer, and a substantial fund to care for it. "It was always going to be your house, Maya. Take time to heal. I love you so much."

After my freak-out and relapse—"A one-hour relapse is pretty good," Deborah said—I realized how shaky my sobriety could be, and with regret, I told Ayaz I couldn't see him. Not even as a friend, because we saw how that went. I had to take the full year to do the work, find out who I am, and grow a baby. He took it with both grace and disappointment. He sold the house down the road, and we keep in touch via email, writing letters as if we're conducting an old-world love affair. We talk about everything, sometimes at length, about our lives and our hopes and our disappointments. He's taking his boards in California, living in a more modest house in town.

"Are you all ready?" Meadow calls.

"Ready!" Rory is carrying a small speaker attached to the phone in her pocket, and she holds it up.

"Grab handfuls, everybody." Meadow tilts the urn so we can reach in and grab handfuls of the bones and ashes of the man we all loved. I fill my hands and pause while she starts to pour it out. "We love you, Augustus," she cries, and we fling him into the Pacific.

Rory starts the music, slow strumming strings that pluck all our hearts. Slow, slow, anticipation building. "Zorba's Dance," the only possible eulogy song for my father.

The sea is cold and the sun is warm. We fling his ashes into the air and spin around, faster and faster and faster, swinging each other around by the elbow, dancing.

Alive. Grateful.

Epilogue
Maya

One year later

I'm nursing Gus, my greedy little boy, when the doorbell rings. Cosmo, all seventy-five pounds of him, leaps to his feet and barks impressively.

"Norah? Can you see who that is?"

No answer. "Norah?"

I debate whether to ignore it. No one ever comes to the front door. It's probably a salesman. But Gus detaches and sits up, curious as ever, and I pull myself together to go answer it. Cosmo trots along beside me, serious about his job as Gus's eternal, ever-present companion and protector. I spy Norah at the desk in the study with her noise-canceling headphones on, and grin to myself. She waves distractedly, and that's a good sign—her book is almost done, and although I'm not expert, I think it's really good.

"Shall we see who it is, little one?"

He grins, clapping his hands, and I kiss his little nose. As far as we can see, he is completely unaffected by the alcohol early in my pregnancy. He's a round-faced, black-eyed child with thick black curls just like mine. He's definitely not Josh's baby, but whoever his father was, he was a good-looking guy. My boy is so beautiful people stop and coo over him in the street. Meadow says we have to teach him not to take himself too seriously.

I open the door and standing there is Ayaz. He looks good—his hair has been cut into a short professional style, and all the weariness that haunted him when we first met is gone. He's carrying a bouquet of flowers. "Ayaz!" I exclaim, surprised and flustered. "How great to see you!"

His smile is very small and he says nothing for a moment. The faintest flush touches his temples, and my skin ripples in reaction. "You look wonderful."

"Thanks! So do you. Come in, come in!"

"This must be your son."

"Augustus. We call him Gus." I bounce him a little on my hip. "Can you say hi, Gus?"

He waves cheerfully. "Hi!"

"Good!" I laugh.

Cosmo swings his entire backside, trying not to break training and slurp at him, but eager to greet him. Ayaz notices and squats down, scrubbing Cosmo's ears and chest. "Haven't you grown into a fine dog?"

Cosmo lets go of a soft whine of happiness.

"Norah!" I call. "Come say hi."

She swings around the corner and slides in her socks. "Ayaz! How great to see you!" She kisses his cheek and takes the flowers and reaches for Gus. "You guys go sit down. I'll take everything. You want some tea?"

"Sure." He pauses, looking a little nonplussed.

It makes me feel shy. "Is everything okay?"

"Yes." He smooths a hand down the placket of his shirt and stands up straight. "It has been one year to the day since we agreed to take some time and heal before we . . ." He shakes his head, struggling for words a bit. "Try again."

I smile, my heart opening like a sunrise. I hear "Zorba's Dance." "A year to the day, exactly?"

"To the day." His smile is slightly larger. "Would you like to go to dinner with me?"

"Oh yes," I say, and take his hand.

He leans in and kisses my cheek. "I'm so glad to see you."

"Me too."

We walk to the patio and sit down.

And begin again.

About the Author

Photo © 2009 Blue Fox Photography

Barbara O'Neal is the *Washington Post, Wall Street Journal, USA Today,* and Amazon Charts bestselling author of more than a dozen novels of women's fiction, including *Write My Name Across the Sky, The Lost Girls of Devon, When We Believed in Mermaids, The Art of Inheriting Secrets,* and *How to Bake a Perfect Life.* Her award-winning books have been published in nearly two dozen countries. She lives in the beautiful city of Colorado Springs with her husband, a British endurance athlete who vows he'll never lose his accent. To learn more about Barbara and her works, visit her online at www.barbaraoneal.com.